Waters 10-2003

Dark

'The ability to create believable heroes out of policemen is rare, and Lindsay's Detective Inspector Jim Meldrum is both credible and endearing'
The Sunday Times

'Lindsay isn't interested by police procedure . . . The novel becomes more an investigation of the victim than of the murder. As such it is compelling'
Allan Massie, *The Scotsman*

'The British crime novel is enjoying a second "golden age" – an age of realism – with literate writers using the form to say important and necessary things about contemporary life and the darker workings of the human mind. Frederic Lindsay is playing his part in making readers sit up and take notice'
Ian Rankin, *Scotland on Sunday*

'An intriguing and intelligent thriller. Lindsay's detective, DI Jim Meldrum, and his taciturn sergeant make an unusual pair and the mystery is more complicated than it first appears'
Sunday Telegraph

'An entertaining read, to be savoured for its wry, literate dialogue and compelling noirish atmosphere'
The List

Also by Frederic Lindsay

Death Knock
Idle Hands
A Kind of Dying
Kissing Judas

About the author

Born in Glasgow, Frederic Lindsay now lives in Edinburgh. He has served on the Literature Committee of the Scottish Arts Council, and is actively involved with PEN and the Society of Authors. He has written for the theatre, TV, radio and film, and is the author of seven previous highly-acclaimed novels. His earlier novels featuring Detective Inspector Jim Meldrum are all available as Hodder & Stoughton paperbacks.

Darkness in My Hand

Frederic Lindsay

NEW ENGLISH LIBRARY
Hodder & Stoughton

First published in Great Britain in 2001
by Hodder and Stoughton
First published in paperback in 2002
by Hodder and Stoughton
A division of Hodder Headline

A New English Library paperback

2 4 6 8 10 9 7 5 3 1

A CIP catalogue record for this title
is available from the British Library.

ISBN 0 340 76573 9

Printed and bound in Great Britain by
Mackays of Chatham plc, Chatham, Kent

Hodder and Stoughton
A division of Hodder Headline
338 Euston Road
London NW1 3BH

For Cameron

Here at the head of the precious stair I stand
With darkness in my hand.

'There was a time when I used to envy flies: that's a
good way to live, I used to think; but then one night I
heard a fly whining in a spider's clutches, and I
thought: No, they've got to watch out, too.'

Marfa Timofeyevan in
Home of the Gentry by Ivan Turgenev

CONTENTS

Dead Man's Morning

The taller of the two, broad shouldered with the build of a boxer, had come out of the house first, and he was the one who marched ahead, full of purpose it seemed, heels ringing across the stones of the terrace, until at the steps down to the lawn he came to a sudden stop. The other man moved softly to his side, soundless as a pacing cat.

'A refrigerator full of heads, Archie,' he said, smiling up. 'I talked with a man who'd seen them. I'd no reason to disbelieve him.'

Ahead of them, the night air shone, pale, almost luminous. It was early summer, and as he glanced up the speaker saw an unclouded sky and half a moon balanced on his companion's shoulder like a white parcel.

The taller man was wondering how it had happened, what had been said in what order to involve him in this stupidity. Turned twenty, he had the notion that falling for a dare in schoolboy fashion — face-your-fears crap — was something he should have outgrown. Even that they'd been drinking wasn't an excuse. The first touch of night air had sobered him, or so he felt. He turned half round intending

3

to go back, but the French windows were being drawn shut. A moment later the light in that room went out and the house was dark. As if signalled, he started down the steps.

Crossing the lawn, he couldn't see the break in the hedge, which stood over head height, black and solid as a wall. He edged forward cautiously, stretching his hands out in front to protect his face. When Rannie came there, however, he followed without breaking stride; though strange to the place went as if by an open door, as if he'd known about that gap for ever.

As Archie came through the hedge, cloud came off the moon and showed a field of wheat moving like water beyond a stock fence. Behind him, he could hear Rannie whistling softly through his teeth. He slowed, forcing him to catch up. There was enough of a space between the fence and the hedge to let them pace along side by side.

'They use this for walking horses,' he said. 'There's a riding stable over there.'

Rannie continued his tuneless whistling without response.

As they turned the corner of the field, there was a snuffling, and a bulking of shapes came at them.

'What the hell—?' It comforted him that Rannie could be startled. But then he heard him laughing. 'Just cows. Somebody left a gate open?'

Ignoring what Rannie was saying, with one arm he pressed him back against the hedge. A wary eye gleamed at them, then half a dozen beasts went by in a rush, so close he smelled their heat.

Where the field ended, they climbed over a gate into the wood. They went along a narrow path and Rannie tried for a pace or two to take the lead before having to fall back. It was dark under the trees, so dark Archie followed the path by instinct, not hearing Rannie behind him, resisting the temptation to turn and see if he had lost him. Mud sucked at his shoes as if trying to hold him back; it had rained heavily the night before. Thinking about that, he almost walked into barbed wire, stopped barely in time. A post hammered in at either side, three lines of wire strung across the path. And it occurred to him, of course it did, the barrier gave them a reason for turning back. Go back to the house, have a last whisky, go to bed. That made sense, except that Rannie didn't say anything, just stood watching him as if curious to see what he would say. Made sense; except that the barrier wasn't much of a barrier at all: on either side, there was space to get by between the trees and the posts. Show the bastard then. A couple of steps was all it would take, up on to the bank at the side of the track and squeeze round. But when he tried it, in too much of a hurry, his leading foot slipped on a slick of leaves. He was falling and one hand would catch the post by the top, but if with the other one he hit the wire in the wrong place his whole weight would drive a barb into his palm. In the split second of seeing the danger, he made it safely between the barbs, and with a heave threw himself upright and swung round the fence down on to the path on the other side. Before he could recover his breath, Rannie had joined him.

'That's new since the last time I was home. Absentee landowner and to hell with rights of way.'

Rannie said softly, 'If I had him here, I'd wrap his face in it.'

Ten minutes later they came out on a scrap of shingle beach at the edge of the water.

'There is a boat,' Rannie said, with a faint pleased

emphasis as if it wouldn't have surprised him if after all there hadn't been. Not much of a boat, large enough for three, or two comfortably, used probably for a few hours' fishing now and then, but there all the same and with its oars stacked inside.

He was the one, unaided, scorning the indignity of seeming to hesitate in front of Rannie, who dragged the boat forward until it slid into the water, shuddered and came alive under his hands. Now from the front of the boat, as they left the shore, he watched the broad wedge of Rannie's back recede and approach as the blades dug in. The expanse around them widened with every stroke. Rannie was pulling hard. The night was so still he could hear the engine note of a car change as it took a hill. A beam of light swung at the sky and fell. The oars rose and fell, but straining to listen he couldn't hear Rannie taking breath. He fell into a kind of dream in which he imagined all the dark length of the loch hissing under last night's downpour.

Far out, Rannie stopped. As the boat drifted, he began to pull off his jersey.

'What are you doing?' He heard the note of panic in his voice, and hated himself for it.

'Lacing my shoes round my waist.'

'If that's a joke, it's not funny.'

'Quite right,' Rannie said. 'Going to see your little sister then.'

He laughed and slipped over the side.

In the same moment, the man in the boat spotted the oars floating away in the water. The thought came to him that, after all, it must have been his sister who had closed the French windows on them as they left and switched off the lights. And that she must have been the one, it could only have been her, who had betrayed his terror of drowning to Rannie. But had she also told Rannie of the part she had played in his learning to be so afraid?

He felt the boat under his feet, and where his hands gripped it on either side. The boat was planks of wood on the crawling surface of deep water. Adrift, he could not unclench the grip of his hands. When morning came, earlier at last, for it was spring, first light found him bent forward as if praying in church and the boat, drawn by currents under the surface, turning a long slack circle on the dark water.

When at last he came home, his mother and father met him at the door.

'Isn't your sister with you?' his mother asked.

'Rannie's taken her,' Archie cried. 'She's gone to London with him.'

'I don't understand,' the father said, looking up at his son. 'If you knew, why didn't you stop him?'

BOOK ONE

Choke the Hammer

Chapter One

Jim Meldrum knew how it could be between fathers and sons. As a young man, his father had quarrelled with his own father and fled for the city, abandoning younger brothers to the endless labour of a sour-soiled upland farm. Till his dying day, they had never forgiven him. Meldrum had wondered if his father ever felt guilty about that. Not that he would have said, that would have been a sign of weakness, and anyway he never spoke about the past. All the same, he was a man to whom happiness never seemed to have come naturally, as if he had not ceased to carry inside him the expectation of stony acres. When he'd been told by Meldrum aged sixteen he wanted to take an apprenticeship as a joiner, he'd erupted so violently that Meldrum, repeating history, had left home. Later he'd responded with contempt to the letter written to tell him his son had joined the police. Long afterwards, clearing out a desk after his father's funeral, Meldrum had come across brochures from universities, different courses in maths and science, collected over six years, stopping in the year he'd left home at sixteen. As late as that, and for the first time, he'd had a glimpse of the dreams his father had for him, the hopes he might have invested in him. It was an insight he could have done without.

Himself he had only one child. His daughter Betty and he had been close when she was small. Afterwards not so much. Even before the divorce not so much. The endless hours he'd given to his job had cost him more than his marriage. A clever girl, Betty had gone to university. At her graduation, sharply, unexpectedly, Meldrum had missed his father, as if he might have been the one who could have shared and understood his complicated pleasure in her achievement. Yet if his father had been spared to see his granddaughter graduate, almost certainly he'd have kept whatever he felt locked inside. Running true to form, chances were he'd have pointed out Betty's mother was a head teacher, and so any credit due should be Carole's with her being in the education business.

Whatever the truth of that, it wasn't less true that Meldrum, history repeating itself this way also, in his turn had made an investment in dreams.

Now, looking round the flat Betty shared with her husband Sandy Torrance, Meldrum remembered his hopes for her. Sandy and she had fallen in love; he was going to be a great painter; she'd got pregnant; he'd gone to training college and got a job as a teacher so they could marry. When the child was old enough, maybe Betty would follow the same route into teaching. She seemed happy enough. Sandy was a good man, even an admirable one. If he regretted the travelling scholarship to Italy he'd given up to get married, Meldrum had never heard him complain.

'Sandy's late.'

'How would you know?'

12

'What?'

'How would you know what time Sandy gets home?' She collected her cup and sat opposite him. 'Have you any idea how long it's been since you've been here?'

'When did you last ask me?' It was his instinct to go on the attack.

'Plenty of times. A month ago. All right, maybe longer. You get tired of asking someone who always finds an excuse not to come.'

One difficulty with Betty was that, being too like him, she was prone to attack mode herself. The other was he was too fond of her to have his heart in arguing.

'Work,' he said feebly. Added, 'You know what it's like,' and wished he hadn't.

'Hmm.'

Silently they matched memories of when she'd been a child.

He said, 'Well, I'm here now,' trying for cheerfulness.

'I wanted to talk to you,' she said. 'I told Sandy to take his time about getting the wine.'

'Is anything wrong?' His tone sharper than he'd intended. Debt or a lover, husband's or wife's, that kind of possibility occurred to him on automatic pilot. He'd been a policeman for a long time.

'I think so.'

He waited. 'I can't help if you don't tell me.'

As she hesitated, chewing her lip, he decided it had to be something to do with Sandy. *If he's got himself a girlfriend*: the thought, as he pictured his grandson sleeping next door, coming on a wave of anger and pity and near panic.

'I don't need help,' she said.

He raised his eyebrows and waited. In the interview room, he was good at waiting. It was one of his strengths.

13

'You're the one who needs help,' she said.

She'd regretted starting to tell him whatever it was, he decided. Don't change the subject, he wanted to tell her.

'I don't think so,' he said.

'You must feel it yourself. Don't you feel it? How you've changed in the last year.'

Suddenly, he realised he was the intended subject after all. Taken by surprise, automatically he put up his defences. If he had been able to lose his temper with her, that would have been helpful.

'Changed? But you've just finished telling me, we haven't seen much of one another for a while. Make up your mind.'

Instead of flaring up in response, she looked at him, then shook her head. 'Daddy.' She sounded sad.

He had no defence against that. 'I'm fine,' he said.

'When I phoned, I thought you'd been drinking. And the time before, too, you sounded—'

Drink, he could talk about. Everybody drank.

'I'm a policeman,' he said, his smile inviting her to share the joke.

'Not you. That was one of the things about you. I'm not saying you didn't take a drink, but not so we ever saw it at home. That was one of the things . . .'

'What?'

'Made me proud of you.'

'God's sake, Betty. I was looking forward to my dinner. This is like a meeting of the Band of Hope.' He didn't like the tone of that. He tried again. With a smile: 'If we're going to sign the pledge, Sandy didn't need to bother about wine.'

'Don likes a glass with his dinner.'

'Don who?' He couldn't believe it, but she met his stare

without flinching. Raising his voice in disbelief: 'Don who-I-think? *That* Don? *He's* not coming here, is he?'

'And Mum.'

He got to his feet. 'I'll be off.'

'I wish you wouldn't.'

'I've only met the guy two or three times. The last time he was getting married to your mother.' His tone was quiet and reasonable. *What the hell gives you the right to pull a stunt like this?* 'What gave you the idea I'd want to have dinner with him?' His job had taught him to hide his feelings.

'No point in losing your temper.'

She knew him too well.

'Fine, but I don't feel like it. Maybe another night, when it isn't a surprise. Okay?' He went into the lobby. 'I promise next time you invite me, no excuses.'

He was reaching for the handle when the bell rang. Nothing for it but to beat a retreat and hope it was Sandy with the wine, when he could make some excuse and complete his leave-taking. He'd his back to the fire in the front room when Carole came in, followed in a moment by her new husband.

It could easily have been an embarrassing meal. With five of them, the table was slightly crowded, the plates were a shade too close together, occasionally elbows bumped. The table was set, too, at the end of the long narrow kitchen, which though it meant Betty didn't miss anything as she cooked and served, also meant it got too warm for comfort. Add awkward silences to complete a hellish evening, Meldrum thought, and waited for them, in vain as it turned out. With Don Corrigan, silence wasn't an option. If he had an opinion on anything, it seemed he liked to share it; and if there was something on which he

15

didn't have an opinion, it didn't turn up from soup through to coffee.

On wine: 'It's a useful tip to have a look at the Portuguese corner in Oddbins or wherever. If you can find a bottle the Aussie flying winemakers haven't got their hands on, chances are you'll be getting a bargain. Made from one of the local grapes, I mean. The outside world doesn't appreciate those varieties as it should. For one thing, they're harder to pronounce than Cabernet Sauvignon and Chardonnay. But you can get tired of the whole world bottling *them*.' They were drinking a Chardonnay from Chile. On politics: 'I met this charming woman at a conference in Dundee. She's head of a very good private school for girls, and she said to me, Never mind two parliaments, why should we have two different education systems? This is a small island. What on earth is the point?' On education: 'I was in a school – oh, yes, I do know what the inside of a classroom is like!' He had just been made Director of Education in one of the neighbouring authorities. 'It was a special needs class. I asked this boy, Do you know what special needs means? He said to me, It means you're good at nothing. But when I chatted on to him, he told me he'd spent the Sunday helping his dad to build a shed. You can imagine the conversation I had afterwards with that teacher!'

On religion: 'Carole's back in the classroom.'

'What?' Betty exclaimed, turning to her mother.

'I'm enjoying it,' Carole said.

'Teaching,' Betty said, the single word flat and incredulous.

'It's what it's all about,' Don Corrigan said. 'The chalk face. Over twenty years since I stopped teaching and I still miss it.'

At a table that size, ignoring him wasn't easy. Betty managed it. She asked her mother, 'How many times have I heard you saying that being a head was a different job from being a teacher? A job you liked. I've heard enough people talking to know what a difference you made in that school. I can't think why you'd want to give up a job you did so well.'

'In a word, parents,' Don Corrigan said with a smile.

Betty waited.

'Some of them,' Carole said. 'About half of the School Board wanted me to go. Half were sorry about it, though – under the circumstances, I took that as a compliment.'

'What circumstances?' Sandy asked.

'Register Office weddings don't go down well with the Catholic Church.'

'When I was seventeen,' Don Corrigan said, 'you know what it's like at that age, I was troubled by doubts. I took them to our parish priest. He told me, It's not your business to ask questions, it's your business to have faith. I've never set foot in church since.' He laughed. 'Fortunately, I'd the sense to get out of Glasgow to make my career.'

'Teaching where?' Betty asked her mother.

'No problem with that,' Don said, 'if you've a friend at court.'

Before Betty could respond to that, Carole said, 'My poor parents. For some of them, you were a problem, Jim.'

'Cuts both ways,' Meldrum said. 'If I hadn't married you, I could have joined the Masons. I might have been Chief Constable by now.'

'Not you,' she said.

It was an odd little moment of intimacy and suddenly felt by all of them as such.

Sandy said, 'Let's take our cups and go through. Make

ourselves comfortable. And if you'd like something else to drink—'

'Can't,' Don said. 'Didn't you say, Carole? Oh dear.'

He waited.

'Say about what?' she asked.

'Oh, for God's sake!' said with a certain pleasant impatience. 'The Mitchison presentation.' Explaining round the table: 'It's at the City Chambers. One of those duty calls affairs, I'm afraid.'

'I thought,' Carole said, 'that was tomorrow night.'

'No, tonight.'

Ten minutes later and they were gone.

Meldrum stood in the front room and listened as Sandy and Betty made their hosts-saying-farewell noises. He heard the outer door close.

Coming into the room, Sandy made a face and said, 'I don't believe that thing, whatever it was, is tonight at all.'

'It must be. What would he say to Mum?'

'Can you imagine him at a loss for a word?' Sandy asked. A gentle young man, being sardonic wasn't his style. Meldrum guessed he was offended for Betty's sake. The meal had been surprisingly good; cooking not being one of Betty's strong points, she must have made a special effort. 'He never stops. This is a modest little wine – did you get it at Oddbins? – I get mine rowed in from Portugal. Britain's a small island – what do we need two education systems for? Can you imagine his face if I'd said, Oh, it would be a shame to ask the English to give up theirs? He'd probably just have been baffled. Scotland's full of clowns like that. Head counters. I always want to tell them, Go and catch jaundice then, there's a hell of a lot of Chinese in the world.'

'Sandy! Let it go.'

'Sorry. It's just . . .'

'Let it go. Please.'

'Didn't mean to go on.' He put an arm round her shoulder and hugged her. 'I got excited at the sound of my own voice.' He grinned. 'First time I've had the chance to hear it all night.'

'Made a nice change for me.'

'Funny girl. I'll put more coffee on and wash some cups. Be back in a minute.' But he paused at the door and said, 'It's just, I don't know, your mother's job, you'd think she'd know how to handle a bully. Sorry,' he said again, and added as if in explanation, 'I've always liked your mum.'

Betty sighed and dropped heavily into the chair by the fire.

'Sandy lets fly sometimes.'

Looking down at her, Meldrum said, 'You looking after yourself? You're looking tired.'

'The wee one's teething. We were up half the night.'

'Hmmm.' After a pause, he said, 'Sandy's all right.'

'Of course, he is. But that stuff about bullying. Can you imagine Mum letting herself be bullied?'

Maybe. Because she thinks the sun shines out of his arse, Meldrum thought. He didn't say it, though, because there were certain words he didn't use in front of his daughter, since even now he wanted her to think well of him.

Perhaps because he'd hesitated too long before answering, she let out a little groan. 'Remember when I said you were seeing Mum too often?'

'When was that?' But he knew. In the long interval after they'd separated and even after the divorce, he'd developed the habit of dropping in on Carole. They'd sit and talk, sometimes have supper together. He'd tell her about his work, which he'd never done when they were married. That work which had taken up so much of his life, no wonder she'd tired of what was left to her. They'd been married young, though, and for a long time; and somehow the habit of friendship had stayed with them. No doubt he'd been stupid, but he'd been shocked, taken absolutely by surprise, when Betty lectured him. *You've got to let her get on with her life. She gets so upset after you visit her.* No doubt he'd been stupid. He'd stopped going to see her, and the day came when she and Don married.

'Do you blame me?' Betty was asking.

'What for?'

'I might be going to blame myself.' She put up a hand. 'I'm being stupid. I'm tired. Pay no attention. I told you I was tired.'

'I'm off.' He stood up. 'I'll say cheerio to Sandy on my way out. Let you two get to bed.'

'You don't have to.'

'I need a drink,' he said.

Chapter Two

———◆———

The grass needed a cut. Meldrum felt guilty about that. On the other hand, it always needed to be cut. The smell of cooked meat hung on the warm air. Across the fence, they were having a barbecue. The house next door was the same size as his, so was the one on the other side. All the houses were much the same size, built to much the same plan, in that street and the streets round about. Tidy houses, not too big, behind barbered hedges. All the same, it was taking him a long time to walk along the path at the side of his neighbour's house, as though at some point when he hadn't been paying attention the house had got bigger, a lot bigger, big as a church. The windows were different too, round at the top. What did you call churches with windows like that? The grass in the back garden was neatly cropped; he noticed that, then that a lot of people were standing around on it. All of them invited to the barbecue. Except him. Carole had been the one who made friends, and Carole was gone. When the laughter and talk stopped, suddenly it was so quiet he could hear from the far end of the garden fat sizzling through the grill on to the fiery coals. Everybody but the man in the chef's hat had turned to look. What was Chef Hat's name? He should know his name. Why should he know his name? A neighbour for ten years was why. Too bad. Meldrum headed for him through the staring crowd, brushing people out of his way. Bent over the barbecue, Chef Hat didn't seem to realise how quiet it had gone. To catch his attention Meldrum took out his prick and pissed on the grill. He did it matter-of-factly and shook himself when he'd finished. For as long as it took, it seemed the natural thing to do. A cloud of pungent steam obscured the grill, and as it cleared he was looking down into an open grave. At the foot of it was an unlidded coffin, and the man who lay in it, a man he almost recognised, and then thought might be himself or anyone, opened his eyes and winked at him. Horrified, he thought, I've let Carole down in front of all our neighbours. Oh Christ, what have I done? But as Chef Hat turned, holding a steak on a fork, he was smiling and Meldrum saw it wasn't his neighbour (Jimmy, that was the neighbour's name, not that it mattered, not now) but Neil Heuk. Seeing the child killer, a wave of relief broke over Meldrum. Since Heuk was dead, then this had to be a dream.

For confirmation, he opened his eyes.

He was lying in a strange room, looking at a dressing table with a tilted forward mirror reflecting what looked like sheets of notepaper; a room in a hotel, not a cheap hotel, but a hotel room. Somehow you could always tell. Blue drapes across the windows were drawn and the lights were on. As he pulled himself upright, he caught his breath and pressed a hand to his side, stifling a groan. His ribs ached more badly than when a mob had thrown him down a flight of stairs. He'd been a beat constable then and only in the police a matter of months.

There was the sound of a lavatory flushing, and a woman came out through an open door in the corner of the room, pulling up the zip on her trousers. When she saw he was awake, she smiled and asked, 'What was your name again, darling?'

She had a pleasant voice, the voice of an educated woman. While he thought about that, she sat on the bench seat in front of the dressing table and began to pull on her shoes.

He stared at her and licked his lips. They were dry and rough and his tongue felt too big for his mouth.

'Is this London?' he asked.

'I've been asked a lot of things in the morning,' she said. 'It was a strange night, but not that strange.'

She stood up and drew the curtains. Grey light and streaks of rain on the glass.

'No, still Edinburgh. Just the way it was when we went to bed.'

It seemed they'd shared a bed. Looking at her, not to remember what had happened seemed a waste. She had blue eyes and dark hair, hair its own colour with a rich sheen to its blackness. It was a very smooth, young face, oval in shape, the forehead high, not beautiful but striking. She was slim with small high breasts under a white top. When she'd turned from pulling back the curtains, the top had ridden up so that he'd seen a tattoo, dark blue-green like a bruise, curled under her navel. Too quick a glimpse, before she tugged the top down, to make out the design on her belly, flat, sleek, and olive brown, though her face was pale. She was the kind of woman men would turn to look after in the street, a desirable woman. Late twenties, at a guess, old enough to have broken some hearts. Twenty years younger than him, whose heart was made of tougher stuff.

He cleared his throat. 'Who the hell are you?'

'I asked you first.'

'Did we sleep together?'

'You must have been even drunker than I thought.' She shrugged. 'But if it matters you managed all right – what did you say your name was?'

'Jim.'

She smiled. 'Good boy.'

'What?'

'That was what you told me last night. Maybe it is your name.' She smiled as if thinking about something. 'You did better than all right.'

Meldrum hitched himself further up against the headboard till he was half sitting. Wincing at a stab of pain in his side, he felt behind him for a pillow.

'They're on the floor,' she said.

Big fat pillows, half a dozen of them, scattered across the floor at the side of the bed.

'I was going to make you sleep down there,' she said. 'But you barked so nicely I changed my mind. Like a good dog.'

'You're mixing me up with someone else,' he said, unruffled in his certainty.

'I don't think so.'

'Not me.'

She came over from the window and pulled the sheet down, uncovering him. He had an erection.

'Maybe I know who you are better than you do.'

A stab of pain went through his skull. Involuntarily, he put up a hand and found a lump at the back of his right ear. Ignoring his ribs, he swung his legs over the side of the bed. The movement of getting up was sudden, but she didn't

24

flinch. As he stood over her, she asked, 'Are you in pain?' glancing up slyly at him.

She raised a hand as if to touch his head.

He went to pass her, and when she didn't get out of his way took her by the shoulders. He held her lightly, a big man, four inches over six feet, hardly exerting any force, and she let herself be moved aside without the slightest resistance. He went to the door she'd come through earlier. In the bathroom, he spat out the taste in his mouth, brown like rust into the washbasin. He felt the lump behind his ear and twisting his head saw that the hair round it was stuck together with blood. Nice to pretend it was a stranger staring at him from the mirror, but he knew that face too well. For a detective, drinking was part of the job. Over the years he'd done his share, no more than his share, less than most. After Carole left him, taking Betty with her, it was only to be expected he'd drink more. Wasn't that natural? Since he was too proud to show weakness, he did the extra drinking on his own, sometimes at home, which he hadn't done before. One night, celebrating a conviction, he heard a DC called Chalmers boast about never suffering from a hangover. Meldrum had smiled to himself, not saying anything as he emptied his glass, for he could have claimed more or less the same luck. Next morning, Chalmers was in hospital, a diabetic coma his first indication something was going wrong. Not so lucky, after all. Round about then, Meldrum had cut back on the drinking, and things had gone on that way for a long time. In the last few months, though, he'd lost his grip on himself. Not for one reason alone, an accumulation of things, and one last that had been one too many. The truth was he was disappointed in his life. Violently, since self-pity disgusted him, he threw up handfuls of water into his face. The water came tepid from the cold tap and ran down his face like tears.

He heard her voice, but couldn't make out the words. When he went out, she was standing by the door.

'Past time you should be dressed,' she said. 'It's getting late.'

Ready to leave, she was wearing linen trousers of a colour like fresh cream, wide linen trousers, and a jacket to match. Dressed like that, more than him she belonged in a hotel like this, even the little bag she held looked expensive. They'd shared a bed, unless he was being lied to they'd shared a bed, and he had no idea what she would look like naked or how her body would have felt under him.

He didn't know her name.

He heard himself asking, 'The room. Is it paid for?'

'Not by me,' she said.

For a while then, he stood motionless, head inclined to the side. If she hadn't gone as soon as the words were out of her mouth, closing the door softly behind her, she might have thought he was waiting for a different answer, one to some other question that would have told him everything he needed to know. He wondered later if there was a question like that, anything was possible, but if there was he couldn't find it, even after later turned into too late.

He started to get dressed, finding his jacket in a crumpled heap dumped on the floor under his trousers with the rest of his stuff scattered around. Only his socks were on a chair, side by side and neatly folded. Pulling them on, he wondered if that was because he'd taken them off first; usually even drunk he took them off first, but then usually in the morning he remembered the night before; maybe last night he'd taken them off last. Suddenly, he wanted urgently to get out of this room, the bill for which might or might not have been paid. For a moment he imagined himself down at Reception, asking about it, offering to pay. Even a man with an ingrained habit of honesty could see that was a stupid vision. It wasn't going to happen.

Ready to leave, he knew the smart thing would be to make sure there was no one in the corridor, but didn't. Peeking round the corner of a door offended his sense of who he was. Fortunately, when he opened the door and stepped out, the corridor was empty except for a house-keeper's cart piled with laundry parked against the opposite wall under a watercolour of a farmyard.

At the end of the corridor he went through a frosted glass door and came on to a landing. Glancing up, he saw a cupola of yellow glass spread above an enormous double chandelier. Now he recognised where he was: the cupola was a feature of the Hamilton Hotel. He looked over the stair rail. No one in sight. All the same, less chance of encoun-tering anyone, if he took the lift down. Maybe he should go back and find the lift. Instead, he started down the wide curving stairs two at a time, only slowing to a walk on the last flight. As he came into the hall, voices murmured from the far end where morning coffee was being served. He passed the bar on his left, early morning empty. There was someone behind the reception desk, maybe more than one, he didn't look. The doorman, whom Meldrum had ques-tioned at times over the years, was lifting a case into a holding area by the door. The man didn't look up. Next moment, he was out in the street, dazzled by the sun, the sudden uproar of traffic, safe from the scandal of a voice calling behind him. Being morbidly honest, *scandal* was how he thought of it, though he'd been a policeman for a long time and knew there were worse things, many worse crimes, than ducking a hotel bill.

Even although he was already late for work and his flat was half an hour's walk away, he needed to shave and change his shirt. All the same, when the paper vendor in Leith Walk waved he crossed the road to him.

'You've been in the wars,' Old Jimmy said, deftly folding the paper one handed.

Meldrum stopped himself from putting a hand to the clotted mass of hair behind his ear. He'd have to wash that, clean it up, something else to do before he went into work.

'You want paid for that?'

'Just for the paper. I've nothing else you'd want at the minute.'

'I should tell you to fuck off,' Meldrum said, handing over a coin. 'I don't have time to waste.'

He was turning away when Old Jimmy said, 'Anyway, looks like you gave as good as you got.'

'Come again.'

'Some mess.'

At the old man's nod, Meldrum saw that the knuckles on his right hand were cut. Same with the left, with the addition that two on that hand looked as if they might be broken. In a fight, that had always been his vulnerable hand.

'Looks like you've given somebody a hell of a doing,' Old Jimmy said.

Chapter Three

Meldrum was able, after changing and cleaning himself up, to arrive at work not more than an hour and a half later than usual. As he made his way through reception, the desk sergeant made a careful point of being busy so as not to have to see him. Since he had a habit of observation Meldrum noted this, and was puzzled by it. Through the swing door, he started to lope up the stairs, on the theory life was too short to wait for the lift. Anyway, it wasn't his day for lifts. Going along the second floor corridor, it occurred to him that he'd had no breakfast. Immediately, as if it had been lying in wait, he was ambushed by hunger. He thought of getting a bacon roll from the canteen and broke step; then changed his mind and carried on. Bobbie Shields, who was laying a bundle of folders on Meldrum's desk in front of the window, turned round startled.

'Is it finished already?' he asked.

'McArdle in among that lot?'

'He's there.'

Meldrum sat down and stared at the folders. A bacon roll and coffee, that would help. 'What's finished?'

Shields looked suspicious, like a man who suspected a trap was being laid for him. 'What?'

'You said something was finished. When I came in.'

'The budget panic. I thought the meeting would go on longer.'

Christ! Meldrum thought.

'That meeting,' Meldrum said.

The one Fleming had called to explain management thinking on the budget overrun. The one Meldrum had forgotten about.

'What happened?' Shields wondered. 'Did he pass the hat round?'

'No idea. I missed it.'

'Christ!' Shields said. Tone suggesting, what a bad idea.

Later that morning, Assistant Chief Constable Fleming struck the same note.

'Did you ever hear the expression, his coat is hanging on a shoogley peg?' Originally from Glasgow, Fleming, of the variety of accents possible to that city, had one of the genteel variety, a grudging emission out of a button mouth in a round face under an edge of thinning red hair. 'That was a top priority meeting this morning. I'm talking about the one that finished half an hour ago. No excuses accepted, people with a heavier caseload than yours were there, because they knew they had to be.'

Meldrum looked thoughtful. 'Jacket,' he said. 'The way I heard it was, his jacket's on a—'

'Not his, *your* jacket, coat, whatever you like. On a *very* shoogley peg. Half out the wall, right now, at this moment in time.'

Wary of Meldrum, whom he'd no idea how to handle, Fleming had unthinkingly acquired the habit of avoiding him as much as possible. As a result, once started he'd difficulty in stopping. At one point, he asked, 'Don't you think money matters?' Taking the question as rhetorical, Meldrum said nothing. They looked at one another for a while. For want of a more forceful tactic, it seemed Fleming had settled for waiting him out.

Tired of the silence, Meldrum said, 'I'd like to take another look at Hugh McArdle.'

'What for?'

Meldrum was surprised. It wasn't in his scheme of things that the ACC could be sufficiently on top of his job to recall McArdle without prompting. Could someone have warned Fleming it might come up? But the only one who knew about his renewed interest in McArdle was DS Bobbie Shields. So QED? Equals paranoia, Meldrum told himself, and said, 'For one thing, Harkness's attitude doesn't add up.'

'Harkness?'

Reassured by this display of ignorance, Meldrum explained, 'The hotel manager.'

'I know who he is. Attitude? What attitude?'

'He hasn't fired McArdle.'

'Why should he?'

Meldrum suppressed the first answer that occurred to him. Asking your boss not to be a stupid cunt wasn't ever a good move. Instead he tried to keep it simple. 'Because he's confessed to murder?'

'Which we know, I mean know perfectly certainly that he didn't commit.' Fleming's frown suggested Meldrum's tone might have been too consciously patient.

'Which one would that be, sir?'

'What?'

'He's confessed three times.' Meldrum raised his fist and

31

put up a finger for each name. 'Sylvia Marshall. Madge Chambers. Kitty Grant.'

'And we're as certain McArdle didn't do the last two as we were certain he didn't do the first one.' And when Meldrum hesitated, 'Or have I missed something?'

'He had an alibi for Sylvia Marshall. I was told about it within an hour of him making the confession. We checked it and he was out the door with a warning about wasting police time. I wasn't involved with the other two. But it's my impression that he wasn't taken seriously when he made his confession to the Chambers killing. And when he came in again after Kitty Grant was murdered—' Meldrum shook his head. 'McArdle was a joke by that time. The only way to describe it. You only had to listen to the way Barry Gowdie and his team talked about him to know that.'

'I'm not clear what point you're making. Maybe I should say I'm trying not to see it. If it's what I'm afraid it might be. For your sake, afraid, you understand.' Fleming's button mouth was puckered tight with disapproval. Like a tiny pink arsehole, Meldrum thought. 'Are you suggesting Detective Superintendent Gowdie was negligent?'

'Not for a moment.' That came quick and pat. Tactically, Meldrum even managed to inject a touch of righteous shock into the denial. This wasn't the first time in his career he'd been involved in a scene like this. 'All I'm saying is that these are open files. No one's been caught for any of these murders. I'd like to take another look.'

'Why?'

'To check out McArdle one more time.'

'We've been over that! What possible reason could you have?'

Meldrum took the plunge. 'The alibi McArdle had for

the Marshall girl's death. Harkness gave him it.' And added incautiously, 'The hotel manager.'

'Oh, *that* Harkness!'

'It looked perfectly straightforward at the time. But that was eight years ago.'

'You didn't like not getting a result,' Fleming said. 'You think any of us do? I'd like nothing better than to keep every case active. But you've said nothing that would justify me deciding to commit man-hours to an eight-year-old murder. And whether you like it or not, money matters,' Fleming said, repeating himself. 'At the end of the day every decision I make is a budget decision. You know how much the new computer data base is going to cost over the next five years — or you would, if you hadn't missed the meeting.'

And so it went on, too long for both of them, so much too long for Meldrum that, grilling over, he was out of the building like a claustrophobic, drawing DS Shields in his slipstream.

'Where we off to?' Bobbie Shields didn't ask so much as ponder the question, as if challenged he might claim only to have been thinking aloud.

As Meldrum searched for a plausible destination, he was distracted by the fat sergeant easing one haunch up off the passenger seat to leak a slow-time-passing fart.

'For God's sake!'

'What's up?'

'Global warming.'

'I'm not with you.'

'I should be so lucky.' He checked the traffic from his left and pulled out into the street.

After a pause, Shields said again. 'Where we off to then?' But without waiting for an answer exclaimed, 'That looks a sore one.' He nodded at Meldrum's left hand where it gripped the wheel. There was a livid swelling around the big knuckle at the root of the second finger.

'Hamilton Hotel,' Meldrum said. As soon as the words were spoken, he was pleased with the idea. Why not? he thought.

'How you mean? You hurt your hand there?'

'Of course not,' Meldrum said calmly. He felt better, coming awake on a buzz of energy. As far as he knew, he'd got out of the hotel this morning without being seen. He'd have to go back to it some time. Why not today? 'We'll go and talk to McArdle.'

Chapter Four

Not too long ago, the Hamilton, though a taxi ride from the centre, had been the most expensive hotel in the city. It had slid gradually down the rankings since then, and with the *Scotsman* newspaper building, a monument to Victorian self-confidence, being made over into yet another hotel and one in which rumour had it a penthouse suite would cost £800 a night, it was set to slip still further. Its reputation too was tarnishing, scarcely perceptibly still perhaps, but always edging towards the watershed moment when the change would become one more fact of the city's life. In the meantime, its bars in the evening had too many expensively dressed women drinking on their own, languid, alert.

It still, however, could boast of kilted Hugh McArdle, resplendent from the cascade of white ruffles at his throat to the high polish on his brogues. Holiday albums and video cassettes in the Far East and across North America recorded him alone in his splendour, typically with head thrown back after the fashion of the stag at bay, or posed with guests, often two young women, one giggling on either side, or in the midst of a glee club or quest of golfers; and more often than not *HAMILTON HOTEL* could be discerned in the background etched in a script almost heraldic on the glass panels of the entrance. Over six feet, barrel-chested, still with a full head of red hair though somewhere in his fifties, with the thick pale skin that goes with that colouring and a drinker's nose for contrast: the doorman was an institution.

As they got out of the car in the park at the back of the hotel, Shields said, 'Are you sure it's all right talking to him here?'

Meldrum hit the remote and watched the lights round the car flash as it locked. When he'd done that, he dropped the key ring in his side pocket. He put his head on one side and studied the detective sergeant.

'Come again.'

'The man's at his work.'

'So?'

'So what are we going to do? Try talking to him while he's showing the bus parties in?'

'Fancy doing that, do you?'

'Fuck's sake!' Shields said.

Meldrum let him go half a dozen steps then said, 'Other way.'

Shields looked round. 'What?'

'We'll go in the back.' He nodded to the entrance at the rear of the park. They walked towards it in silence. As they went up the steps, he said, 'Sneak up on him.'

Shields, well liked in the canteen, a man who enjoyed a laugh, glanced at him sharply. One of his difficulties was that he'd never cracked the code of when Meldrum might be joking, if he ever was.

Through the swing doors, they came into a dully lit empty area with a row of lifts facing them and a corridor to the left that, according to the sign, led to one of the function suites. They went the other way, passing the health club complex and a flight of stairs down to the basement. Through another set of doors where, emerging into the lounge, to weave between leather couches among the discreet clatter of morning coffee, felt like coming from the wings on to a stage flooded with light.

McArdle was in the reception area. He was leaning across the desk as if trying to whisper in the ear of the blonde receptionist. Waiting for him to turn, Meldrum felt a touch of bravado at being back in the hotel so soon, a tightening of the stomach. At once, that he should feel like that annoyed him, struck him as stupid. After all, what had he done? Slept with a woman. Even for a policeman, all of them paranoid about such risks, what could it matter?

Shields said, 'He's not going to be happy.'

As he spoke, the receptionist saw them.

McArdle turned. He looked surprised, which was understandable. It was the look of excitement they hadn't expected.

'How did you manage that? We're just this minute off the phone!' He'd been born in Glasgow, but years of role playing the Highland body servant had given him just the suggestion of a lilt. 'Mr Harkness is waiting for you.' He lowered his voice to a discreet rumble. 'He's upstairs with the body.'

Chapter Five

A little dapper man, an under manager called Simms, whose usual responsibility was for the bars and function suites, went up with them in the lift. He'd reminded Meldrum, who, as it happened, hadn't forgotten, that they'd met before.

'A sudden death is always sad,' he said.

Meldrum grunted. He was watching the floor numbers and trying to remember how many flights of stairs he'd run down when he fled the hotel.

'How do you mean sudden?' Shields asked. 'What happened?'

'They're always sudden. Seriously ill people don't book into a hotel. Not in my experience, and that goes back to just after my sixteenth birthday.'

The lift doors opened. As they came out, Shields said, 'How many deaths do you reckon you've come across then?'

'Oh, it's not a common occurrence. All the same, having said that . . .'

But Meldrum had stopped listening. It was the same corridor he'd walked down that morning. He hadn't memorised any door numbers, but there wasn't any doubt about it. There were paintings at intervals, little landscapes in pastel shades, and as he approached the third one he could make out a farmyard with a tractor and a cow looking over a byre fence. The door opposite was the room he'd wakened in that morning.

'. . . There was one man who took tablets. He didn't want his family to find him, so he did it in a hotel room.'

Could the woman have come back? Was she the one who was dead? His stomach tied itself in a knot of apprehension.

'It didn't occur to him staff might have feelings. The girl who found him—'

Him.

'Who found him?' Meldrum asked. They were almost at the door. Number Four One Six. Without thinking, he stopped, waiting for Simms to open it and lead them in.

Turning in surprise, asking, 'Sorry?' Simms paused.

'This it?' Shields asked. Puzzled, he glanced from Simms to Meldrum.

'No, no,' Simms said. 'Four One Seven. Didn't they say?'

'I don't think so,' Shields said.

Simms led the way to the next door and after giving it four spaced knocks, firm yet unassertive, ushered them in ahead of him.

Harkness, the hotel manager, had been looking out of the window. As they came in, he turned and said, 'Thank you for being so quick.'

'We didn't—' Shields began, and broke off, as if deciding it wasn't his job to explain they hadn't been called to this death.

Same colour of curtains, same decoration, same furniture: to Meldrum the room was horribly familiar. Even the bed

40

looked the same, except that it was made, the covers drawn tight; and that neatness was disconcerting, too, for it was where he might have expected to see a body.

'How is Mrs Torrance?' Harkness was asking.

'I haven't seen her. I was in the Islay Suite when McArdle passed on your message,' Simms said; adding with just a touch of the busy man's sense of grievance, 'We've a wedding there at two and after last night, as you know—'

'She was badly shaken,' Harkness said.

His voice quivered, which surprised Meldrum. Previous meetings had suggested the manager kept everything, including his own emotions, under control. Word was he ran a tight ship. Certainly, he looked the part. In his late forties, tall, well dressed, the expense not in the discretion of the suit so much as in the shirt, tie, shoes, the watch on his wrist. Now, however, sweat shining on his upper lip, he appeared crumpled, like a man who'd slept in a chair and been shaken awake. Yet it was hardly possible that he hadn't encountered situations like this before. He was another whose whole working life had been spent in hotels.

'This Mrs Torrance — she was the one who found the body?'

'One of our housekeepers. She supervises this floor.' Harkness looked at his watch. 'I came up at once. She was in a dreadful state. Under the circumstances, not surprising.'

And again, Meldrum wondered where the body was. No question of it not being here, they would have known better than to move it. He glanced in the direction of the bathroom, and looking back at Harkness found the manager nodding in confirmation. With that, he had a vision of a fat man dying on the toilet. A big hotel breakfast, sausages, bacon, fried mushrooms, plenty of butter on the toast, that could do it after a business dinner the previous night and a drinking bout before turning in; it happened all the time. Nothing to do with what might or might not have been going on in a neighbouring room. Life was full of coincidence.

'In there, yes.' Harkness wafted the back of his hand in indication. 'Do you mind if I don't? Once was enough.'

So he was a man who didn't like bodies; that was all right; it explained the sweat.

Meldrum nodded reassuringly, went over and opened the bathroom door.

Unprepared, he stared at a rusty brown splash on the shower curtain, seeing the same colour slashed on the mirror over the basin, and then in streaks and smears high on the wall. Last of all, by some self-protective reflex, saw a stiffened pool of it, recognised from the first as dried blood, spread out from the head of a man lying on the floor. The body, fully dressed, wearing a jersey and jeans, lay on its back with the legs twisted round the toilet pedestal. One arm had been thrown up and might have protected the face, except that it bent away at the wrong angle as if broken just above the elbow. In the same instant that Meldrum took all of this in, he realised that he'd opened the door without gloves.

Turning back, gesturing Shields not to go in, he demanded of Harkness, 'Why the hell didn't you say it was a murder?'

'But I did. I told your lot when I phoned. And about the fight.'

'What fight?'

'Last night. Coming up for midnight, as far as I can gather. A guest entering from the car park saw two men fighting outside the lifts. I mean physically. I'm told she was almost hysterical. It seems to have been a real battle.'

A perverse impulse made Meldrum rub a hand along his jaw, the left hand, so that the broken knuckles showed.

'If one of the two was—' Harkness gestured towards the bathroom, 'the other one is the murderer.'

Before either of them could say anything else, there was a tap on the door and a stocky man in a worn leather jacket took a step into the room and stopped so abruptly he was bumped by the taller man behind him.

The police who'd been summoned had finally, it seemed, put in an appearance.

Chapter Six

However puzzled to find a senior officer already on the scene, DS Cobb and DC Stratton made the natural assumption that he had a right to be there.

'Violent death, no question,' Meldrum told them. 'Give me a minute,' and he turned back to Harkness. 'This room was occupied last night? Right. Who by?'

'It was registered to a Patrick Hennessy. Just for an overnight stay. That's all I can tell you. When I was told – what had happened – I checked quickly before I came up . . . to see for myself.' Though he still showed signs of shock, his colour had come back and his voice was firm and business-like. With a glance towards the closed door of the bathroom, he said, 'Poor man.'

'Has anyone identified the body? That it is the man who took the room.'

Harkness shook his head. 'I took it for granted – who else could it be? It was a single reservation. Just for a Mr Hennessy.'

'Perhaps we could confirm that, sir. If you would go down with Sergeant Cobb, he could check the address given for Mr Hennessy. It would be useful if there was a phone number, too. Depending how the booking was made?'

'Yes, of course.' Harkness by now seemed fully recovered; recovered sufficiently to exert himself. 'If Mr Simms comes with us, he can help the sergeant with all of that.' He glanced at his watch. 'A place like this doesn't run by itself, I'm afraid.'

'Of course,' Meldrum said drily. 'And if Mr Simms finds us a room to talk to people we can make a start.' To Cobb, he said, 'We'll need a list of all the guests who were here overnight. The names of the reception staff who were at the desk yesterday. Bar staff last night, porters, waiters – anyone who might have come in contact with the murdered man. Once we get a photograph, we can try them with that. Restaurant staff, too, if there's any dinner booking.'

Harkness said, 'This is going to cause so much disruption.' He made a small distressed gesture.

As if he hadn't heard, Meldrum went on, 'There's breakfast staff, too, of course, downstairs or bringing it up to the room. But I've a feeling he was dead by then.' He nodded to Shields. 'ME and the technicians – get them here, then you and DC – what is it?'

'Stratton, sir.'

'You and Stratton start knocking doors along this corridor. Any disturbance from yesterday evening through to this morning. Any contact with the occupant of this room – at any time, did they see anyone going in or out of this room. You know the drill.'

'Can I ask—?' Harkness began.

'Chances are, this time of the day,' Meldrum said, 'the rooms'll be empty. Guests away seeing the sights or paid their bills and moved out. But anybody we catch in now, saves time later.'

'I know it has to be done, you don't need to tell me how serious this is — but, even so' — Harkness tried to appeal directly to Shields — 'without too much of a commotion? Please?'

Shields, however, frowning, chewing his lip, still had his gaze fixed on Meldrum.

As for Cobb and Stratton, like most of his colleagues, they found Meldrum formidable. When he started issuing orders, they'd come to an unspoken decision to keep their heads down and get on with it. If it occurred to either or both of them that there had been some kind of muddle, after all that wasn't unheard of in the police. As with most organisations, muddles got sorted, in their experience, sooner or later. Meantime, they let themselves be shepherded out with the others into the corridor. For the specialist teams when they arrived, dealing with a hotel room with its misleading traces of irrelevant previous occupants would be difficult enough. Already the crime scene had been compromised by all of them tramping round it without protective clothing or overshoes.

For the moment at least, the death in the hotel was Meldrum's to investigate.

As the others went off, he was left with Shields and Stratton. The fat detective sergeant, having finished his phoning, was knocking on the door of Four One Eight. Getting no answer, he gave up and came past Meldrum to try Four One Six. Instead of knocking at once, he turned and asked, 'What the hell are we doing?' Stratton, who'd been sent to the far end of the corridor and was working his way back, was out of earshot.

'You're seeing if anybody's heard anything,' Meldrum said. 'I'm going back in here to check the place out.'

'You know what I mean.'

'Put it another way. You're doing what you're told.'

'Absolutely,' Shields said. 'If there's any shit over this, that's exactly what I've been doing. Just what I was told.'

Meldrum nodded. He knew he should do what he'd said, go back in and check the bedroom. Shields hesitated, then finally knocked the door. Still Meldrum waited. That morning in the room behind that door he'd wakened naked in bed and seen a woman by the window. Even though Shields kept turning his head to glance at him, he couldn't move. He was waiting for the woman to open the door, turn her head and recognise him. Is the room paid for? he'd asked her. Not by me, she'd said and walked out, which didn't mean she hadn't come back, wasn't still staying there.

'No one there,' he heard himself saying aloud.

At his voice, Shields looked at him, then at the door.

'Don't waste time. Try to the far end, that way.' He jerked his head in the direction opposite to Stratton.

Grudgingly, Shields passed him again and knocked the door of Four One Nine. It had made sense to check the doors on either side first, now they would try the rest of the doors on either side of the corridor. So far, there had been no reply.

Meldrum went back into the murder room, closed the door behind him and stood with his eyes shut. The movement was involuntary, a sign of the tension he was under. He'd seen a lot of people with their heads in the sand and their arses in the air at one time or another. The world rolled on; like a juggernaut sometimes, not least over the ones who tried to shut it out.

He pushed the bathroom door forward, holding it by the edge, till he could see the body. Knowing who the dead man

48

was would help. Without going inside, it was hard to be sure, but there looked to be enough of the face left for identification.

Using a handkerchief, he opened the wardrobe, expecting to see clothes and perhaps a case. It was empty. He started round the room sliding open every drawer he could find. Apart from one holding the usual set of letters and envelopes, guides to the city and hotel information, all of them were empty. He'd reached the little stand by the bed, and was looking down at the Gideon bible in the drawer, when there was a tap on the door. Before he could respond, it opened and Bob Ross, the medical examiner, appeared. Behind him came three scene-of-crime officers.

'In there.' The photographer nodded and went into the bathroom.

'Morning, Jim,' Ross said. 'When I saw Sergeant Shields, I thought it might be you.' He smiled cheerfully. 'Tampering with the evidence?'

'If you can find any, I'll try.' Meldrum gestured around. 'Nothing in the wardrobe. Drawers are all empty.'

'Bit odd that, is it not? Unless somebody's dumped the body in an empty room.'

'No. Somebody was booked in for last night.'

'Same someone who's been killed?'

'Seems a reasonable assumption, but he hasn't been identified yet.'

As the SOC team started on the room behind him, he stood in the doorway of the bathroom watching as Ross crouched awkwardly in the narrow space beside the body.

'Somehow,' Ross said, 'I hadn't expected him to be fully dressed.'

'Wrapped in a bath towel, you mean?'

49

'Something like that.' Stretching, he felt with his gloved fingertips round the skull.

'Just as well he wasn't. I'm hoping he'll have something in his pockets. After you've finished with him.'

'Strange,' Ross said.

'What?'

'There's been more than one blow to the head. But the damage isn't as bad as I'd expected.'

'Bad enough. There's blood all over that wall. And on the mirror.'

'One blow took him in the middle of the face. My guess, a lot of the blood up there sprayed out of his mouth when he was hit. I can feel broken teeth. Given a weapon heavy enough to break the top of the skull, I'd have expected even more damage.'

'Not much room in here.'

'To take a full swing, you mean? I suppose that's true. All the same . . .'

'I remember my father saying, Don't choke the hammer, when I held it too far up the handle. That way you don't get the full power of the blow.'

'It could have been a hammer,' Ross said. Red cheeked, healthy and cheerful, he grinned up at Meldrum. 'Don't quote me, but if you want a bit of the art as much as science approach, this wasn't a frenzied attack. For my money, someone did just enough to kill. Enough and no more. As if it had been planned, wouldn't you say?'

Chapter Seven

———◆———

Journalists called it monstering, getting on the doorstep and demanding a story. A lot of times, surely, it must need a hard heart. But then, apart from the rich and the useless, people preferred to earn a pay packet, and what job didn't have its drawbacks? The way sensible folk looked at it, compromise made the world go round. And so on and so forth. As for hardening the heart, practice did that, and so well that on a doorstep genuine through-to-the-bone bastards and professional bastards would not be easy to tell apart.

When Meldrum came down into the lobby of the Hamilton Hotel, however, a lengthy history of previous encounters identified the man in the blue suit talking to the doorman just inside the entrance as one of those who owed their compassion by-pass to nature not nurture. In the same moment of recognition, dapper Dougie Stair tacked out from under the decorative bulk of Hugh McArdle and headed for Meldrum.

'Anything for me?' It was his standard greeting.

The toe of my boot up the crack of your arse, Meldrum thought, as he'd thought before.

'Not a thing,' he said, heading for the reception desk. 'Bob Ross is up there just now, that right?'

'Up where?'

'A man's been found dead, isn't that right?'

'You shouldn't believe everything you're told.'

He'd reached the reception desk. As he went behind it Stair's last question followed him. 'I take it you're the gaffer on this one?' The tone was perfunctory, that of a man who'd encountered the big detective too often to expect a response.

Meldrum looked back at him, breaking step, giving it a moment. Then he nodded, just once, the smallest of acknowledgements. He registered Stair's response, more puzzled than gratified at getting an answer, nodded to the receptionist and went into the narrow corridor that led to the administrative area.

Room Four One Seven was registered to a Patrick Hennessy. With the under manager Simms hovering at his back, Meldrum seated in front of a computer made a note of the details from the screen.

'I'm right it wasn't an advance booking?'

'That's right,' Simms said.

'Is that unusual?'

'Not really. Though most bookings are in advance.'

'He hasn't charged anything to the room?'

'If he had, it would be shown. Drinks, a meal, papers. We make the bill up from that.'

'And no telephone calls from his room.' It was a statement not a question. 'Do you note the time of registration?'

Simm indicated on the screen. 'Entered automatically. He signed in at eight minutes after five.'

Came in off the street, asked for a room. And then what

Went on the town, met someone, came back and got himself killed? Or went up to his room and stayed there, without a meal, waiting. Waiting for what? Someone to come? Only one thing sure, the end of the story: And got himself killed.

'Who booked him in?'

'The initials there.' He pointed to them. 'That's Theresa – the receptionist who dealt with him – Theresa Connors. She's not on this morning.'

'I'll have to talk to her.'

'She comes on at twelve. I could try her at home, but—'

'Twelve will be fine.' Part of being a good detective was knowing how to be patient. Meldrum looked at his watch. He didn't have time to be patient. 'I want to talk to the woman who found the body. The housekeeper in charge of the floor.'

'Mrs Torrance. I'm not sure where she is.'

'Could you find out? Please.'

Simms managed to look accommodating and displeased at the same time. Not an easy combination, but maybe it went with the job. 'Of course.' He hesitated as if waiting for Meldrum to get up and come with him. 'And I'll arrange a room you can use.'

'On the ground floor would be easiest.'

Under Meldrum's stare, Simms wilted and headed for the door.

'One other thing.'

'Yes?'

'What was the name of the woman who claimed she saw two men fighting last night?'

'I've no idea . . . I'll ask Mr Harkness.'

When he'd left, Meldrum turned back to the screen, scrolled up slowly, then sat back and thought for a moment.

He wasn't particularly comfortable with computers. He'd never felt any interest in having one at home. Nice thing about using them at work, if you hit the wrong button, a technician would fix it. Fortunately, without creating a crisis in police relations by wiping the Hamilton's records, he found what he was looking for straightforwardly referenced under the room number.

Four One Six. Unlike the murder room, it had been booked in advance. Occupied last night. Paid for this morning. The booking made on the Monday of that week by someone called George Rannie.

Meldrum had been expecting a woman's name. He'd been looking for the name of the woman he'd wakened up with that morning. A woman who'd behaved as if she was on her own. Apart from himself, there had been no sign of a man's presence.

In that case, who was George Rannie?

Chapter Eight

Time running out and the body not even identified yet. A phone call to the number given by Patrick Hennessy got a woman's voice on the answer machine: 'Sorry, Patrick and Lena aren't available at the moment. Please leave a message after the tone.' DS Shields had given his own name and rank and, as instructed, asked her to call the number of Meldrum's mobile as a matter of urgency. 'Great sexy voice,' he'd volunteered. 'Sounded young.' So far there had been no call back from the woman, presumably Hennessy's wife.

The narrow, meanly furnished room Simms had put at Meldrum's disposal was used by porters and kitchen staff for break times. Across a table carrying a scatter of used ashtrays, a plump woman of about thirty divided her attention between Meldrum and the clock prominently positioned on the wall to her left. It was just after twelve.

'I don't think I can tell you anything else,' Theresa Connors said. 'Mr Hennessy was alone. He came to the desk and asked for a room. I didn't see him again. Not to notice at least, so I couldn't tell you if he went out of the hotel later. If you do you're supposed to leave your key, but not everyone does.'

'Any room in particular?'

'Sorry?'

'He came to the desk and asked for a room. Was that all? He didn't have any preferences? Front or back of the hotel? Or for that floor?'

She hesitated. 'I asked him about a non-smoking room. Some people are fussy about that. He said it didn't matter.'

'And how he looked. Would you go over that for me again?'

He ignored her frown. Getting someone to repeat a description could be useful for what was added or omitted. He knew the unreliability of memory.

'Not as tall as you, but not small. Middle-sized. He'd a tan and a nice smile. Brown hair, or maybe black, I'm not sure.' As she spoke, Meldrum tried to check these generalities against his image of the dead man lying on the bathroom floor. 'And beautiful hands,' she added unexpectedly. 'Long fingers with the nails buffed and polished, you know? No rings, except a broad gold one here—' She displayed the ring finger of her left hand. 'Don't tell me, I know it's silly, all this about his hands when I can't remember the colour of his hair. But I watched as he filled in the form. I notice hands.' Getting no response to her smile, she waited, then said again, 'I can't tell you any more.'

Had the corpse worn a wedding ring? To Meldrum the hair had looked fairer than brown, but he'd seen it matted and stained with blood and that might have modified his impression. As for a tan, well perhaps, death made for other things to remark in a face.

'Is that all?' she asked. 'Saturdays are busy for us.'

He made a show of referring to a piece of paper.

'Room Four One Eight was empty last night,' he said. 'But the room on the other side, Four One Six, it was occupied.'

She shook her head. 'Was it?'

'Booked in advance by a George Rannie. He signed in last night – according to Mr Simms.' As if it was any of this woman's business how he'd learned about Rannie; why was he explaining to her? And with a lie as it happened.

'Rannie, yes. I remember, about nine o'clock.' She smiled. 'Just for the one night.'

'Was he alone?'

'He'd his wife with him.'

Husband and wife? In the same room he'd wakened in? None of it made sense. He heard himself saying, 'Obviously, we're wondering if they might have heard anything. In the next room. During the night.' His voice he thought, as if listening to someone else, was admirably steady.

And again she took this explanation at face value, not realising how uncharacteristic it was to be given one.

'It's too horrible to think about. But if they'd heard screaming, wouldn't they have phoned down, or at least said something when they checked out this morning?'

'Maybe not as definite as screaming.' Meldrum shrugged. 'But you can never tell what people will do.' And as she nodded agreement, 'What were they like? An older couple or what?'

'He was middle forties, somewhere in there.'

'And her?'

He felt his stomach tighten in expectation.

'I never saw her. He said she was waiting for him in the bar.'

'His wife.'

'So he said.' She smiled again, a small involuntary twitch of the lips.

'Not his wife, you mean?'

'Wouldn't be the first time.'

'Apart from her not coming to the desk with him, did you have any reason for thinking that he wasn't telling the truth?'

'No.' She frowned. 'I'm being silly. Of course not. No reason at all.'

He watched her for a moment in silence. 'So what happened?'

'Happened?'

'You gave him the room key. Did he have luggage?'

'A bag over his shoulder.'

'Did he go to the bar?'

'I suppose so.'

'You didn't notice?'

'There's always something, you have to answer the phone, someone else comes to the desk. Always something to distract you. Like I said, we're kept busy.'

'He didn't eat dinner in the hotel.'

She misunderstood, thought he was asking a question. 'I'd have to check the computer. If he ate in the restaurant or had room service, it would be on his bill.'

'There's nothing about dinner on the bill.'

'I suppose he didn't then.'

'Nine o'clock isn't late,' Meldrum said. 'You'd think he – and his wife – would want to eat something.' And catching her little private smile. 'Even if they ran upstairs and jumped into bed. That can work up an appetite.'

'Maybe he paid for dinner in the restaurant. It wouldn't be on his bill, not unless he charged it to his room.'

58

'Maybe.'

'Right enough, it wouldn't be usual. Usual thing with a guest having dinner would be to charge it to the room.' Offering that with the air of someone going the extra mile to be helpful, she followed it with a hint of impatience, 'Does it matter?'

It did to him. Investigating a murder at the same time as trying to make sense of what had happened to him that day was disorienting.

'Probably not.' Catching her glance again at the clock, he said, 'Forget Mr Rannie. Come back to Patrick Hennessy. That description you gave of him wasn't much good, was it?'

'It's not so easy!'

'I'm a policeman, I know that. That's why we have ways of helping people remember—'

'You mean someone to draw a picture or those photographs they use?'

She sounded interested, almost enthusiastic. She must have seen it on television. He wanted to say to her: We're not looking for Mr Hennessy, you stupid bitch. We have a good idea where he is, like upstairs, dead.

He said: 'It's surprising what people remember. They can't give you a description, but it doesn't mean they couldn't recognise someone. If they saw the person again. We meet somebody, we take a photograph, carry it around in our heads, don't even know we've done it.'

'I know what you mean.'

'Like Patrick Hennessy.'

'Oh, if I saw him—' She broke off, suddenly uncertain.

'Would you try?'

'But he's *dead*.'

'That's what we have to establish. There's been no identification yet.'

'Someone else must have seen him. When he paid his bill—'

'No one's paid the bill for Four One Seven.'

'I've never seen a dead body. There's no way I'm going to look at one that's had its head bashed in.'

Jungle drums. The speed with which bad news travelled could still impress him.

'His head? Who gave you that idea?'

'Mr McArdle told me about it soon as I got here.'

'He shouldn't pass on rumours.'

'And that you'd want to speak to me.' A light broke on her face. 'He could do it.'

'Do what?'

'Hugh McArdle never forgets a face. It's a trick of his. Guests love it. He'll say, nice to see you again, even if it's been years. He'll identify your body.'

'As Patrick Hennessy?' Meldrum wondered sceptically.

'Yes,' she said. 'He spoke to him. I don't mean just, Good afternoon, sir, I mean a real talk. Standing in the hall, before Hennessy came to the desk.'

'As if he knew him?'

She hesitated. 'Know? Maybe, if he'd been here before as a guest. I mean, he might have been. Hundreds of people come in and out, I don't remember everyone who comes here. But what I'm saying is, Hugh McArdle talked to him – and even if it was only about the weather, *he'*d remember.'

Chapter Nine

'Sweet fleshed,' Hugh McArdle said of himself, in explanation of why despite the kilt and the heavy wool jacket which went with it and the heat of the lift into which the two of them were crowded, he gave off not a trace of an odour to cause offence. He held his jacket back with two hands, showing his shirt unmarked under the arms. 'Not that guests think about it, but it's one of the reasons they like me. They'd notice quick enough if I needed a deodorant. Size I am, I'd have to ladle the stuff on. You know that deodorant smell, brothel smell I call it, makes some people feel sick. Thank God, I don't sweat. I asked an American doctor about it once and he said I'd bet you don't have any body hair. If I bet against you on that one, I'd lose, I told him. Thought so, he said. He was an endocrinologist, one of their top men, they were here from New York for a conference. Do you know what an endocrinologist does, Mr Meldrum? . . . I didn't till he told me about it. Working in this place is an education.'

Meldrum disliked the man the way a dog dislikes a cat. As they stepped out of the lift, he asked, 'What were you talking to Patrick Hennessy about? Yesterday, when he arrived. Don't shake your head, you were seen.'

'Seen? That would be Theresa. That little girl has eyes in the back of her head.' He waved Meldrum ahead of him through the swing door into the fourth floor corridor. 'Talking about? It's a cold day or a warm one. Nice to see you again, sir, or enjoy your first visit. He's looking very well or I never change. *About* the usual things.' He patted the thick swag of his belly complacently. 'People like to talk to me.'

Meldrum stopped. They were halfway along the corridor to the murder room. Turning his back on the uniformed constable standing guard outside it, he said softly, 'Don't play the fucking ghillie with me. How well did you know Hennessy?'

McArdle made a face, the corners of his mouth turning down, so that for an instant he resembled a vast, curiously bloated child. 'He's stayed here before, more than once. Like I always say, I remember faces. No need to get on to me.' But then, as though a thought had struck him, his expression altered. The child smiled. 'You know I only kill lassies.'

Meldrum stared at him. 'Plenty of time,' he said, 'I'm going to make plenty of time for you.'

As they went into the room, the constable shut the door behind them. Scene-of-crime officers were still at work in the bathroom and gathering fibres from the carpet around the bed. The medical examiner Bob Ross was looking down into a long box of brown plastic open and placed on the floor at his feet. The body lay on its back inside, the face turned to the left profile.

'I'd almost given up on you,' Ross said.

'We've been trying to contact the wife.'

'If she's out shopping, I hope she's enjoying it. She'll have a nasty surprise when she gets home.'

As he was saying this, Ross had to step back to make room. Even slightly crouched, head bent to peer down at the body, Hugh McArdle dwarfed the medical examiner with his bulk.

After a glance, he looked up and asked Ross, 'How do you mean shopping?'

'A joke,' Ross said. 'Not funny if you know him. I take it you know him?'

'Oh, I know him,' McArdle said. 'But he doesn't have a wife.'

Chapter Ten

Meldrum watched the shop fronts go by, and wondered at his reaction to the body being taken out of the Hamilton Hotel in a brown plastic shell. It wasn't something he hadn't seen before, this manner of transporting a body from the place of its violent death to where it would be sawed, sliced and ransacked in pursuit of some part of whatever the truth might be. Yet now, showing no emotion, eyes on the changing street, he grued at the memory of the plastic container. First job after school, he'd worked as a joiner. He'd served his time and become a craftsman, and might still have been in that trade if there hadn't been a slump — one of the sort that hits the building industry at regular intervals even in reasonably good times. That was when he'd joined the police. Though that had changed his life, his knowledge of good and evil, his way of looking at the world, the world's of looking at him, he'd never forgotten what his first job had taught him. Under your fingertips as you worked, good wood of the kind the best furniture was made of reminded you that it came from the living tree. Plastic was numb under the fingers; smelling of nothingness, it smelt of something worse than death.

'How come?' Shields asked, slowing the car to catch the lights on green as he turned into Frogston Road.

It was a good question. Since wakening in the hotel bedroom that morning, he'd been on a roller coaster with no time to think. Coming back to the hotel to interview McArdle, he'd stumbled into the killing in room Four One Seven and, without any authority for doing so, had taken charge. Once ACC Fleming caught up with what he'd done, there had to be more than an even chance he'd be taken off the case as a matter of discipline. Certainly, if he were in Fleming's shoes, Meldrum thought, that's what he would do. You couldn't run an organisation without discipline. Anyway, he believed in the need for authority, all that stuff, to the extent that his daughter Betty at some point during her university years had called him 'a typical fascist policeman'; in the heat of an argument, of course, but he'd been surprised at how angry it made him, not that he'd shown it, and hurt too, though admitting that had come much later and naturally only to himself. So how come? How come five years ago this 'typical policeman' had got the idea into his head that a prisoner halfway through a life sentence for murder was the victim of a miscarriage of justice? Call it being in the wrong place at the wrong time: call it integrity: call it his lousy luck. He'd broken ranks. A political naïve, he'd taken on a politician with something to hide and learned, whoever else suffered, the whistleblower always would. He'd been grateful to keep his job, and only gradually understood he'd risen as far as he ever would.

'What's the joke?' Shields asked.

'What?'

'I ask you how come I'm driving, and suddenly you're having a smile to yourself.' It was an old grievance of Shields that Meldrum, who also hated being a passenger, always pulled rank and drove himself.

'Was I?'

'A sour wee smile.'

'Can't think why,' Meldrum said, in a tone that closed off any follow-up.

Glancing to the side, he saw that they were passing the Princess Mary Rose.

Nodding at the hospital, Shields said, 'I'm going back for more physio. They were great the last time.'

'What last time?'

'After the car crash! I told you. I had to have physio.'

'Right,' Meldrum said vaguely.

'Christ!' Shields muttered soft indignation to himself. 'I've fixed up to go back. My neck's been bothering me.'

'You should lose weight,' Meldrum said.

A second set of lights and they were heading towards IKEA at Straiton and out of town.

After miles of silence, Shields who'd been whistling, more or less softly, less rather than more tunefully, almost as if inviting a protest, gave up and remarked, 'I've always hated this bit. I can still remember the first time. This old sergeant gave me a bit of paper with an address and told me what I'd to do. I went on a bike, you believe that? Can't remember why, short-handed, royal visit in Edinburgh, some bloody crap or other. I cycled up the hill into the scheme in Tranent, parked the bike at the kerb, went up the path and chapped the door. This old guy came to the door and when he saw me he gave me a big smile. I don't know why. Anybody with any sense knows a policeman at the door's bad news. And how many folk do we knock up don't hate you on sight, doesn't matter what you've come for? I think it was that big stupid grin of his that's stuck it in my head. As if I'd come to tell him he'd won the lottery. Not that there was any lottery then. Got his coupon up more like in those days. It was a nice day too. I could smell the flowers in the garden. Mr Johnson? *Yes.* Still with the grin. I've bad news for you. His son had been killed on his motor bike. Do you know what he said? *But we bought him it for his birthday.* Turned out he was only seventeen.'

Calling at a house to tell a father his son was dead. A death knock job, the newspaper guys called it. The kind of job that went more often than not with a day of bright sunshine, a day like this.

They came off the main road on to a secondary road and then at a junction went left along a road between thick straggling hedges.

'Better not meet somebody coming the other way,' Shields said.

'It's wide enough.'

'See the ditch?' On the passenger side, narrow but deep at the foot of the hedge for winter drainage. 'Get two wheels in that and we're in trouble,' and mumbled as if to himself, 'even more trouble.' It was the first indication he'd given since the hotel of his unhappiness with what they were doing.

Meldrum said nothing. He knew as well as Shields he'd put the sergeant in an awkward spot. Just obeying orders hadn't worked too well as an excuse at Nuremberg. On the other hand, shopping a fellow officer to the powers that be . . . Back to the fate of the whistleblower . . .

'You're smiling again.'

Meldrum folded the map on his knee. 'From here we keep our eyes open.'

Not that there was much to see: hedges, an occasional glimpse of fields, at the crown of each rise a view of low rolling hills. They went by a field of stubble waiting for the plough and then one with jumps laid out and a blanketed horse grazing under a tree.

'Left now.'

An even narrower road which after a hundred yards went between two stone posts that must once have held a gate and widened at once into a parking space set before the low frontage of a single storey house. They pulled in beside a car already parked there, an H registration Granada badly in need of a wash. Meldrum got out of the car expecting to see the door open or a face at a window. To his right stood a barn-like construction with ancient whitewash peeling from its walls and a roof of rusted corrugated iron. Two sagging doors, one pushed half open, added to the air of dereliction. From what he could see, the dim interior was empty apart from what looked like a stack of logs piled in the middle of the floor. He was struck by the silence.

'You wouldn't think we were only half an hour from Princes Street,' Shields said.

As if in answer, a voice called, 'Round here!'

Walking to the end of the house, Meldrum saw a thickset man with a shock of white hair about twenty yards away. The garden stretched down to a high hedge and there were enough trees to make a small orchard, which must have hidden him from them as they pulled into the house. He was dragging a wheelbarrow over brick edging on to the path. Seeing them appear, he nodded over his shoulder, got the barrow where he wanted it and came towards them wiping his hands on his trousers.

'You'll have to get someone to bring me back.'

'I'm sorry,' Meldrum said; 'you are Mr Wemyss?'

There was an odd brief pause, then the man said, 'Hector Wemyss.' He put the faintest possible stress on the given name. Close up, though he had a healthy outdoors look, a touch of yellow in the eyes and loose skin under the neck suggested a man much older than he had seemed at first glance. The neck was always a giveaway.

'Of course, someone will bring you home. I wouldn't want you to drive under the circumstances.'

'Under one set of circumstances, it wouldn't be a problem.'

He seemed very calm. So much so that Meldrum wondered what the relations had been between father and son.

'Circumstances?'

'If this dead man you want to show me isn't Archie.'

Something in the tone of instruction brought back to Meldrum a schoolmaster he'd suffered under as a child, a beak-nosed pedagogue who came from some windswept bare place about Aberdeen.

'I hope not.'

'But you believe it is.' It was rapped out uncompromisingly like an accusation.

'The doorman at the Hamilton Hotel claims to have identified him.'

'Archie hasn't stayed in a hotel, any hotel, for years. How could this man know him?'

'I gather there are sometimes articles about you in the papers. In one of them recently, there was a picture of your son. This man seems to be interested in you, and he has an unusual memory for faces.'

'I never heard such damned nonsense in my life.'

70

Not getting an instant denial, Wemyss set off round the house, taking it for granted they would follow. At the front door, saying, 'I'll get a jacket,' he went in and shut the door on them.

'Who does he think he is?' Shields asked.

'He'll be frightened.'

'He doesn't sound it.'

Meldrum shrugged and walked back to the gable end. It was a fine day. The land was flat all the way to the hills in the distance, and from this low elevation he could see over the garden to where trees went away in a long curve to the left. As he turned to go back, a little breeze stroked his face and with it he caught the sound of voices and a stir of movement, horses and riders passing close by on the far side of the hedge. Distracted, he bumped against the wall, knocking off loose flakes of yellowing whitewash.

He was brushing at the shoulder of his jacket as he came round the corner and saw that the door had been opened. An old woman bent over a stick was leaning out. Yellow white hair hung in long unbrushed strands around her face. The hands clutched on the top of the stick were twisted in arthritic knots. She was confronting Shields, who'd retreated back a step. Her face had the deep lines of someone in habitual pain.

'This one,' she nodded at Shields, 'tells me you're police. Is that true?'

Her eyes startled him, very blue, fierce and alert, not faded at all, the eyes of a young woman.

'Detective Inspector Meldrum. Mrs Wemyss?'

'Did he know you were coming? Is that why he was waiting outside? What's it about?'

71

Fixed by those young eyes, he could find nothing to say. Wemyss came into the corridor pulling on his jacket. When he saw his wife in the doorway, he became excited. He hurried towards them, struggling to free an arm entangled in a sleeve.

'They've come to see me about the car,' he said.

'About the car?'

As an excuse, it was absurd. What could there be about his car, presumably the old Granada beside which they'd parked, that would make two policemen in plainclothes come to see him? All the same, the fierce eyes wavered from Meldrum's, drifting it seemed to his shoulder, perhaps to the patch of white from the wall, before she turned and pulled with one knotted hand at her husband's sleeve as if in a futile effort at helping him.

'I'm going into town with them. I'll tell you about it when I get back. You'll be all right on your own?'

'I'm not helpless.'

'I know.' He buttoned his jacket. He hadn't taken off the bulky jersey he'd been wearing in the garden. He unfastened the jacket again.

'How will you get home?'

'They'll give me a lift back.'

His wife looked to Meldrum for confirmation. He nodded.

'Yes,' she said.

And all this for an old Granada? Those fierce intelligent eyes made Meldrum wonder how she could accept this absurdity, and then wonder if accepting it was easier for her than asking what other reason there might be.

'I won't be long,' Wemyss said. He got into the back of the car and Shields went in on the driver's side again.

The old woman asked, 'Do you have the remotest idea who you are taking off with you?'

Looking at her over the car, his hand resting on the roof, Meldrum waited.

'A great poet,' she said. 'I know you are only a policeman but, oh, it's a Philistine land.'

Not having any opinion on that, he got into the car.

Chapter Eleven

Hector Wemyss identified his son's body more like a soldier than a poet. Depending on which soldier and which poet, of course: stereotypes made for stupid thinking. In a police morgue, though, staying focussed wasn't always easy; stupid thoughts sometimes helped. Too often before, Meldrum had come here on the same errand, getting more accustomed with each visit, always with one part of him hating the last time as much as the first. If that part ever went, he'd told himself he'd get out of the job, though whether, lacking it, he would want to was a question he preferred not to think about.

'That's my son.'

Meldrum looked down at the dead man from the hotel. The mouth was closed, and some kind of dental prosthesis supplied the broken teeth. Blood had been wiped off the forehead and cheek, and a towel folded round the head hid the worst of the injuries. Even if the only intention had been to assist with identification, the effect was humane. He was struck by how dark the hair was, that kind of glossy black that keeps its colour into old age. At a guess Archie must have been about six feet; the shoulders were broad under the sheet; the neck muscular. The features of the face were strong too, a big, well-shaped nose, wide mouth. Meeting him in life, what impression would he have made? A good-looking man, yes. A determined man, a strong character? Maybe. So much depended on the eyes, the look in the eyes, the steadiness of the gaze, the expressions of the face, the mouth in repose, the readiness or the reluctance. And with all of that gone, no amount of looking would tell you anything of what the dead man had been. From this moment, Meldrum knew, a process began which at best, if you were lucky, might end in some monochrome image made out of an offered accumulation of looks, of expressions, all of them seen through someone else's eyes. It began with a name.

'Archibald. It's a family name. I had a brother Archie who died. My grandfather was called Archibald. I need to get home. You've seen my wife. I need to get back to her.'

'I have to ask you some questions.'

'Could you not ask them in the car?'

'There might not be time. You've had a shock. We don't have to sit in a police station. We could go somewhere, you could have a drink while we talk.'

'Jesus Christ, man, what are you saying? Do you think I could sit in a pub drinking whisky with you? While my wife's at home not knowing our son's dead?'

'I'm sorry.'

'. . . I think you meant well. If there wasn't time for your questions on the way back, we could stop the car and sit till you'd finished. I just have to feel I'm on my way back to her.'

Whatever Shields made of what was going on, he had at least the option of concentrating on driving. In the back Meldrum, suppressing his own anxieties, began with the basics. Archie Wemyss was thirty-seven years old. He was unmarried, didn't have a partner or regular girlfriend, had no job; at the time of his death had been living with his parents.

'What made you think it was Archie?' Wemyss asked suddenly. 'You didn't say. I never thought to ask you how you knew.'

'The doorman at the Hamilton Hotel recognised him.'

In fact, Meldrum had explained this when he'd first made contact, but it didn't surprise him to be asked again. Like a hospital doctor, he was familiar with the inattention and forgetfulness that came with shock.

'That's where he was killed?'

'One of the hotel staff found him this morning.'

'He went out early yesterday. Did I say he lived with us?'

'Yes.'

Wemyss rubbed a hand down his face. Though an old man's hand, heavy veined, it was square and strong. With arcs of black under the fingernails from working in the garden, it was more like an artisan's hand, stereotypes again, than a poet's.

'I know how it sounds. At home with his parents. That could give the wrong impression. He was my only son, I was proud of him, he captained the rugby team at school. He did well at university, took a good enough degree that he went to Cambridge afterwards. We'd no doubt he'd get his PhD. I thought I saw his life laid out in front of him. One night in November, in his second year down there, he turned up on the doorstep. He'd a case — you know, one of those Samsonite cases, his mother gave him it for his birthday the year before — with books and clothes in it. He wasn't wearing a coat, though, and it was cold that night. We woke up to snow in the morning. And that was it. I never could get to the why of it, but he never went back.'

Watching the back of Shields' head, glancing occasionally at the old man by his side, it occurred to Meldrum as he listened that the impression of his son Wemyss had disclaimed wasn't so far off the mark after all. For Archie Wemyss, something had gone badly wrong.

'That must have been what, when he was in his early twenties?'

'Yes.'

'And has he stayed with you? Since then?'

'Off and on . . . More or less.'

Meldrum tapped Shields on the shoulder. 'Can you pull over?'

'Where am I going to do that?' Shields jerked a finger one way, the other with his thumb, at the hedges so close on either side.

They were almost there. As they turned into the last narrow road, Meldrum said abruptly, 'Just stop.'

'What if somebody comes?'

'Worry if it happens.'

They stopped in sight of the entry to the house.

'Don't come in with me,' Wemyss said. 'I want to be alone when I tell her.'

'I will have to speak to your wife—'

'She couldn't tell you any more than I can.'

'All the same—'

'But not today! You could come back.'

'Not today,' Meldrum agreed. After a moment's silence, he said, 'If your wife comes into the yard, she'll see the car. We can reverse back.'

'No need. Since she had a fall, she's lost confidence. She could manage out on her own, but she won't unless Archie or I – unless I'm there.'

His battle won, the energy had drained out of Wemyss. Each word came as if against a tide of sudden overwhelming weariness.

'There are some things I have to ask.' It was an apology. Meldrum almost said, You've done well, but that would have been crass. The truth was if the old man had broken down, if he'd been less stoical, the questions would have had to wait. 'I won't keep you long.'

'If it helps to find . . .' Who killed him: Meldrum expected. Instead after a dragging pause came, '. . . why he died.'

Shields cracked the driver's window open. Somewhere in the distance a dog was barking. The sun was shining, the car was warm, but it was an autumn sun and the outside air brought a faint chill.

'You say Archie went out early yesterday. About what time would that be?'

'I didn't see him leaving, I was in the garden. But it couldn't have been much after ten. The bus goes by the road end at half past.'

Shields turned half round. It was a tight squeeze for him against the wheel. 'A bus gets along that road?' He sounded incredulous.

'Of course not. I meant where the road we left joins the one to Roslin.'

'That'd be some walk in half an hour,' Shields exclaimed, hitting the sceptical note this time.

Meldrum made no attempt to hide his irritation. This was vintage Shields. The fat sergeant would drift along, semi-detached from an enquiry until something snagged his attention, rousing him from his torpor to set off in vigorous brief pursuit, typically of an irrelevancy. Do that again,

79

Meldrum had told him, and I'll charge you with imperso-
nating a police officer. When he'd first been assigned
Shields, he'd regarded him as another signal of authority's
displeasure and been too proud to object. Then, it seemed
he'd hardly time to turn round, and three years had gone by,
and he'd got used to the fat man as he'd got used to too
many things. If that big red face, craning round to pursue the
vital question of the bus stop, had been intended as his
handicap for the Police Stakes Promotion Cup, fine by him;
he'd run his own race.

'There's a path across the fields to where it joins the
other road. It's a stiff walk, but not for Archie . . .'

Meldrum waited a moment, then asked, 'Did he tell you
where he was going?'

'It's the Edinburgh bus.'

Meldrum's scowl was involuntary; Edinburgh was a big
place. 'Would he have told your wife?'

'He was a grown man. He didn't need to tell us where he
was going.'

'So you weren't worried, when he didn't come back?'

Wemyss opened his mouth as if to speak, then fell silent.

Meldrum watched Shields easing back round, making
himself comfortable again. No doubt he'd be able to hear as
well facing front. 'He didn't have a coat when he was found,
which seems strange. It got cold later on yesterday.'

Wemyss stared. 'He had his anorak. Not one of those
cheap things. It's a Berghaus.'

'I thought you didn't see him leaving.'

'I didn't have to. It's what he wore all the time. That and
a jersey and jeans. But he wouldn't have his anorak on
indoors. Was he in a room, didn't you say he was in a room
in this hotel?'

'Nothing in the wardrobe. Come to that, there was nothing in the drawers either, nothing that could have belonged to him. As I told you, it was the Hamilton Hotel.' He waited, giving the old man time, wanting to see if he would ask the obvious question. At last, he asked it himself, 'What was he doing there?'

'I don't know.'

'You'd never heard him mention staying there?'

'No.'

'You've never heard him mention it in any connection, arranging to meet someone, anything like that?'

'No.'

'Did he often spend a night away from home?' Then forestalling Wemyss' objection, 'I know he didn't have to account for himself. But he did live with you. Most of the time, you said.'

'Most of the time,' Wemyss said. He paused, then said quietly, 'I never minded him being with us.'

It didn't answer whether Archie had been in the habit of staying out overnight. Meldrum decided to leave it. He took another tack. 'Does the name Patrick Hennessy mean anything to you?'

The old man cocked his head sharply and was still, as if listening.

'Why?'

'Obviously you know the name.'

'You could call him my son-in-law.'

'Could call him?'

'He's married to my daughter Lena. So yes, then, my son-in-law.'

The old man's tone was dry and impatient; and that was familiar, too, the way in which habits of character couldn't

81

be suppressed for long even by the trauma of grief. Oddly then he paused, not at once asking again why the name had been raised.

Meldrum took his opportunity. 'You sound as though you dislike him.'

Wemyss shook his head. 'No, that won't do. Like him or not, tell me why it would matter?'

'It was in his room in the hotel your son was found dead.' If it had been Meldrum's aim to shock, he'd succeeded. Staring at the old man's trembling lips, he smothered a tremor of shame. He said, 'We've been trying to contact him. He's not at home.'

'Was Lena with him?'

'The room was booked for Mr Hennessy. As far as we can learn, he came into the hotel alone yesterday.'

'I'll tell you where to find him.'

'You know where he works?' Involuntarily, Meldrum glanced at his watch.

'He killed Archie. Get him to admit it.'

In a familiar tingle along his nerves, Meldrum felt the blood thrill of the hunter.

'What reason have you for thinking that?'

'My reasons are my business.'

'You've made a serious accusation. You must tell me why.'

'Must? I've never taken kindly to that word.'

'You're asking me to get someone to confess to murder. Unless—'

'I've nothing more to say.'

'Unless I get help, that won't happen.'

'Is it your intention to keep me from my wife?' Wemyss made a gesture of dismissal. 'I don't think you can do that.'

Chapter Twelve

———◆———

Approaching Princes Street, Meldrum belched up a mouthful of sour acid. The last time he'd eaten had been the previous evening at Betty and Sandy's. He loved his daughter and liked her husband; so as far as that went, so far so good. The trouble had lain with his ex-wife and her new husband, two guests he hadn't expected. Before Carole's remarriage the year previously, Meldrum had met Don Corrigan only once. Finding how much there was to dislike about the man had come as a shock; and an unwelcome one since, despite everything, he'd never managed to fall out of liking with Carole; maybe even not out of love, though that was harder to assess.

'So what about it?' Shields asked, driving one-handed and scratching his crotch with the other.

'What about what?'

'Are we for the hotel again?' An unstifled yawn indicated it had been a hard day. 'Or back and start on the paperwork?'

Meldrum shook his head in disbelief. 'We,' he said slowly, a space round every word, 'are going, of course we're fucking going, to see Patrick Hennessy. Just in case

he's our murderer. Christ, man, were you listening back
there? Hennessy is the victim's brother-in-law. You no*
think that makes him worth a visit?'

'It's Saturday afternoon,' Shields said stolidly, a side-
glance checking whether the point had struck home. He
continued, if not quite with a space round every word, with a
more pondered air than usual, 'The old fellow told us where
Hennessy worked, but chances are he won't be there. Most
folk don't work on a Saturday afternoon.'

True. It was, as Shields had pointed out, Saturday
afternoon. To be even more exact, more or less in the
middle of Saturday afternoon. So, Meldrum thought, if I
left Betty and Sandy's between nine and ten o'clock last
night, that means I haven't eaten for about eighteen hours.
It was always possible, of course, that somewhere during
the lost hours, he'd had a bag of crisps; the taste left by the
acid in his mouth had a tang of salt, a touch of vinegar.
Superstitiously, he felt if he could remember the first pub,
the rest of the night might come back. On an ordinary
evening, the first would be in Leith Road, one of half a
dozen within minutes of his flat. Chances were, however,
after a couple of hours of Don Corrigan, he'd made for the
nearest bar to Betty and Sandy's flat. He thought about it
and remembered noise and smoke. Very useful for distin-
guishing between one pub and another; call it an intelligent
guess; call it an unintelligent guess. He needed time on his
own. If he could sit quietly, maybe something would come
back to him.

'There! You've missed the turn. Take the next right.'
'Eh?' Shields protested.
'Hennessy's office. It's worth a try.'
A stamp on the brake and jerk of the wheel took Shields

through the traffic lights at an amber pause in the oncoming traffic; hard to tell if it was good reactions or bad temper.

Thing was, Meldrum brooded, he never had, never before, he'd never blacked out in his life. So there was a mystery. On the other hand, there had been a few mornings these last months when he hadn't wanted to remember the night before. Would he have been able to if he'd tried?

From Shandwick Place, they wound their way into the New Town, where office space was getting scarce again after the flourish of development in and around the financial district had been absorbed. From Queen Street, they went down Hanover Street and into a cross street, heavily parked on both sides, where Shields reversed the car into the first available space.

As they got out, Meldrum said, 'I don't want to tell him for openers who was killed. If he already knows, he's our man. Let's make it hard for him. See how he reacts when we do tell him.'

The nameplate beside the entrance would have been easy to miss.

'Schwert,' Patrick Hennessy explained. 'It means sword in German.'

He was tall and good looking, with the build of an athlete and the fleshy neck of a man who ate and drank well. The young woman who'd answered the buzzer for Schwert Associates had let them into a hall with uncarpeted stone slabs and a wide stair leading to the upper floors and, presumably, the other firms listed on the nameplate. The room she'd taken them into on the ground floor, double windows looking on to the street, had a row of filing cabinets along one wall and was big enough to hold three computer stations. At one of them, a man with shirtsleeves rolled up over thick biceps glanced round and swung his chair slightly to put his back to them. It was casually done, the action glossed by making a show of reaching along the table for papers, but it reminded Meldrum of reactions he'd seen before. It was possible the man might have recognised Shields or himself; or maybe had an eye for police and preferred not to be noticed. He was wondering about that as the girl led them into a passage, past a galley kitchen visible through an open door, and showed them into a room on the left. Not as large as the room at the front, this one was still big enough to hold an oval table with eight chairs round it. Hennessy had been working at the head of the table with papers in front of him. 'I come in here for a bit of peace and quiet,' he'd explained. Charm was hard to define, but you were never in any doubt when someone had it. 'We use it for talking to clients.'

Clients for what? The name didn't give much away. Not even when Hennessy, without being asked, offered his translation.

'There isn't a Herr Schwert. Or a Mr Sword. It's an invention; you have to call a firm something. Schwert Associates has a certain air of authority and just a touch of menace, useful in our business. Wonderful language, German. Think how much more exact Ersatz Labour would be than New Labour.'

All of which was less interesting to Meldrum than its being offered at all. Hennessy, told who they were, instead of asking why they were there had launched into his explanation while seating them on a couch set between the windows and turning his chair to face them. That arrangement put them with the light behind them, him with the light on his face. A man with nothing to hide? Or perhaps a man who fell automatically into this act, including the gratuitous stuff about the firm's name, because it was what he did with clients, like a stand-up doing his routine.

'What business is that?'

'I could give you some elaborate euphemisms for what we do. The accountancy is complex more often than not. Basically, we're high-class debt collectors. We're very good. Money with menaces, you could say.' When Meldrum, still trying to decide between something-to-hide and man-in-the-grip-of-habit, made no response, Hennessy, happy it seemed to be his own straight man, went on, 'Except, I hasten to say, that the menaces are psychological, which is to say, illusory, unless we've to resort to the courts, which we regard as a *last* resort.'

Meldrum smiled and, as Hennessy smiling back waited for his response, asked, 'Why did you book a room in the Hamilton Hotel last night?'

The smile froze, the surprise was so well done only its implausibility prevented Meldrum from taking it as genuine. In any case, he'd long since come to the conclusion it was getting harder, as film and television ran an unending seminar on the human face, to tell genuine from fake emotion.

'Is that what this is about?' Hennessy asked. 'I must say that's a bit cheeky.'

Shields, bulky beside Meldrum on the couch, gave the effect of growling soundlessly. It happened, unpredictably, that a word would pierce his indifference and offend him.

'Why would you think that?' Meldrum asked.

'Because nothing happened. I can see if something had happened, you people would be entitled to take an interest.'

'You expected something? What were you expecting to

happen?' Questions asked in the same mild tone as before. Meldrum was curious to see how long the man could go without asking a question of his own. The longer, the stranger, and he didn't think for much longer without seeming very strange indeed.

But at last Hennessy got round to it, the obvious question. 'Why are you here?'

'A man was found dead in Room Four One Seven at the Hamilton Hotel this morning,' Meldrum said.

'One of the staff? How awful. Four One Seven? Is that the room I'd taken? I see why you might want to talk to me, but I can't be of any help. I decided after all not to stay the night. What was it? A heart attack?'

'This is a murder investigation.'

Could you fake going white? Meldrum wondered, watching Hennessy go over to a cabinet against the wall. He held up a bottle of Glenmorangie. 'I need a drink. Can you? No, on duty, of course.' He poured three fingers of whisky, sipped, gave a sigh and came back to his chair.

'You didn't stay the night?' Meldrum said. 'Would you explain that?'

'I suppose you know my home address?'

'We did try to contact you there,' Meldrum said.

'Half an hour's drive from here. Twenty minutes, if the traffic's reasonable. And I've a fold-down bed hidden away here in the office – do an overnight if things get hectic. Modern times. If you have stuff to finish, you work on a Saturday afternoon. It's the way things are.'

Meldrum took the point. 'So why book into a hotel?'

Hennessy finished his whisky and stared into the glass. 'This doesn't reflect well on me.' Meldrum put him in his late twenties, no younger, maybe even early thirties. Some people, though, could pull the boyish charm trick into old age. 'This won't go any further than it has to?'

'Of course not.' Confidentiality? No need to worry. Apart, that is, from most of his colleagues being gossipier than a WRI bus run. Leave aside the ones who had a mobile number for journo Dougie Stair hidden in their wallet.

'I appreciate that.' He sighed. 'Best to come out with it. There isn't any easy way to say you thought your wife was having an affair. I booked the room at the Hamilton because I thought that's where they were planning to spend the night together. I was going to catch them. Simple as that.'

Shields asked, 'And did you catch them?' The fat sergeant had a good response time on the infrequent occasions his interest was aroused.

Meldrum closed his mouth on the question he'd been shaping.

'Yes and no,' Hennessy said. 'I slipped the receptionist a tenner. Shouldn't tell you that, should I?'

He waited for an answer till, 'We've other things to think about,' Meldrum said drily.

'I wouldn't want to get her into trouble.' Such a *nice* guy, Meldrum thought, so sincere. He was beginning to be intrigued by Hennessy. 'I got the room I wanted.'

'Four One Seven.'

'Yes.'

'Why Four One Seven?'

'Something I'd overheard. I went straight up. It was five o'clock, round about that time. I had no idea when they'd come. It's going to sound stupid to you two, being professionals at this kind of thing, but it was only when I'd gone into the room and shut the door that I realised there was a problem about checking if they came at all. I even thought of boring a hole in the wall. Naturally, I didn't have a clue about how thick the walls were or what they were made of. I imagined the two of them sitting up in bed in the next room as a drill came crashing through the wall. Not that it mattered in any case since I hadn't thought to slip a Black and Decker in the overnight bag. In the end, I got the chair from the dressing table and cracked open the door into the corridor. I sat peering out until I got a sore neck and then I sat back and listened for a while. And I did that turn and turn about for hours until it got to ten o'clock and I went down to the bar. Don't get me wrong, I hadn't given up, I'm not the type to give up, I just needed out of that bloody room. As it happened, bit of luck, there was one place in the bar where you could see the entry from reception into the main hall, so instead of going back up, I sat there drinking and waiting. I decided that when I went back up, I'd knock the door of Four One Six. That way, if I'd missed seeing them come up, it wouldn't matter, I'd still confront them. There are a few flaws in that plan, I know – like two people in bed not bothering to get up to see who's knocking. Never mind. Just when I'd got it all worked out, I saw him coming through the arch and heading straight for the bar—'

'Him?'

'The man I suspected. If he'd been looking, he'd have seen me. I shot across the bar, out the side door into the street. From there, I could see him and he did meet a woman. But it wasn't my wife. So I went home.'

'And when you got home, your wife was there?'

'Oh, yes. She was surprised to see me. I'd told her I had to stay overnight in the office.'

'You told your wife you wouldn't be coming home last night. When did you tell her that?'

Hennessy's face went still. Eyes blinking, he considered the question, then said, 'I can't give you it to the minute. A few days ago I told her it was on the cards.'

'How do you mean? Tuesday? Wednesday?'

Room Four One Six had been reserved on the Monday. Meldrum didn't believe in psychic adulterers.

'Probably earlier. To give them a chance to get together,' Hennessy smiled, 'which they didn't. Thankfully, never intended to. I was being a bloody fool. As she told me this morning. Are you married?'

'Yes,' Shields said promptly.

'You'll know how it is then. You feel ashamed and affectionate, so next thing you're confessing. Bloody fool again for telling her. I'd forgotten the number one rule of married life – confession may be good for the soul, but it makes for an unpleasant breakfast. I had a hellish breakfast.'

Meldrum held his eye until the smile faded, then said, 'Last night you took a room in the Hamilton Hotel. You intended to spy on your wife. You kept watch for some hours, and then you went down to the bar – at what time did you say?'

'About ten.'

'How long were you sitting in the bar before you saw this man coming into the hall?'

'Does it matter? Half an hour, something like that.'

'So it would be about half past ten when you saw him?'

'I suppose so.'

The receptionist Theresa Connors, however, had said that Rannie came into the hotel at nine o'clock.

'But, instead of your wife, you saw . . . this man you suspected of having an affair with your wife, meeting another woman. Did you recognise this woman?'

'No. I didn't get much of a look at her. As I said, I got out into the street before he saw me. From there, I saw him come into the bar. He looked round and then went across — I lost sight of him. She must have been waiting for him, because he came back in sight more or less at once and this woman was with him. A glance told me it wasn't my wife—'

'You were sure of that?'

'Hundred per cent. You know your own wife, right?'

'Right,' Shields volunteered.

'Anyway,' Hennessy said with the air of a man making a point, 'I looked round when I went into the bar. If my wife had been there, I'd have seen her.'

'So this woman, whoever she was, she must have seen you.'

Hennessy frowned. 'I don't suppose she paid any attention.'

'If she was waiting for this man, she'd be taking a look at everyone who came in, wouldn't you say?'

'. . . I suppose so.'

Meldrum couldn't have explained why he'd raised the possibility and then pursued it. The pat explanation would have been instinct. In fact, it was more a finely tuned sense, developed over the years, for unease.

'Anyway, whoever was involved, to your relief it wasn't your wife. So you went home. So if a man was killed in Room Four One Seven some time during the night, you know nothing about it. Have I missed anything?'

'That's what happened.'

'We'll have to talk to your wife.'

'Of course.'

'What time did you get home?'

'I don't know exactly. Certainly before eleven o'clock.'

It had been midnight when, a guest claimed, two men had been fighting outside the lifts at the hotel.

'Your wife will confirm that?'

'Yes. We watched the news on television together.'

'I'll need the name of the man you thought might be involved with your wife.'

'Is that necessary?'

'For your sake.'

'I wouldn't want him to know. Couldn't you check he was there without bringing my name into it? You must see how embarrassing it would be for me.'

'You're a suspect in a murder inquiry. It's worth some embarrassment.'

Hennessy winced. After a moment, he said, 'His name's George Rannie. I can give you his home address. Go there, if you want.' He tore a sheet from a pad and scribbled a few lines. 'You won't embarrass him. He isn't married.' As he passed it across, he burst out, 'Someone I've never heard of gets killed and my private life has to be dragged into the open.'

'How do you know?' Meldrum wondered.

'What?'

'That you don't know the victim.'

'Don't be ridiculous. There's no earthly reason why I should. Didn't you say he was a member of staff?'

'No. He didn't work in the hotel. He wasn't staying there either. But he was identified. His name was Archibald Wemyss.'

'Oh, God,' Hennessy said. 'Not Archie.'

Chapter Thirteen

Beautiful hands, the receptionist at the Hamilton Hotel had called them. Not an adjective Meldrum would have used, but he was getting plenty of opportunity to look at them. Sitting beside him in the back of the car, Hennessy rubbed his hands down his face and sighed at intervals. Well-tended hands, long fingers, the nails carefully manicured. He was wearing a wedding ring too, just as Theresa Connors had remembered, a chunky band of gold.

'I don't know how I'm going to tell her,' he said, and sighed again.

He was speaking of his wife Lena. He'd given every appearance of being in shock as he explained that the dead man, Archie Wemyss, was her brother.

'Coincidences happen,' Meldrum said, 'but this would be a strange one. I'm not much of a believer in them.'

'Not in this job.' Glancing in the driver's mirror, Shields offered his support.

'I don't give a damn what you believe! You tell me Archie's been murdered. Why would anyone want to kill Archie? What in God's name was he doing in that hotel anyway? I can't begin to imagine. I'm almost home, and somehow or other I've to tell my wife her brother's dead.'

Hennessy slumped back after this outburst, and used a hand to shield his eyes.

Meldrum studied him in silence. When no sign came of the hand being lowered, he asked, 'Come to that, why were you in the hotel?'

That did the trick. The hand was snatched away. 'You know why!'

'You suspected your wife might be meeting a lover. But—'

'I don't suspect her. Not now. I was wrong. I see that now.'

'Fine. But when you were wrong, why the Hamilton Hotel? You said you overheard something, did you hear the name of the hotel?'

'No.'

'So what made you think they'd be meeting there?'

Before the younger man could answer, as the car slowed Shields asked, 'Which one is it?'

'Other side of the road,' Hennessy said. 'Not that one or the next. It's the third house. Parking's a problem.'

Parking was a problem everywhere in Edinburgh.

'Don't worry about it,' Shields said, pulling up on a double yellow line.

They were in one of the streets between the open space of the Meadows and the complex of buildings that housed the oldest of the city's four universities. As Meldrum got out of the car, a cloud slid off the sun. He screwed up his eyes against a dazzle of light. By contrast, the terrace on the other side of the street was thrown into darkness. As they crossed the street into its shadow, the air was colder. Hennessy was making for a light of half a dozen steps up to an arched door set in a frame of stone. A carriage light over the door and the heavy stone balustrade on either side of the steps gave an impression of solidity. In an earlier period, it might have belonged to a judge or prosperous merchant. Now a close at the next entrance suggested the upper floors might have been turned into flats, and looking over the balustrade as they followed Hennessy up the steps he saw a silt of wrappers and torn paper in the area below and basement windows, unwashed behind a guard of iron bars, blank with drawn blinds.

The hall they were led into, though, panelled in dark wood, oval brass mirror, long sideboard, gave an impression of well doing comfort. Neither it, however, nor the front sitting room, leather chairs, paintings in heavy gilt frames, struck Meldrum as having much to do with Hennessy's age or the image he projected. He wondered if the difference might be accounted for by the house having been inherited from his parents, perhaps, or his wife's or (come to that, taking a second look at the paintings) grandparents.

Hennessy came back shaking his head. 'I was sure she'd be here.'

'She didn't answer when you phoned,' Meldrum reminded him.

'She could have been having a bath. Or just decided not to answer. She does sometimes.' He looked from one policeman to the other unhappily. 'We're supposed to be going out tonight.'

'On the other hand,' Meldrum said, 'you could come back with us and answer some questions.'

'The police station? I don't think so.'

'Until we see your wife, we only have your word for it that you came home last night.'

'I'm not going to a police station. Unless you're going to arrest me?'

'Helping with our enquiries, that's what you'd be doing.'

'You're not going to arrest me.' He sat down in one of the leather chairs. 'Ask whatever you want. Poor Archie, of course, I want to help. But you must see, if my wife comes back, I have to be here. I wouldn't want her to hear about Archie from anyone else.'

'She'd better not buy a paper then,' Shields said.

'It's in the paper?'

Falsely helpful, acrimonious, Shields said, 'It'll be on the street now. And in all the Sundays tomorrow.'

Meldrum understood Shields, maybe too well. He'd seen the cramped house on an estate outside Musselburgh, met the defeated wife, the recalcitrant children. Most times in their work, policemen dealt with people poorer than themselves. If they had to cope with country gentry, touchy types with influential friends, or the seriously rich, one eye on the crime and one on damage limitation was only common sense, part of the survival kit. Come to a house like this, though, on the wrong day in the wrong mood, an edge of acrimony was understandable.

'Soon as my wife gets back, I'll phone you,' Hennessy said. 'That way you wouldn't waste any time. Isn't it better I'm here in case she comes back?'

He seemed to have lost confidence. Meldrum had observed before that Shields' skew interventions could have that effect.

'You could leave a note,' Shields said, still helping.

'I've given you Rannie's address. Talk to him why don't you?'

'We will.' Meldrum took the chair opposite Hennessy. 'But first there are some questions I'd like you to answer.'

'Like why I went to the Hamilton Hotel?'

Meldrum nodded. From the corner of his eye, he saw Shields giving up on the drama of taking a suspect in and reluctantly settling himself down into a chair.

'That and some others,' he said.

Chapter Fourteen

On the way into the hotel, they met Dougie Stair coming out. He took a folded copy of the evening paper from under his arm and spread it out for Meldrum to take a look.

CITY HOTEL MURDER, the headline read.

'Don't tell me I don't do you proud,' he said. 'Nice write-up.' He tried to hand it to Meldrum, who shoved it away. Stair grinned as Shields took it and went inside. 'Anything for me?'

'Not a thing.'

'And what about the picture?' he asked, following Meldrum back in through the revolving door. Blown up to the right of the report, it showed Meldrum coming out of the Hamilton Hotel. 'Taken at the time of the Sylvia Marshall murder. I got it out of the library. Eight years ago. Makes you look fresh as a daisy, not a care in the world.'

Still married. Whistles unblown. Not a care in the world.

Fuck off, Meldrum thought, and headed for the reception desk.

Theresa Connors, plump and smiling, glinting recognition denied her two colleagues, phoned then took him into the narrow administrative corridor. Passing the room where Simms had helped him check on the guests, he glimpsed screen savers looping strings of colour. Connors knocked on the manager's door and opened it at once.

Harkness looked up from his desk. Not getting up, he nodded Meldrum to a seat. The choice lay between two upright chairs. Like a lot of these places, money tended to be spent only where it could be seen: public opulence, private squalor, a commercial variant on the political philosophy of the last twenty years.

Without preamble, he began to complain. 'I don't care for the way some of your people are conducting their enquiries. Mrs Torrance, one of our housekeepers, was in tears after they talked to her. Since she found the body, I was surprised you didn't feel you had to talk to her yourself. I told her that.'

'Why was Mrs Torrance upset?'

Harkness made a face. 'I've told you.'

'Not why. Is she making a particular complaint?'

'No, nothing like that. I'm sure she wouldn't want a fuss.'

'A complaint against a named officer?'

'Certainly not.'

'Was it something she was asked that upset her?'

'Can we get on to something else?'

'My sergeant's arranging for me to talk to some people. I'll add her to the list,' Meldrum said. 'Did Simms ask you for the name of the woman who saw two men fighting by the lifts late last night?' And when Harkness didn't respond at once, 'He was supposed to ask you.'

'Mr Simms' job is to help me to run this hotel. Today's been enormously difficult for us.' Abandoning the defensive tone, he added, 'Your colleagues have been gathering

tatements all day. And now you want to talk to more
people. They'll all have been interviewed.'

'And may have to be again. Sometimes that's necessary.'

'I know how these things work!' The exclamation came
sharply. But when the silence ran on, Harkness became
uncomfortable and started to fiddle with papers on his desk.

When he looked up, Meldrum said, 'Eight years is a long
time. I thought you might have forgotten.'

'The death of that unfortunate young woman. It's not
something I'd forget.' And Harkness, as though afraid he
hadn't made the point sufficiently strongly, added solemnly,
'I'll carry the memory with me to my dying day.'

The muscles of Meldrum's face sagged, so that it took on
a peculiarly dull, almost vacant look. He had a weak stomach
for sentiment.

'I remember her too,' he said without emphasis. 'Sylvia
Marshall. She was nineteen. I remember all the unsolved
ones. The other ones I can forget.'

'That must be hard,' Harkness said, man to man, the tone
firm but not excluding a diminuendo to do with male
bonding.

Unexpectedly, Meldrum smiled. 'No,' he said, 'it's useful.
It means no matter how much time goes past, I never stop
wanting to catch the bastard.'

It wasn't a nice smile.

Chapter Fifteen

'She's a witness in a murder case. She should be here. Why isn't she here?'

'Out on the town, sight-seeing, I don't know. It's a Saturday night, she'll be enjoying herself,' Shields protested. 'That's what people do on a Saturday night.'

Held down by an act of will, like the pain from his ribs, from the moment he learned of her existence Meldrum had been waiting to confront this woman. Leaving the hotel to find Hennessy had made sense, but it was also true that he'd left without finding even the name of the woman who claimed to have seen two men fighting the night before. He had dreaded meeting her then. Dreaded meeting her now. Imagined her look of puzzlement turning to fear. '*But you were one of them.*'

They'd been looking through statements, reinterviewing, catching up the ones missed earlier as people came on for the evening shift. In one of the ashtrays, a badly stubbed out cigarette leaked a curl of foul smelling smoke. The room had no windows and the air tasted stale. When no one was talking, Meldrum could hear the faint wheeze of ineffectual air conditioning. Its usual occupants, porters and kitchen staff on a break, had been excluded all day. God knows, Meldrum thought, what it was like normally.

At least now he knew the woman's name.

'Is there a Mr Kravitz?'

'If there is, he's at home,' Shields said. 'She's over here with her daughter and son-in-law. Home's New York.'

'Nobody knows where they've gone?'

'They've been out all day.'

'You'd think they'd come back to freshen up, get changed for dinner.'

Shields shrugged. 'I checked. They didn't take dinner here last night either.'

'Did you *check*,' Meldrum asked with a scowl, 'they haven't gone home and nobody's noticed?'

'Monday. They're due to leave Monday morning. Coach'll be out front seven thirty sharp to take them to the airport.'

I've done what I can, Meldrum thought.

He said, 'We'll see her tomorrow.'

'No problem. What time?'

'Let Simms have my mobile number to give her. Tell him to ask her to check direct with me tomorrow.'

'That wee arse licker. I'll put a rocket up him.'

Shields left, a man on a mission.

Alone, waiting for the next knock on the door, Meldrum sat staring at the clock on the wall. He was tired and beyond hunger. The clock on the opposite wall, plastic case painted to look like wood only it didn't much, hung askew. It annoyed him and he thought of getting up and straightening it, thought of it then thought of Mrs Kravitz. Monday morning she'd be on her way to the airport. He wondered how long the clock had been off centre. Chances were, ever since some cackhanded bastard slid it on to the nail. Monday she'd be on a plane; New York was a long way away.

Before Shields came back, a tall pale man wearing a barman's white jacket put his head round the door.

'You wanted to see me? I was on in the Sleat Bar last night. The one beside the restaurant.'

Meldrum checked his list. 'Mr Thompson?'

'Right.' Taking a seat facing Meldrum across the table, he wrinkled his nose and asked, 'Mind if I put that out properly?' Without waiting for an answer, he rubbed out the cigarette in the ashtray. The last twist of blue smoke faded above them. By way of apology, he explained, 'I'm not a smoker.'

'Neither am I.'

'I hate the smell. You'd think I was in the wrong job, eh? Funny thing is, when I'm working I just tune it out.'

'How long have you worked at the Hamilton?'

'Eight years, coming up for nine.'

'You get to know people.'

'The ones that like a drink.'

'Do you know a man called Patrick Hennessy?'

'Hennessy? I thought the dead guy was called Wemyss? I told the policeman who spoke to me earlier I'd never seen Wemyss before. He'd a photie of him. I said to him, there's something queer about that photie. He said, no wonder, he was dead when they took it. But, right enough, it showed you what he looked like. Like I said, I'd never seen him before. But Hugh McArdle – you know, the doorman? We've all been talking about it, of course. McArdle says this Wemyss's never stayed here before. And if McArdle says so, it'll be right. He's a walking encyclopaedia, that fellow.'

Bombarded by words, Meldrum, hunger headache getting worse, was finding it hard to take his usual grip.

'Forget Wemyss. A man called Patrick Hennessy. That mean anything to you?'

'Not by name, maybe by sight. Is he one of the guests?'

Meldrum nodded.

'So maybe I would know him, but I'd need to see a photograph.'

Should have got a photograph from Hennessy. That had been a mistake. Start making mistakes, no telling where you'd end up.

'We'll get one.'

'A live one this time, eh?' Thompson laughed at his own joke. Stopped abruptly, 'He's not dead as well, is he?'

Meldrum shook his head. Thompson essayed a smile, which faded as the silence went on.

With a breath like a sigh, Meldrum asked, 'What about a George Rannie?' He waited for the answer almost indifferently. 'I don't have a photograph for him either.'

Thompson's smile flooded back. 'You don't need one. *Him* I do know.' The slight tension he'd been put under dissolved in relief. 'He's in and out all the time.'

It hit Meldrum like a dash of cold water in the face. He wanted to yell, *Who the fuck is he?* He'd got only vagueness and evasion from Hennessy.

Instead, quietly, he asked, 'In last night?'

Thompson frowned, tapping his tongue on his palate as he pondered. 'I think so. Couldn't have been for long.'

'Can you put a time on it?'

'You've got me there. I don't remember him buying a drink. But I've a feeling I saw him.'

'Any idea where? At a table? Coming in? Going out?'

'We were busy. Maybe I noticed him and expected him to get a drink and he didn't, so I'm remembering that. But there's waitress service at the tables, right enough. Maybe I saw him coming in by himself and thought he'd come up to the bar.' He shook his head. 'Honest to God, I've no idea.'

'Could you get any closèr on the time?'

'Well, it wasn't early on. Don't think it was all that late either. There was a bit of excitement late on. This American woman came in the back entrance and walked into a fight. Two guys hammering away at one another.'

'I heard about that,' Meldrum said carefully.

'Came up to the bar, eyes popping out of her head. Told me, I didn't think that kind of thing happened in Edinburgh. Happens everywhere, I told her.'

'You got that right.'

'Knocked back a double gin. So I don't lie awake all night, she said. She was on a talking jag with excitement. Gave Hugh McArdle an earful.'

'McArdle? What was he doing there?'

'Having a drink. He wasn't on duty. I mean, he was out of the fancy dress. But after he'd listened to her, he went out to see what was going on. I don't know why. She'd already been to reception – so probably the fight club had scarpered by then.'

Not long afterwards, it was time to call it a day. Instead of going through the hotel to the car park, he led Shields out through the revolving door at the front and walked round the building in silence. When they came to the side entrance into the Sleat Bar, he stopped and looked inside.

'Fancy one for the road?' Shields asked. He sounded faintly surprised, not very enthusiastic. They weren't drinking buddies.

'Stand on that side over there,' Meldrum said. 'Can you see folk coming through into the bar from there?'

In theory from where they were, it should have been possible to see the entrance from the hall of the hotel into the bar. At the moment though, people blocked any chance of a view. Yet Hennessy had said that from here in the street he'd seen Rannie coming into the bar, which was interesting, but unfortunately didn't prove him a liar. From one hour to the next a bar could get quieter. A gap could open in a crowd to give a view. All the same, it had been busy last night too according to the barman.

'No,' Shields said. 'But I can see your friend McArdle.'

Surprised, it took Meldrum a moment to locate him, sitting at the bar in a suit instead of a kilt, talking to a woman.

'You get the car,' Meldrum said. 'Bring it round here. I'll only be a minute.'

As he went in, Meldrum, tall enough to look over the heads of the crowd, found himself catching the eye of the barman Thompson. The man ducked his head and as he moved along the bar must have said something, for McArdle looked round and waited expectantly.

Before Meldrum could speak, McArdle said to his companion, 'I'd like you to meet an old friend—'

'Cut it out,' Meldrum said.

The woman, a tanned blonde who looked about eighteen, lost a smile wide as a pillar-box, very white teeth disappearing as her mouth drooped in surprise.

'Please,' McArdle said. 'Annie isn't used to people being rude. She's from New York.'

The girl's smile made a tentative comeback.

'You should find somebody your own age,' he told her.

'Hugh?' The smile had gone away again.

'Annie doesn't need to find anybody,' McArdle said solicitously, a little grin tugging the corners of his lips. 'She's a married woman.'

The grin did it.

'Then she should have more sense.' Meldrum the diplomat.

'Oh, there's Desmond now,' the girl said in a little breathy relieved voice, getting down from the stool. 'Thank you for your company, Hugh.'

Meldrum, resting a haunch on the stool she'd vacated to prevent anyone else taking it, watched her being met by a plump man in glasses. She said something to him and they left.

'He'd only gone for a pee,' McArdle said. 'They're a nice young couple. I don't think you have any idea how important the tourist industry is to this country.'

The barman Thompson set down a tumbler with three fingers of amber liquid. 'Glenfiddich,' he said to Meldrum. 'No ice, no water, right?'

'You do an educated guess,' Meldrum said. He watched the barman move off. Nothing had been said about paying.

McArdle said, 'I told Mr Harkness you'd been having a go at me.'

'I could tell something was wrong with him. Does he get nervous when he remembers he gave you an alibi eight years ago?'

'You've a long memory. He's just the nervous type. But he's good at his job. A lot of your gaffers come here, I've seen the Chief Constable at a function here, more than once. Bertie Harkness knows them all.'

Meldrum rocked the tumbler gently, watched the whisky tilt one way and then the other, set the glass down untasted.

'You spend a lot of time in here?'

'How do you mean?'

'I'd have thought the guests would prefer the help to do their drinking somewhere else.'

Giving the impression of a man responding to a compliment, McArdle said, 'I'm different. You know, like an institution.' Well pleased with himself, he nodded smugly.

'Aye, Carstairs,' Meldrum said.

McArdle looked blank for a moment. 'For the criminally insane? That's not nice. I was thinking of the Scott Monument.'

'Think of last night,' Meldrum said. 'An American woman saw some men fighting at the lifts through there.'

'You should have asked Annie.'

'What?'

'Annie — Mrs Kravitz's daughter. Her and Desmond were thanking me before you turned up. They said I was a big help to her mother, getting her calmed down, like.' The lumpy expanse of his face split in a childlike smile. 'Her and me had a real good talk.'

Chapter Sixteen

———◆———

Hennessy came to the door in his dressing gown.

'We've come to talk to your wife,' Meldrum said.

The air was full of Sunday bells tolling come-and-pray. He and Shields had come from a meeting with detectives in the mobile incident room that had been set up in the hotel car park. Already, this early in the day, he was tired. Despite a sleep, and ten minutes under a cold shower watching the bruises go dark purple, his ribs ached.

'She's not here.'

'Gone to church, has she? Were you waiting till she came back before you phoned me?'

'I haven't seen her since she walked out yesterday morning. I told you we quarrelled.' Hennessy shivered suddenly. The dressing gown was silk, presumably expensive, yellow in colour with red on the pockets and collar. It only came to his knees, though, and seemed to be all he was wearing. 'Do you want to come inside?'

'So where is she?'

'She's done this before. But don't worry, she'll be back some time today.'

'You're the one who should be worrying,' Shields said.

'I'm getting chilled.' He shivered again and pulled the collar of the gown shut. 'I really can't stand out here.'

'You don't seem to understand how serious this is.'

'I was going to phone around her friends, but I slept late.'

'You'd better start doing it now.'

'Like I say, she'll wander in some time this afternoon. And that'll be the end of it. She's got a terrible temper, but she doesn't bear a grudge.'

Meldrum looked at Shields and shook his head. Shields took a moment to think about it then shook his. The general effect aimed at a sort of incredulous disbelief.

'I'm about this,' Meldrum held up finger and thumb barely parted, 'off taking you in.'

'She'll come back, she always does. I'll phone you at once.'

Meldrum stood for a long moment as if weighing the options.

'Don't lose my number,' he said.

Hennessy started to close the door, then asked, peering out through the gap, 'Have you seen George Rannie?'

'After your wife, he's top of the list.'

As they came down between the heavy stone balustrades into the street, it was suddenly quiet. The church bells had stopped ringing. No shortage of churches, Meldrum thought, kirks and chapels, the Quakers over at Victoria Terrace, Unitarians in the shadow of the Castle, and a mosque, not as grand as the one in Glasgow, just up the road from here, which the Saudis had promised to clad in gold till Saddam Hussein invaded Kuwait and gave them something else to think about, but there all the same and calling the faithful to prayer. Meldrum, a congenital disbeliever, envied them their optimism.

At least Shields seemed to be amused, chuckling to himself as they crossed the road to the car.

Settling into the passenger seat, he said, 'If he gets the flu, he could have you for police brutality.' He held up finger and thumb almost in contact. '*That* close. Fuck me, I enjoyed that.'

Meldrum cracked a reluctant smile. 'There was more to it than that.'

'I know. Guy like that. Posh voice. Running his own business. Got a big flat. So you give him a lot of shit to see how he takes it, and he takes it like a lamb. I'm not a complete dummy.' He paused. Meldrum checked both ways and took the car out from the side street. On the dummy question, it seemed he'd no opinion. 'Makes you wonder if he's guilty.'

'Of something,' Meldrum said. 'Maybe he fiddles his taxes.'

'All that class of cunt fiddles the tax. They don't get a bad conscience. They get an accountant.'

No, Meldrum thought, an idle sod, but not a dummy. You couldn't be in this game for as long as Shields without picking up some of the angles. At whatever point along the line, though, something had made Shields decide there was only one thing that he really wanted to pick up. Since then, his motto, mantra, prescription for living: Roll on the pension.

'Off to Rannie's?' he was asking. Which made a nice change from, Where to now? The fat man was on good form this Sunday morning.

They went past the Royal Infirmary to Tollcross and down Lothian Road. Meldrum liked driving in the city on Sundays, not that it was ever really quiet, just quieter. No flag was flying above the Castle. Princes Street showed a perspective of near empty pavements. In Charlotte Square, from the corner of his eye at the last moment, Meldrum glimpsed a figure like a hallucination among the douce grey buildings. Ten minutes later, getting out of the car he was still wondering if he'd really seen a white-haired man flying a kite behind an iron fence in the middle of the grass enclosure. Looking at the handsome curve of high terrace building facing him, he recalled reading that one of the flats there had sold not long ago for more than a million. So why not a kite flyer, he thought, or a minister walking up Waverley Steps on his hands whistling 'Dixie'?

Hennessy had given them Thirty Eight as the address, but it was good to get the confirmation of seeing Rannie's name in the list by the entryphone. When they rang, however, there was no answer. Shields nodded at this, a man who'd been clear from the beginning that it was always a good idea to phone first. Meldrum's anxiety meant he needed to keep on the move; he didn't feel inclined to explain why. He leaned on the next button, then the next without a pause and the next again. There was a click and as a metallic voice squawked, 'That was quick!' he pushed the door and it gave way.

The hall was papered; the stair carpeted from side to side. As they went in, a man came running down taking the steps two at a time. He teetered to a stop. 'Looking for someone?' His tone hovered between helpfulness and challenge. When Meldrum told him, he grinned and said, 'He's along here. Everybody is. Come on, and I'll show you.' His relief suggested the challenge had been more out of duty than conviction.

They went after him down the entrance hall, where he opened the door to the ground-floor apartment, apparently left unlocked. Following him in, Meldrum heard voices and laughter coming from the back of the flat. He caught the distinctive smell of cooking meat, and for some reason thought of a barbecue, unlikely in a flat and it not even summer. At the end of the passage, there was a sizeable living room with half a dozen people standing around, drinking and chatting. They followed the main source of the noise through to the kitchen. It was empty except for a woman taking stuff out of a microwave and another cutting sandwiches at the table. At the end of the room, however, patio doors opened on to a space under glass, a conservatory in carnival mood. Out of habit, Meldrum estimated the crowd: twenty or more adults in casual gear with children weaving in and out. All of them invited to an autumn barbecue. He'd found the party.

Some special quality of light from the glass roof, dazing no doubt in summer, glittering this late in the year, added to the air of well being. Looking out, Meldrum saw a stretch of neatly cropped grass, walls dividing off back lawns and buildings looming all round. He had the impression everybody in the place was clutching a drink and talking at once. Behind a long table a man in a chef's hat and a tall redheaded girl were setting out plates of meat and salad bowls. 'That's George,' the man who'd brought them in said.

Meldrum headed for him through the crowd, brushing people out of his way. Laying out chicken pieces on a platter, Chef Hat didn't seem to see him coming.

'Mr Rannie?'

He looked up puzzled but smiling. 'Yes?'

Meldrum leaned closer. 'Detective Inspector Meldrum.' Although he'd spoken quietly, the nearest of those lined up in front of the table were distracted from the serious business of loading food on to paper plates. 'I'm sorry about the timing, but I really have to speak to you.'

'Detective?' Rannie asked, straightening up. 'You mean you're a policeman?'

He made no effort to keep his voice down. The noise level dropped. Behind him, Meldrum sensed attentiveness rippling back through the crowd.

'Could we have a word in private? It won't take very long.'

Rannie took off his hat and gave it to the red-haired girl. 'Can you manage without me, Liz? Get somebody to give you a hand.'

The girl put on the hat. She was very pretty and it suited her.

Rannie took them into a small room equipped as a study that led directly off the living room. He didn't offer them a seat, perhaps because he assumed they wouldn't take long. Without the chef's hat he was about five ten, a broad shouldered healthy looking man in his mid-forties. He had thick curling hair of that energetic glossy blackness shared by descendants of Spanish Armada crews wrecked on Hebridean islands. Closing the door, he smiled and said, 'I don't know what the odds are against it, but two of my neighbours share a birthday today. I thought any excuse for a party. Naturally, I didn't expect a visit from the police. I'll have to explain what it's about before they suspect the worst. What *is* it about?'

'We shouldn't keep you long from your guests. Do you know a man called Patrick Hennessy?'

'I might have guessed. What trouble's he got himself into?'

'Has he been in trouble before?'

'It depends what you mean by trouble. Back to the same question, eh? What's this about?'

'It's about the death of a man called Archibald Wemyss.'

'Archie Wemyss?' Rannie gave every appearance of being in shock. 'But he's only a young man. For God's sake, what happened?'

'He was found yesterday morning in a room at the Hamilton Hotel. He'd—'

But Rannie interrupted, 'In the Hamilton? But I was there on Friday night. What was it? A heart attack? He was only half a dozen years younger than I am— Dead at thirty-seven? That's too young.'

'He'd been beaten to death.'

'Oh, Jesus! Have you got who—?' He broke off. 'What's Patrick Hennessy to do with it? Has he been hurt as well?'

Meldrum couldn't be sure, but imagined he had caught the slightest of pauses between the two questions, which made him wonder if there was some element of calculation or seeking an effect in asking the second.

'What makes you think he might be?'

'You asked about Patrick. And he's Archie's brother-in-law. Didn't you know that?'

'But why should he be hurt? Did you think they might have been fighting one another?'

'No, of course I didn't! It was because you—Why *did* you mention him?'

'He took a room at the hotel on Friday evening. Wemyss was found dead in it the next morning.'

Rannie's mouth opened in astonishment. 'You amaze me. Was Patrick there? Have you spoken to him? I can't imagine what could have happened. What have I got to do with it?'

'You've said you were at the hotel that night.'

'So?'

'You'd taken the next room—'

'To where he was killed? That can't be true!'

'Archibald Wemyss was found in Four One Seven. I take it you did spend the night in Four One Six?'

'All night, all night. And neither of us heard anything. Not a sound.' He made a face. 'It's too awful to think about.'

'You're certain your wife didn't hear anything?'

'I'm not married.'

Rannie spoke casually, then seemed to be lost in thought. In the small silence, Meldrum listened to the muffled sound of the party. There was a jagged spike of laughter. He wondered if someone had thought of a funny reason for their host going off with two policemen.

'Poor Archie,' Rannie said. 'I can't even imagine him at the Hamilton Hotel. No job, he lived with his parents, doesn't that say it all? A nice, ineffectual man. A bit of a hopeless case. I've known him off and on for years. His father and mine were friends.'

'Did you know his daughter too?'

'Lena? Not until later. She was younger than Archie, so when his father visited us it was always Archie he brought with him. What about her?' He frowned. 'You know she's married to Patrick Hennessy?'

Meldrum nodded. 'Can I ask what your relationship is with her?'

'Relationship? A friend. A family friend, I suppose you could call me.'

'You knew her before she met her husband, I take it.'

'I introduced them. What's this about?'

'According to Mr Hennessy, he thought you and his wife were having an affair. The idea was to catch you in the act.'

'The bloody fool!' For a moment, it looked as if Rannie

would burst out laughing, but that changed at once to anger. Angry, he seemed like a man it might be dangerous to cross. 'He doesn't deserve her.'

'There's no basis for his suspicions?'

'None.'

'But you were with someone. You've admitted that.'

'And if I was?'

There was a curved table with a computer and printer and scanner lined up in a row. Above the table, there was a painting of a low range of hills with a little moon like a yellow nail paring nestled on top. Without asking, Meldrum turned the office chair out from under the table and sat down. If he'd been giving a seminar at Police College, he could have invented some elaborate justification for doing that. The truth was simpler: his tiredness was getting worse.

'If you were,' he said. He started again. 'All right, let's suppose . . . Hennessy thinks you're having an affair with his wife. He tells her he's going away for the weekend. He decides the two of you will take advantage of him being away to go to the Hamilton Hotel. Anything strike you as strange about that? I thought it was strange. I asked Hennessy, why the Hamilton Hotel? What made him think you'd go there? Would you like to guess what he told me?'

'I bloody well wouldn't. What do you think you're playing at?' Rannie glanced savagely from the seated detective to the impassive Shields. 'What kind of question's that?'

'Quite right. It's not a game. You don't have to guess. The way he explained it to us, Hennessy went to the Hamilton Hotel because that's where you like to go for an overnight.'

'Isn't that my business?'

'Not if you were with Hennessy's wife.'

'I wasn't. Not with anyone's wife. I was with a friend.'

'Why sign in as husband and wife then?'

'You mean now there's so much screwing around, no-body bothers any more with the Mr and Mrs Smith routine? That's why I do it. It's a joke.'

Meldrum thought about that. It was true he was tired and that he wasn't known for his sense of humour. All the same, it didn't seem to him much of a joke.

'I'll have to know who you were with.' And as Rannie scowled and hesitated, went on, 'Unless, of course, you don't want to tell me because you feel it's a matter of defending a lady's reputation.' That seemed to him like a better joke. He had to resist the temptation to smile as he said it.

'Wait here,' Rannie said.

He came back almost at once with the red-headed girl. She still had the chef's hat on. It suited her; she still looked very pretty. She looked like a lot of fun.

'This is Liz McKinnon,' Rannie said. 'We spent the night together at the Hamilton Hotel on Friday.'

'Oh, God,' she said, 'they've passed a law against it.'

'Not yet,' Rannie said. 'Someone was killed in the next room, and they want to know if we heard anything.'

'That's *sick*. While we were – I don't want to think about that.'

Shields cleared his throat. 'We don't have a precise time of death,' he said. 'It could be round about midnight. Would you have been asleep by then?' Another gentleman of the old school, Meldrum thought. It was one name for it.

'No,' she said, 'but we weren't listening for anything. If we'd thought about it, we'd have been more worried about what the people next door might be hearing.'

Fuck it, Meldrum thought, in every sense of the word

naturally. Everybody seemed to be doing it, thinking about doing it, making bad jokes about doing it. From now on if anybody asked his advice, which nobody was likely to, he'd advise taking up a hobby: archery or watercolour painting, something that got you out of doors, into the fresh air, used up your energy, gave you something else to think about – other than fucking, that is. But then, with bruised knuckles, sore ribs, a spongy lump behind his ear, and lost hours matching too exactly those in which a man had been murdered, it could be he was prejudiced. He wondered if he could have a cracked rib. That was another possibility. With a kind of detached interest, he watched Shields take up the questioning. Filling the gap wasn't something Shields did, not as a general rule, but at the moment he was going in for it with animation. Meldrum suspected this red-headed woman might make a lot of men bend the rules. He wondered if Rannie was taking it as an example of police technique: alternating hard cop with soft cop, lean cop with fat cop, tall cop with squat cop, libidinous cop with clapped out cop.

Liz McKinnon lived in Stockbridge. A nice part of the city, Shields said judiciously. She had a degree in fine arts, and had met Rannie when he came for advice to the interior design firm where she worked. Why go to a hotel? She smiled at the question. Of course, they'd made love in her flat and here in Rannie's. But if he wanted to go to the Hamilton Hotel, it was fun there too. So why not?

When Meldrum spoke at last, it was to Rannie. 'When did you say you booked into the hotel?'

The question seemed to take all three of the others by surprise, not least Shields, who'd been intent on questioning the girl. Not getting an immediate answer, Meldrum stood up. Emphasised by the room's lack of space, his height gave an unintended effect of menace.

'About ten,' Rannie said. 'Isn't that right, Liz?'

'I'm terrible about times,' the girl said. 'I suppose so.'

Meldrum nodded. 'That would more or less fit the time Mr Hennessy claims to have seen you.'

'So?'

'The receptionist puts your arrival earlier. Quite a bit earlier. According to her you booked in at nine o'clock.'

'If she says so. That'll be right then.' Rannie seemed entirely unruffled. 'Like Liz says, we weren't watching the clock.'

'It's not that simple. You arrive at nine—'

'That still feels early,' Rannie said. 'But does it matter?'

'You sign in and go through to the bar where Miss—' He paused, making a question of it. The girl nodded.

'I told you,' Rannie said, 'not anybody's wife.'

'You go through to the bar where Miss McKinnon is waiting for you.'

'Yes. That's about it.'

'And then you went up to your room.'

'Yes, again.'

'The thing is, Mr Hennessy says that he saw you come into the bar and leave with Miss McKinnon, but not at just after nine. He puts it after ten.'

Rannie smiled. 'Liz and I sat in the bar for a while. Then I'd a phone call to make so I left her to finish her drink in comfort. I came back and we went up to the room. By that time, it probably was after ten.'

'That clears that up,' Meldrum said. He thought of asking for the name of the person Rannie had phoned, then decided against pushing it. Time enough later, if he had to;

after he'd talked to Hennessy again and to his wife. 'Oh, one other thing. When I asked if you knew Patrick Hennessy, your first thought was that he'd got himself into trouble. What made you think that?'

Rannie said, 'I suppose because of the business he's in. Whatever fancy name you give it, he's collecting debts. I imagine some people won't be happy with that.'

'You're not in the same business, by any chance?'

'Christ, no! I went to London in the 'Seventies. For the best part of twenty years I was in partnership buying and selling property. We did well during the boom and not at all badly when the bubble burst. If you know what you're doing, you can make money whether a market's going up or down. I came back to Edinburgh five years ago. I'm still looking round.' He laughed. 'I don't have any debts, and I don't have any to collect. So, you see, there's no urgency. I've worked hard and now I can find time for the pleasant things in life – like giving parties for my friends.'

Listening to this compact energetic man, self-contained, self-sufficient, self-satisfied, Meldrum found him enviable enough to want to get away from him as quickly as possible.

As they came into the hall, Shields said, 'Nice girl. No, that's all I mean, nice.'

There was a clatter of feet and the man who had let them into the apartment came trotting down the stairs again carrying a birthday cake balanced on a tray. 'All done?' he cried. 'Can't have George missing the cake being cut.'

Shields headed for outside, but Meldrum paused. 'He throws a good party. Does he do it often?'

'This is the first. Hopefully, not the last.'

'Well, don't worry, Mr Rannie's back at the party.' He pushed open the door, held it as the man started to back in, guarding the contents of the tray. 'And Miss McKinnon, of course.'

The man grinned. 'I said to George, Where have you been hiding her?'

As he drove back up to Queen Street, Meldrum thought about Liz McKinnon. He wondered if Rannie should have been more curious about what could have brought Archie Wemyss to the hotel. After all, even if Hennessy had thought his wife was having an affair, would he have involved her brother? If his story was to be believed, though, he'd left the hotel almost as soon as Rannie arrived with Liz McKinnon.

Why had it been Archie who was killed? There was a lot to think about.

It took him a moment to pick up on what Shields was saying.

'. . . good job he didn't.'

'Didn't what? Who?'

'Rannie. I'm saying it's a good job he didn't take a bet against two of his neighbours sharing a birthday. I was on a bus run once where the driver did that as a kind of game. Turns out you can't have more than about a dozen or so folk without two of them having a birthday on the same day.'

Meldrum said, 'We're going back to the hotel.'

It was Shields' turn to ask, 'What?'

'I thought I'd save you asking Where to now?'

'Fine.' Short and clipped.

'Then,' Meldrum added helpfully, 'we're going to collect Mr Patrick Hennessy. Time we got some answers out of him.'

Chapter Seventeen

Even with the incident room set up in the car park, it was still more convenient to use the room in the hotel. To Meldrum's surprise, a plate of sandwiches and a pot of coffee appeared just as they were settling down. As he was looking at them, the manager Harkness put his head round the door, and said, 'Your sergeant mentioned that you hadn't eaten.'

When he'd gone, Meldrum said, 'Pour yourself a coffee. Then find somewhere to drink it. Come back when you're finished.' He pointed at the plate of sandwiches, 'And take that with you.'

'What about you?' Shields asked, more truculence than concern edging the question.

'I'll be interviewing a witness. It's better doing that without chewing, just so nobody gets the impression we're arseholes.'

Shields looked at him, then poured a cup out of the pot for him with careful deliberation, picked up the tray with the coffee and sandwiches and said, 'I'll be back in no time.'

The witness was Mrs Torrance, the second-floor housekeeper, who'd found the body. As he took her through her account of the previous morning, he sipped coffee and ignored successive rumblings of protest from an empty stomach. He'd have been surprised to learn anything useful, and he didn't. It was necessary but routine, even down to the show of sympathy.

'A terrible shock, of course it was. I'm glad you're feeling better.' He risked another sip of coffee. 'Oh, one thing. How was it you were in the room first? Wouldn't it usually have been one of the maids?'

'Mr Harkness asked me to check the room.'

'Why?'

Mrs Torrance, whom Meldrum placed in her early fifties, struck him as being competent and sensible. Odd then that she should be flustered by the question.

'Isn't that silly? I can't remember. He must have said. I just can't—'

'It's all right,' Meldrum said.

'But he must have given a reason. I don't know why I can't remember.'

'It's not important.' He made a mental note to ask Harkness.

'I'm not the kind of person who forgets things.' Her eyes filled with tears.

'Don't distress yourself,' Meldrum said. 'It can happen to any of us.'

Alone, he was glancing at his watch, irritated by the length of Shields' absence, when there was a knock on the door. He had started to get up when it opened to admit a plump young man with thinning brown hair and glasses with expensively fashionable lightweight frames. He was wearing a blazer with a club crest on the pocket.

'Detective Inspector Meldrum?' The voice was unexpected, a rich mellow baritone. 'I understand it's your wish
to speak with my mother-in-law. I have to tell you, she's not
very happy about that.'

'Your mother-in-law? Would that be Mrs Kravitz?' From
the time he'd spent in America a couple of years back,
Meldrum reckoned the accent, that of an educated man,
might well belong to someone from New York. 'I can
understand it's not the kind of thing she wants to be doing
on her holiday. I'll make it as brief as possible.'

'It's not that. It's you, Inspector. You were rude to my
wife. And her mother just doesn't want to talk to you.'

The pillar-box mouth girl. Talking to Hugh McArdle in
the Sleat Bar.

'I'm sorry if your wife got the wrong impression.' What
had he said to her? 'But this is a murder enquiry. Mrs Kravitz
should care enough about that to want to help. Even if she is
on holiday.'

Meldrum the diplomat.

The young man was not impressed. 'I certainly see what
my wife meant,' he offered, lowering the baritone in disapproval. 'She was offended not so much on her own behalf,
as because of your attitude to Hugh. If you want her exact
words, she said, Typical cop, he wouldn't have talked that
way to one of the guests.'

Stupid bitch, Meldrum thought. I was rude to her, wasn't
I? At once he could imagine her reply, But you didn't know I
was a guest. Seeing both sides wasn't always a help. All this
going through his mind as a distraction from the dominating
idea: Maybe I won't have to face this woman Kravitz after
all.

It would be so easy. Collect Shields and get out of the

hotel. Go to see Hennessy, who hadn't phoned though he'd promised he'd phone. Making Hennessy their number one priority would make sense to Shields. Tell himself and anyone else who brought it up that he'd attend to Mrs Kravitz later. With so much to do, it would be easy to overlook later until it turned into too late. By the time he got round to thinking again of Mrs Kravitz, it could happen she'd be on her way home to New York on a plane.

'I'm sorry, I really have to speak to her,' Meldrum said. 'A man's been killed. I have to do everything I can.'

'I understand that.' He took off his glasses, folded them and tapped them against his lips. It was a habit that went with his manner, formal for such a young man, almost pompous, but serious and not unimpressive. 'My name's Desmond Tulley. I'm a financial adviser working in a law firm in New York. My work's mostly to do with investing beneficiary trusts and corporate bonuses, all that stuff, but you don't have to be an officer of the court to understand the responsibilities of being a good citizen. When my mother-in-law dug in her heels, I didn't argue. Any time she and Annie think the same way on a thing, they're not either of them open much to being persuaded. But I got a copy of the dead man's picture from your Sergeant Cobb and showed it to her, and then I did say something about what was owing in this kind of circumstance. She asked me to speak to you on her behalf, and I agreed to do that. But first I advised her to tell me everything she could remember. And that's what she did.'

Meldrum was tempted. What had been easy seemed suddenly to have been made easier. Let Tulley tell him whatever the woman remembered: after all, wasn't that what she wanted? First, though, there was a question to be answered. He asked, 'What did Mrs Kravitz say when you showed her the picture?'

'Oh, the dead guy was one of the men fighting in the lobby. She recognised him one hundred per cent.'

Wrong answer.

'Why don't you take it from the beginning?' he suggested. 'What your mother-in-law told you.'

'We had an invitation for dinner on Friday night. For Annie's mother, it went on way too long, which was entirely my fault. Thing is, I hadn't seen Tony – he was our host – since we graduated. He was my best friend back then. But his first job took him to Atlanta and after that he came to Europe. It was the damnedest thing when we met again, as if we'd never been apart. I was having a great time, I just didn't want it to end. He's probably the best friend I've ever had. You know how it is?' Meldrum grunted. 'I should have got the signals. Mother Kravitz got pretty quiet. Then she disappeared for a bit and came back with her coat on. She'd called for a taxi. No, she didn't want Tony to take her; no, she didn't want us to come; no, she didn't want to break up the evening. But she'd had enough. Like I say, she's not a woman you argue with.'

'And this would be some time after eleven?'

'Oh, well after. Tony and his wife have this penthouse flat, very nice, three-year rental, no distance at all from the hotel. Everything's close in this town. Anyway, she gets the taxi to drop her in back of the hotel. She's got a headache, so she's planning to take the lift straight up to her room and go to bed. But as she comes in the door, she sees this big guy pinning the other one against the wall. Right then, the smaller of the two – the murder victim, as it turns out – breaks free. When he does that, he's sliding along the wall,

131

facing her, staring right at her. The other one grabs him, they're tussling, pounding on one another. She didn't squeal or anything, that's not her style. She just got out of there fast. But when she saw the victim's photograph, she wasn't in any doubt about it being the man she saw. It's as if he was asking me for help, is what she's saying this morning. I don't know whether that's true or not. But on the identification, knowing her like I do, you can bet on it, believe me.'

Meldrum took the last sip of coffee from the cup. It was cold, but then it hadn't been all that hot to start with. 'Did she get a look at the other man?'

'I asked her that. Not as good a look at the big guy, maybe not much of a look at all. She just wasn't sure. And, of course, I didn't have a photograph this time.' He laughed. 'If I did, that would solve your problem.'

Meldrum paused for so long that Tulley began to stare at him curiously. At last, he said, 'I have to see your mother-in-law.'

'She's pretty set against that.'

'All the same.'

'Can I ask why? I've covered everything she told me.'

'I'm sure you have. But if there's any chance she can describe the man who was fighting with Archibald Wemyss, I have to talk to her. Under the right questioning, people often remember more than they think they can.'

Tulley looked doubtful. 'As I recall, we've had cases where under the wrong questioning people have remembered more than they should. Have you heard of false memory syndrome over here?'

'We've heard of it. It's something you guard against if you're competent. I've had a lot of experience.'

Tulley had taken his glasses off again. Now he put them

on, and said, 'You're absolutely right, of course. She's with Annie in her room. I'll take you up, then you're on your own. I wish you good luck.'

As they came into the hall, a group of men was approaching. Seeing the two of them come out of the room, Harkness turned back, passing between Shields and Detective Sergeant Cobb who were deep in conversation. It was the fourth man, the one who'd been in front with Harkness, who concerned Meldrum.

Detective Superintendent Barry Gowdie was a thick necked, meat handed brute, who had been an open and a covert enemy since they'd joined the police within a week of one another. The reason for this enmity had never been entirely clear to Meldrum. Goaded in an unarmed combat class, he'd dumped Gowdie on the seat of his shorts. That had been about the first time they met, but they'd shaken hands afterwards: the old no-hard-feelings stuff. There had been, though. He'd put Gowdie down with an open-handed slap, not a punch; and he'd wondered if that might have something to do with it. Gowdie, who'd been to a good school which happened to be situated near the small town where his father had the grocer's shop, had been at first inclined to underrate Meldrum, who'd served his time as a carpenter before joining the force. For his part, Meldrum had come early to an estimate of Gowdie's abilities, which hadn't changed over the years. In trusted company, he might have described him as a bully, the kind who got results by brawn not brains; in short, one of those who joined the police for the wrong reasons. Since he didn't go in for trusted company, however, the odds were high against this opinion being betrayed to its object. All the same, there wasn't much doubt Gowdie had an animal instinct for what Meldrum thought of him.

'I need a word with you,' he said, adding at once before Meldrum had time to answer, 'I mean, now.'

'In that case, you'd better have it,' Meldrum said. 'Could you give me a minute, Mr Tulley?'

'Tell you what,' Desmond Tulley said, 'I'll go and prepare the way. It's Room Two Thirteen.'

Gowdie watched him leaving, then asked, 'Prepare the way? What's that about? KY jelly?'

He spoke with a kind of unsmiling malice. It was Meldrum who smiled. As he did, he reached behind him with his left hand and opened the door of the room he'd just left. With his right hand, he took a grip on Gowdie's bicep. 'We can talk in here,' he said, and pulled. Gowdie had the option of struggling or coming. He chose to come.

Meldrum shut the door in Cobb's face, leaving the two sergeants outside.

'Let go!' Gowdie said. 'You're in enough trouble.' He jerked his arm to free it. Meldrum held on just long enough to show how easily he could, then let go.

'You wanted to speak to me,' he said mildly. 'For police business, we've the use of this room.'

'Those two saw you grabbing me. I could have you for assaulting a superior officer.'

'I don't think so,' Meldrum said. 'Trying to describe what happened? It would sound silly. You don't want to sound silly.'

'Fuck you!' Gowdie said viciously.

Meldrum smiled. 'Just as well there aren't any witnesses for that. And speaking of witnesses, I've got one waiting for me.'

'No, you don't,' Gowdie said. 'Who told you to take this enquiry? What'd you do, appoint yourself? You think that's the way it works?' He pulled a folded newspaper from his coat pocket, and held it up. It was the Sunday sister paper of the evening one for which Dougie Stair worked. Meldrum recognised the picture under the headline on the front page. It was the one Stair had found from eight years back of him coming out of the Hamilton Hotel. 'Did you imagine for a minute pulling a stroke like this would cover your back? It's got Fleming chewing the carpet. If he had his way, he'd hang you up by the balls.'

'If you're finished, I still have a witness to see.'

'Witness? You've a witness to see? I don't think you're the full fucking shilling,' Gowdie said. Flecks of foam gathered at the corners of his lips. 'You're off the case.'

There wasn't any arguing with that. He left the room, Gowdie following, still in full flow. Lengthening his stride, behind him he heard Gowdie call back Shields, who by habit must have started to come with him. The Detective Superintendent would want to question both sergeants, Shields as well as Cobb, in an effort to get up to speed with the investigation before he took it over.

In the reception hall, he caught sight of Hugh McArdle grinning at him over a pile of luggage. In an instant, he'd veered abruptly in that direction, contained temper rising, before common sense restrained him. Turning back, he bumped the elbow of a stout woman emerging from the revolving door with an armful of parcels. As she gaped up at him, parcels scattered around her feet, he fled.

That night, trying to sleep, it was the woman's shocked face that made him sweat in the dark with embarrassment. Least he should have done, he could have picked up her parcels. He remembered tugging Gowdie by the arm; like kids in the fucking playground. Gowdie brought out the worst in him. He wondered if Hugh McArdle was right about the manager Harkness knowing Chief Constable Baird, ACC Fleming and all the others who played the game of politics at functions and dinners, clubs and lodges. Paranoid in the dark, he imagined Harkness dropping a word in the right ear. Later still, however, what came to him was the image of Archie Wemyss before he was taken out of the hotel room, and it seemed the worst thing in the world to lie dead in a cheap shell of brown plastic. He knew the feel of living wood under his fingers. What wood had Christ's cross been made of? Had anyone thought of that? Did anyone know? You'd think it might be one of those legends – like the ones they made up all the time in the old days – the accursed tree, and all the trees of that kind would have some mark or fault from the day of the Crucifixion to the end of the world. But what tree would that be? He lay trying to remember what trees they'd have in Palestine. Cypress? Palm? Cedar? The cedars of Lebanon. But then his thoughts turned to the trees of his own country. Oak and mountain ash and birch and alder and maple and walnut. The hardwoods that grew slowly and were grained and circled to mark the years of their growing. He imagined a slope leading to the brow of a hill and all the way to the summit at intervals a line of crosses, each one made of a different wood and on every cross a man punished for a different sin. What wood for the rapist, the murderer, the thief?

The sky was lightening when he slipped into a last interval of shallow sleep before facing Monday morning.

Dead Man's Noon

One summer day in the year he was fourteen, walking behind his twelve-year-old sister Lena with his father leading the way as they wound between the trees, Archie Wemyss knew that he was happy. The forest path to the loch was his favourite walk, so there was one reason. They were going out in a boat, and that would be another. On a day like this, they would leave the hot still air of the woods and row out to where the air came in cool small puffs across the loch, and the water would be the same blue as the sky it reflected so that with eyes half closed you might be steering among white clouds. His father would cry, 'Stop dreaming, Archie!' but that would be all right, for he would be smiling. And he would be there. His father was so often away. He went to conferences; he went to stay with old friends; he travelled to read his poetry, sometimes to foreign countries. There seemed to be all sorts of different reasons for him being away. When Archie had said that to his mother, she had frowned and seemed angry. She was often angry; angry with him, angrier often with Lena, who had taught herself, by some art he couldn't master, not to care. Companion arts unmastered: knowing when to keep quiet, how to make friends, learning not to miss his father.

Loving his sister? Call it an open verdict. Though he knew that he was supposed to, a powerful incentive for a child disposed to obedience, jealousy of her claims on their father's attention often got in the way.

Even when their father was at home, too much of the time he would be in the office he had made for himself at the far end of the barn that stood beside the house: a secret place tucked under the hayloft, the floor of the loft its ceiling, the stone walls lined with tongued and grooved timber, a window cut in the end wall framing a view of fields and trees all the way to the far hills. It made a snug magic cave. The door to it was kept locked against the children.

As they came out from the shadow of the trees to the side of the loch, sunlight dashing up in sparkling handfuls from the tops of the little waves, for Archie his father being there was the larger part of being happy.

'All together,' his father ordered, taking most of the weight. 'One! Two! Two and a half! Three!' and the boat slid into the water and his father held it steady while the two of them got in and then got in himself and bedded the oars and pulled and they were off.

'Let me row,' Lena said.

'No,' Archie said. 'Let Daddy.'

'Thanks very much. What if I get tired?' his father wondered. 'I might be glad of some help.'

'You don't get tired.'

'Oh, yes, I do,' his father said, laughing.

'Daddy's nearly sixty,' Lena said.

'Prime of life,' his father said. He sang: 'Twenty's plenty, Thirty's dirty, Forty's—' He paused.

'Snorty!' Lena shouted.

'That's not a word,' Archie said. He'd been trying to think of a good one.

'It'll do,' his father said. 'Facility wins over perspiration.' He sang: 'Forty's snorty, Fifty's nifty, And as for Sixty, As far as I can see, Sixty's a very good age to be.'

'Sixty's swixty,' Archie said.

'Now that,' his father said, '*isn't* a word.'

'But—'

'Not when you're fourteen. Time for perspiration and keep your fingers crossed for the other ten per cent. Leave facility to the lassies.'

While he rowed on, brother and sister tried to work out what he meant. Though neither succeeded, characteristically the girl was left feeling complimented, the boy vaguely despondent. Meanwhile the father, unconscious of his effect, hummed a little tune from the pleasure of exercise as he glanced contentedly from side to side.

Though there was an island on the loch, it was small and overgrown so that they made their picnic in the boat, sharing sandwiches from the rucksack, Coke for the children, the father with a flask of tea to himself. The father told a joke and then they took turns, Archie at his turn laughing so hard that the punchline was lost in a spray of crumbs.

'I should have brought the rod,' the man said, shaking the last drops in his cup over the side.

'Fish for tea,' Archie said.

'Better than the shops.'

'And chips,' Archie said.

'It takes a good fisherman to catch a chip.'

'With the right bait,' Archie said. 'A packet of salt.'

'And a poke for a net.'

'You're both being silly,' Lena said.

'Time to go.'

'I want to row,' Lena said.

It happened so suddenly. Afterwards, Archie could never work out exactly how she fell out of the boat. She had stood up, too suddenly, in a temper, of course. Perhaps it was cramp from sitting so long. Certainly, once in the water, though she could swim, she reached for the boat and sank.

Archie went in to save her. Even in summer, even at noon after a morning of sunshine, the loch was too deep to warm. Under the surface, the cold struck into him. He saw Lena, her hair floating up towards him. He kicked hard and reached for her hand. Next moment, she was pulling him down. She was going to drown, they were going to drown, he was going to drown, *he was going to drown*. He tore his hand out of her grip. As he rose to the surface, his father passed him. He smashed up out of the water, and with the first breath drowning seemed as absurd as a bad dream. No surprise that they came up beside him quietly, Lena in his father's arms.

For a week afterwards, he would wake shouting out of a dream in which Lena held him, pulling him down as if she would never let go. After that he still dreamed of it, but kept the shouting inside so that no one knew, except Lena, who came into his room and whispered to him that he was a coward.

BOOK TWO

———◆———

City of Ghosts

Chapter Eighteen

In the opinion of many of his colleagues, Meldrum had been lucky not to be suspended after being removed from the Archibald Wemyss murder investigation; and a few of the canteen lawyers claimed that dismissal would have been the proper option. Fortunately, the decision lay with neither group, nor even ACC Fleming, but with Chief Constable Baird. The interview with him hadn't been pleasant, but, whatever his reason, and that consummate politician always had his reasons, it ended with Meldrum still on duty. It was true, though, it would have been hard to find a task less to his taste than the one to which he was assigned, so to that extent authority got its due pound of flesh.

Meldrum was a detective, trained and practised in the craft for so long that he'd acquired the instincts of the hunter. He talked to people, assessed them, listened for the gaps. Put it a different way, he liked to be kept busy, away from the office, out and about. Instead, on the Monday afternoon following the interview with Baird he found himself in front of a computer wondering how there could be any new path up a mountain of data, or undiscovered route through its maze, considering that the whole extraordinary accumulation had been read over, cross-checked, referenced and sifted by others exhaustively, exhaustingly, innumerable times before. Apart from Lothian and Borders, police forces in Glasgow and Aberdeen, in London and the North of England had contributed to the database held in Edinburgh. Over seventy thousand people had been investigated; thirty thousand statements recorded from those who had seemed, however momentarily, to be possible suspects; statements taken from those cited in support of alibis; statements taken from witnesses of every sort; together with details of enquiries into the best part of forty thousand vehicles similar to the types seen at or near the crime sites. It was the prevailing mode in modern police investigations, and the principle of seeking connections which might unexpectedly yield the right pattern took on a new plausibility given the exponential growth in data handling allowed by computers. The three unsolved murders of young women in Edinburgh had been compared in detail to another five in Scotland – one in Aberdeen, one in Lanarkshire, three in Glasgow – to three in the North of England; and to half a dozen in the Greater London area. DNA testing, because of the killer's caution, bad luck and contaminated samples, had been inconclusive.

As for the Edinburgh killings, two years after the death of the third girl, Kitty Grant, the cases were still open; such cases were never officially closed, but effort on them had reduced until only one officer worked on them fulltime. This had been for the previous six months a detective sergeant who had decided to concentrate on the cases in the North of England, which had involved him in regular visits

o Bradford, where the main incident room records for them
were held. Meldrum started with those three cases and after
a week made up his mind that his predecessor had been
chasing shadows. That the killing of the three women, all of
them prostitutes — one in Bradford, one in Leeds, one in
Manchester — might be linked to one another seemed
possible. They had all been strangled by a man wearing
gloves, a man of unusual strength. That made a connection
of sorts to the second of the Edinburgh murders. Even with
the Chambers girl, however, though again the force used
indicated an exceptional strength, there was the difference
that the strangling had been done with bare hands. Other
differences, too, remained to be taken into account. None of
the women murdered in Edinburgh had been engaged in
prostitution. All were young. All were unusually attractive.
Looking at the photographs, Meldrum was struck by the
contrast between them as a group and the three unfortunates
killed plying their trade in the North of England. The three
prostitutes were older, the youngest in her late twenties, the
oldest nearer fifty than forty. They might have been sisters,
heavy featured, dull eyed, coarsened by drink or drugs,
brutalised by the lives they led. All of them were the product
of broken homes and had alternated time in care with failed
attempts at being fostered; all of them had abusive partners;
all of them had children of their own condemned to repeat
the same wretched cycle. They were marked by the stigmata
of ignorance and poverty; and finally that was the compar-
ison Meldrum settled on between the two groups. One was
of an underclass; the other of young women, two in their
teens, one just turned twenty, educated, better nourished,
with everything to live for. He could imagine the kind of
man who would prey on the first group, and the kind of man

who might seek his victims in the second. What he couldn'
imagine was that it would be the same man.

When he arrived on the second Monday, Meldrum
cleared everything off his desk and spread out in row
seventeen photographs, one from each of the murder victim
in the database, including the three from the North o
England. After a moment, he picked them up, shuffled ther
and scattered them at random face up, seventeen image
smiling, unsmiling, all of them dead by violence. He close
his eyes and remembered the only one with which he ha
been directly involved.

Sylvia Marshall had been nineteen when she died. I
lodgings in the Bruntsfield district of the city, a favourit
area for students, her two flatmates had reported her missin
on the Tuesday following a weekend in the second tern
They hadn't seen her since the Saturday morning, so it ha
taken them three days to get in touch with the police. A
woman journalist wrote a column about the delay i
reporting the disappearance, which incited a lengthy corre
spondence about a modern lack of caring for others and th
dangers of indifference. Some spice was added to thi
exchange by the fact that one of the flatmates was studyin
theology. As it happened, the theologian had herself bee
away for the weekend. Getting back on the Monday evenin
she'd gone to the police the next morning; and so th
deficiencies of a generation boiled down in the event to th
remaining nineteen-year-old, who for what it was worth wa
doing a course on food science. Meldrum's involvemen
began at two o'clock on the Tuesday, and he was so quickl
sure something was badly wrong that, with his encourage
ment, Sylvia Marshall's picture was on the front page of th
later editions of the evening paper. The main source of tha

conviction had been an interview with the girl's father, whom the flatmate, before calling the police, had phoned in case Sylvia had gone home. George Marshall, a gentle, bewildered man, had driven to Edinburgh at once in the certainty something had happened to his daughter. From a close and loving family, she had too much strength of character, too strong a sense of responsibility, to disappear of her own volition. She didn't have any emotional entanglements, no boyfriend at the moment; she had loved her first year at university, exams gave her no difficulty; she was enjoying her second year. Worsening asthma had made Marshall take early retirement from teaching in his middle fifties, and by the end of the interview, he was in such distress that a doctor had to be called. Early on the Wednesday, Hugh McArdle had put in an appearance and confessed to being the murderer. He had seen the girl in the Sleat Bar at the Hamilton Hotel, where he worked as doorman, on Saturday night. She had been drinking on her own, which he had thought odd. He had followed her when she left, talked to her, persuaded her to walk with him, killed her in a lane near the flat where her lived and gone home. When asked why he hadn't confessed earlier, he'd explained that Wednesday was his day off. A search of the lane found no body, no blood, some used condoms, no evidence of violence. On the other hand, a major effort to trace guests who had stayed in the Hamilton Hotel that weekend, accompanied by a public appeal for anyone in the Sleat Bar at the relevant time to come forward, had produced two witnesses who claimed to identify Sylvia Marshall's photograph as that of a woman they had seen in the hotel that evening. As against that, no one on the hotel staff remembered her. 'Not unless she'd her tits out,' as one of the part-time barmen put it. 'Welsh game on, Saturday night was a madhouse in here.' A week after her disappearance, at 12.45 a.m. on Sunday, the naked body of Sylvia Marshall taped around with bin bags was lifted from the boot of a car and rolled into a ditch. It was a quiet side road, and just after midnight a couple in search of privacy had driven into it and found a parking place by pulling in hard against a farm gate. They had recovered from their exertions and were getting ready to continue on towards the main road when, as the man cleared steam from inside the window, he saw a car approaching. It was on dips, then sidelights, then it had stopped and its lights went out. It was close enough for the couple to hear its engine still running, and make out the door swinging open, a shape getting out. A moment later, they saw the boot go up. That was enough for the uneasy watcher. He started the engine and at the same time switched on his headlights. Only as he did so did he realise the car ahead hadn't pulled in to the side. It sat in the middle of the narrow road, blocking it. There was no way he could get past. He saw the boot go down and a man run round into the flood of light, one arm up to cover his face. He scrambled into the car, which at once began reversing at reckless speed. They watched it go back like that for about a quarter mile till without a pause it swung out backwards on to the main road. If anything had been coming, the case would have ended then, but the devil looked out for his own. The couple was sure about the time. They were certain the man had been alone.

At 12.45 a.m. on that Sunday, Harkness the manager of the Hamilton Hotel stood witness that Hugh McArdle had been having a nightcap in his office. There was no reason to disbelieve him. In any case, Hugh McArdle had never learned to drive a car forwards, never mind backwards at speed.

Opening his eyes suddenly, Meldrum, his mind full of the image of Sylvia Marshall, picked up her photograph and then, trying to see all the others as if for the first time, to ignore everything he knew about them, all the details of the crimes committed against them, took up five more from the pictures scattered across his desk.

Six young women. From Aberdeen: Elsie Richards. From Hamilton, in Lanarkshire not far from Glasgow: Frances Deacon. In Glasgow: Margaret Grant. And the three from Edinburgh: Sylvia Marshall, Madge Chambers, Kitty Grant (no relation to the girl killed in Glasgow). After a long hesitation, he picked out another photograph. In London: Sandra Norton.

He bundled the remaining photographs to the back of the desk and laid in line the seven he had selected.

Looking from one to the other, it seemed to him they were alike. Young, dark-haired, attractive, an impression of intelligence, and something else – an eagerness for life. Girls with everything to live for. For a long time then, he sat motionless as if lost in a dream, trying to imagine the man who could have found in each of these girls the thing that matched his need. And at some point every day after that, he did the same thing.

Chapter Nineteen

———◆———

'I had a feeling this was going to be a bad day.'

'You haven't changed,' Meldrum said. 'I tell a lie, you've put on weight.'

'The joys of retirement,' Bannigan said, pulling a branch down and chopping it through with secateurs. 'You should try it.'

Meldrum had rung the front door bell and not been surprised to get no answer, since he'd tried phoning twice from the office before setting out. If he'd come anyway, it was because he'd had enough of sitting at a desk. Getting no response, he'd walked back to the street and hesitated by his car, keys in hand. If he got in, it would be to drive back and start again laboriously going through files and statements. It was unfair that the sun was shining.

Instead, he'd set off for a stroll along the row of bungalows. Behind them, he'd found a path at the top of a flight of steps. He'd seen the same kind of thing before, a path made from a single track railway, shut down as uneconomic years ago. Idling along it, he'd been able to look into the back gardens and was thinking how noisy the trains must have been for the bungalow owners when he spotted Bannigan at his back fence, in shirt sleeves despite the cold, pruning a little straggling rowan.

'What brings you out this way?'

'I came to see you.'

'I didn't think it was for the fresh air.'

'All the same,' Meldrum said, filling his lungs, 'it's not a bad day.'

He thought how pleasant it would be just to wander on along the track enjoying the sunshine. Endless furrows shone brown in the ploughed fields. Half a mile ahead trees had been planted on either side of the track, making an avenue, nothing more peaceful than walking an avenue of trees.

'You'd better come in,' Bannigan said, opening the gate set under the rowan tree.

Meldrum went down steps cut in the bank.

'You've got a nice garden.'

'This time of year, it's just make-work to get out of the house. Be nice when the spring comes.'

He led the way, stopping at a hut against the fence between him and his neighbour. Standing in the doorway, Meldrum watched him press the secateurs into a plastic clip screwed to the wall. There was a line of clips, each gripping some kind of gardening tool: trowels, forks, a rake, shears. Everything was very tidy and workmanlike.

'I never knew you were keen on gardening.'

'My wife's been dead four years.' He spoke casually, his expression veiled in the dim light inside the hut. 'I try to keep it the way she liked it.'

'I'm sorry.'

As they went up to the house, Bannigan said, 'Did you know I was married?'

'Of course I did.'

'Right.' He opened the back door and they went into the kitchen. Bannigan sat on a chair to kick off the old shoes he'd been wearing and put on a pair of trainers. 'Never sure with you.'

Pat Bannigan had been the DI in charge of the investigation into the murder of Madge Chambers. It had been his last case before taking retirement. In the front room, a picture of a woman sat on a table at the window. As Meldrum looked round, he saw another one and then another on a shelf in a wall alcove. Different ages, but the same woman, dark hair, nice face. If she'd been dead for four years, she must have died within a year of her husband retiring. There weren't any other photographs; maybe they had no children. Meldrum tried to remember her name, but he wasn't sure he'd ever heard it.

'Madge Chambers?' Bannigan repeated.

'And Sylvia Marshall and Kitty Grant. Grant was two years ago, after your time.'

'I still read the papers. What about them?'

'I've been given the files to go over.'

'You have? What did you do to get landed with that?'

'It wasn't a prize for perfect attendance.'

They were still standing. Bannigan was studying him in a way Meldrum recognised. He was calculating the angles, trying to work out what was going on. How long would you have to be retired before you lost that reflex, the habit of suspicion? Maybe you never lost it.

'Collating and back-checking files,' Bannigan said, rubbing his chin, 'that's a desk job. The way I understand it, you should be looking at what's already there, not looking for new stuff.'

'It's a nice day for a drive.'

'So who knows you're out here talking to me?'

Meldrum shrugged.

'Fuck it,' Bannigan said. 'You want a drink?'

'Coffee would be fine.'

'You want me to talk about this stuff, I need a drink.' He grinned, 'It's not often I get an excuse in the morning.'

'Okay. But don't forget I'm driving.'

'Don't worry. I've seen too many, you know, you get the habit in the job, be all right if the wife — I'm pretty strict with myself. Drunk in charge of a garden, eh? You could cut your fucking fingers off.'

He came back carrying a bottle of Glenkinchie in one hand and a jug of water in the other.

'You want water?'

'Same again would be fine.'

'Only way to take it. Whisky needs water. Opens it up, changes the smell. It's like walking in a garden after it's been raining.' He nodded Meldrum into a seat, gave him a glass, sat down himself. 'Madge Chambers? What are you looking for?'

'Anything you can tell me.'

'It's all in the files.'

'Most of it,' Meldrum said. 'When could you ever get everything in?'

Bannigan held up his glass as if making a silent toast. 'I remember it, and not just because it was the last one. We didn't get anybody. You don't ever forget those ones, do you?' He sighed. 'She was sixteen years old. Nobody should die that young. Her whole life ahead of her. A pretty kid too. Even when I saw her, you could see that. Christ, she was just out of school. It was her first job.'

'Tell me about that.'

'She'd left school in the summer. Instead of looking for a job right away, she went off rail tracking in Europe for a month with a pal. Too young in my book, but it was her father paid for it. She was their only kid, and he thought the sun rose and set on her. He was destroyed when she was killed. You wouldn't believe it, but first time I saw them the mother was going on at him about letting her go to Europe. If you hadn't known, you'd have thought the kid had been killed on that trip. Tragedy takes folk different ways, pulls some together, breaks others apart. Broke those two apart. They got divorced, I heard later. According to her pal – girl about the same age, same class at the school – the two of them had a great time on that holiday. So at least the kid had that.'

He got up and poured himself another whisky. Meldrum shook his head, he'd hardly touched his. 'And when she came back,' he prompted, 'she got a job.'

'Right. An office in Northumberland Street, half a dozen employees in one room and the boss with a room about the same size all to himself. The firm was called after him – CJM Developments. CJM – Campbell James Michie, that was his name. You asked him, that's what he told you, all three names. Not somebody you called Jimmy. A wee Napoleon.'

'What was he like with the staff?'

'He told them to jump, they asked how high. But that's not what you mean, is it? You're thinking of the Redmond woman?'

'It was in the file. I wondered what you made of it.'

'It looked good – for about five minutes. She claimed Michie had sexually harassed her, he denied it. How do you prove that stuff anyway? The other women in the office—'

'Was it all women?'

'Oh, sure it was. So what? They come cheaper than men. And they all said they'd had no bother with him. Then it turned out she was due the bullet – can't remember what for, but it was genuine enough, I mean he'd told her the week before he'd be letting her go at the end of the month, she admitted that. And she'd never made a complaint or said anything to anybody about getting harassed before. It was a time-waster – we kicked it into touch.'

'I know you did. It's in the reports. I'd probably have done the same. But can I ask you, did you have any kind of feeling about him?'

'Is that what this is about?'

Meldrum looked back at him without saying anything.

'And what do you mean *probably*? No "probably" about it. You would have done the same. There was nothing there. Madge left her work at the usual time, she told one of the women she'd a date, she seemed excited and very pleased with herself. Three days later, they find her in a ditch on a road near Peebles. Like your one, Sylvia Marshall. And she didn't work for Michie.'

'So you didn't have any kind of feeling about him? Off the record?'

'A wee Napoleon. A wee arsehole. Off the record.'

Bannigan got up and reached for Meldrum's glass. 'You want that topped up?'

'I'm fine.'

'If I'm drinking on my own, I'm as well being on my own.'

Meldrum considered him for a moment. 'No problem, Pat. Freshen it up.'

At the sideboard, Bannigan took his time. When Meldrum got his glass back, there wasn't much more in it. Bannigan's tumbler, though, had been filled, and by the colour of it with straight whisky. As he sat down again, he blew out his breath, puffing out his cheeks. 'Don't ask me what that was about,' he said.

Meldrum sipped his whisky, stretched out his long legs at ease, gave it a minute.

When he was ready, he said casually, 'Another thing tied the two murders together. You'd a confession from Hugh McArdle as well.'

But Bannigan instead of answering his smile, leaned forward and said fiercely, 'You know what tied them, and it wasn't that fucking idiot McArdle. It was the way they were *tied*, and what he did to them while they were *tied*. The bastard that killed them took his time. He had them for days. Somewhere he had them for days.' He drained half his glass. 'The things you remember. My wife used to tell me, think about the good things. At night, on your own, the shit that goes through your head.'

They sat in silence. When at last Bannigan got up to refill his glass, he didn't ask Meldrum. Sitting down, he said, 'Know you're driving. Quite right.'

'Nice whisky,' Meldrum said, sipping, the glass almost empty.

'All the best.'

Mildly, after a time, Meldrum asked, 'Why didn't you charge McArdle with wasting police time?'

'I suggested it, but it didn't happen. Same as you, I suppose.'

'I didn't even suggest it. You think it would've stopped him doing it again?'

'I put him through the hoops. I was pretty angry about

159

what had happened to the kid. I sweated him. We went into his flat mob-handed and took it apart. No forensic, of course, nothing. A waste of time, but you'd have thought it would've sickened him. Place was a dump before we started, you should have seen it when we finished. Him out on the landing with the dog, we could hear it barking the whole time we were in there. Wee Tommy Gemmell was windy about dogs, kept saying pity we didn't have a gun. When McArdle got back in and saw what we'd done, he nearly started greeting like a big lassie. And all the time he's struggling to hold the dog on the leash, and it's barking like fucking crazy, it wanted to tear our arses off.' He started laughing. 'And wee Gemmell with his truncheon out nearly shitting himself. You should've been there.'

'I can imagine.'

'The thing is,' Bannigan said, 'after all those years I was ready to chuck it, more than ready by the end; desperate, you could say. I never for a minute thought I might miss it. I'm glad you came. If you're out this way again, give me a knock. I mean, even if there's nothing you want to ask me.'

Chapter Twenty

The days fell into a routine. On the third day after he had gone to see Bannigan, he came out into the corridor to stretch his legs and was surprised to see Bobbie Shields, who broke step then came on at a lingering pace.

'What brings you down here?'

Shields didn't seem to have an answer to that. 'Taking a break?' he asked at last, offering a question for a question.

'This is Siberia,' Meldrum said. 'You don't want to come down here, you might catch a cold.'

'Aye, right.' He nodded vaguely. 'How's it going?'

In Siberia, how does it fucking go? Meldrum thought. You watch the snow falling.

He said, 'Fine.'

'Right.'

'Well, then.'

What else was there to say?

'Am I holding you back?'

'I'm taking a break.'

'Are you going to the canteen?'

Meldrum knew what time it was, but he looked at his watch anyway. 'Too early for me.'

'Just taking a break from looking at they computers, eh? Goes for the eyes.'

Could he be trying to take the piss? Meldrum wondered. Out of me? It would be a stupid thing to try.

'So it's going all right then?' Shields asked.

'You've already asked me that. What's this about?'

'Not about anything.'

'Good,' Meldrum said on a note of finality.

But as he was turning away, Shields said, 'You not want to ask me how it's going?'

'Should I?' Meldrum asked unemphatically, but suddenly he was on the alert. While he'd been checking old files, Shields had been seconded to Gowdie's team investigating Archie Wemyss's death. 'Have you got somebody?'

'No, and you know what they say. Catch somebody early, or chances are you don't catch them at all.'

'Too bad.' He was sincere. Thinking of the old poet Hector Wemyss and his wife, he wished their son's murderer had been caught. Experience had taught him that, without seeing justice done, many relatives of victims couldn't even begin the process of healing. And yet . . . Watching from the sidelines as Gowdie succeeded would have made for a mixed pleasure. 'Nobody in the frame at all?'

'We're going over the same stuff. It should have been easy. Husband in one room, wife next door with the boyfriend. Except that it turned out not to be the wife. All the same but, it was the wife's brother that gets himself killed – and what the hell was *he* doing there? Gowdie's gone through the card – everybody you talked to – seen them once, seen them twice, got nowhere. The hotel staff. Rannie.

Hennessy and his wife. And she's some woman.' He grinned. 'You ever hear of Apple?'

'Apple?'

'It's an escort agency. Hennessy's wife runs it. Apple Agency – it's in the book. We're talking available here. Know what I mean?'

'I assume you mean whores.'

Shields made a face, held out a fat hand and tilted it back and forward in the maybe-maybe not gesture. 'They're not cheap. I couldn't afford them. It's a high-class operation.'

'Hennessy's wife . . . Is he involved?'

'Probably. But he claims it's all hers. And she seems to be the one that runs the business, takes the calls, contacts the girls, all that stuff.'

Meldrum thought of the stair from the street to the Hennessy flat, the broad stone rail on either side of the wide steps, the arched door with the carriage lamp above it. Half to himself, he said, 'This town. You never know what's going on.'

'Tell you for nothing, Gowdie doesn't know.'

'Running an investigation isn't easy,' Meldrum said, on a reflex of solidarity.

Another long-term product of a system of hierarchy, Shields knew exactly the line Meldrum was drawing. He grunted and said, 'This one bloody isn't. Hennessy's wife backs up his story that he was home when he said he was. And they went to bed, she says, and made love. She just came out with that – she said "made love" but it sounded like "fucked". I got a hard on. Don't know about Barry Gowdie, I wouldn't presume to guess, but the temperature in the room shot up. There wasn't a mark on her husband when he stripped – not one little bruise, she says.'

'Why does that matter?'

Shields frowned. Meldrum being obtuse, his look said, was a new experience for him. 'It meant he hadn't been in a fight. But we know from the forensic that Wemyss had used his fists on somebody. It's hard to believe it wasn't the guy that killed him.'

Meldrum folded his arms. Realising what he'd done, he unfolded them. On his ribs at each side he had fading bruises. Rubbing his chin, he said, 'Depends if she's telling the truth.'

'Okay, he's her husband, so you could say she's lying for him. But she's the dead man's sister, for God's sake! And she goes on about loving her brother, so you're not going to get a Procurator Fiscal sending that into a court for a smart defence lawyer to take apart. And as for Rannie and his woman,' he shook his head, 'they were humping – didn't hear a thing. It's driving Gowdie crazy. I tell you, Hugh McArdle better not confess to this one or Gowdie'll have him.'

'Don't worry,' Meldrum said, 'McArdle only confesses to killing women. He told me that himself.'

'Big bastard. Probably confesses to killing lassies, because he's into boys. Poncing around in that kilt and ruffs, when you think about it, he's probably an iron hoof.'

To have Shields turn up for a chat was unexpected. To have him launch unprompted into discussing a case was disconcerting. To have him foray into criminal psychology was too much for Meldrum to handle.

'I'd better get back.'

He had the door open to return to the computer room when he heard Shields say, 'I hear you saw Pat Bannigan.'

'What?' He swung round, a release of the stored energy

he'd built sitting at a desk. Shields blinked and took a step back. 'Where did you hear that?'

'Just around. You know what this place is like. Anyway, take care.'

Meldrum watched him go up the corridor, didn't move till he was out of sight.

What had that been about?

Chapter Twenty-One

Five years ago, it had been Madge Chambers, the unsolved case that haunted Pat Bannigan. What had Bannigan said? *She was sixteen years old. Nobody should die that young.* Eight years ago, it had been Sylvia Marshall. *Nobody was caught: you don't forget those ones.* Three years ago, it had been Kitty Grant. Gowdie's case. Hard to picture Gowdie wakening covered in sweat in the middle of the night, being haunted wasn't his style.

Yet, like the others, no one had been caught.

Kitty Grant had been the oldest of the three. A promiscuous twenty-year-old from a poorer background than the other two. She wasn't a student like Sylvia Marshall or an office worker like Madge Chambers. She had had half a dozen jobs since she left school, and had been pleased to get on the checkout at her local Tesco. That had been her last job. She came from a broken home, and had spent almost a year in care when she was eight. Reading the social work notes, she had been taken from her parents because of persistent neglect, but there was a hint too that the father had been suspected of interfering with the child sexually.

Certainly, once he'd disappeared from the picture, she'd been returned to the mother. After that, there had been the occasional flurry of social work visits triggered off by truancy from school. She'd been caught shoplifting with a group of friends when she was fourteen. There had been a pregnancy at sixteen; the baby had been adopted. More than one boyfriend made a sketchy appearance in the notes, shadowy figures in the background of an abortion or a beating. She should have been a pathetic figure, but wasn't. Her photograph should have looked like those of the victims from the North of England, but didn't. Despite everything, she looked bright and lively, smiling in expectation of some good thing just about to happen. It wasn't hard to imagine that, dressed up on a night out, she might have looked to a stranger's eye like a girl with everything to live for.

Meldrum had taken all he could take. He pushed back his chair and stared unseeing at the screen. For him this was the worst of tasks. Hours of matching and checking. It was a job for a plodder. Too much time to think; too much time to think about dead girls; so much time you suddenly saw your own daughter's image among a flow of images on the screen and felt as if everything clean in your life was being dirtied. Hours spent alone until the walls of the room started to come in.

He usually went later for lunch when it was quiet. Today he couldn't wait. When he went in, the canteen was starting to get busy. He filled his tray and, seeing Jimmy Paton at a table on his own, took the seat opposite. Paton was a big quiet man, not much given to gossip, which normally suited Meldrum. It was one of the reasons they got on fairly well together. Today, though, he'd spent too much time on his own. It would have been a relief to talk about anything as long as it didn't matter. As he chewed, he tried to think of something to say. How's the family? He'd heard a rumour Paton's wife had left him. What about shop talk? Wasn't that what people missed when they gave up a job, or it gave them up? There was always shop talk. Who was up, who was down, who'd made an arse of something. Or the new pay structure. Or money wasted on a new computer system. The difficulty was he couldn't care less what Paton was doing. After his morning at the screen, he didn't want to hear about stupidity or violence. And, out of tact perhaps, Paton didn't ask what he was doing. He wondered what ordinary people talked about. He chewed and wondered what was in the news. To his surprise, he realised he hadn't looked at a paper for days.

It was a relief when someone else sat down. Then he realised it was Barry Gowdie. Looking across the table, he was vaguely irritated to see Paton brightening up.

Gowdie nodded at them both, then took a moment to scatter salt across a sickly yellow mound of chicken tikka and pour a trail of tomato sauce along one edge of the laden plate.

Finished, he said, 'I heard a good one at the rugby club last night. This doctor goes on holiday to the Bahamas. He's in this really great hotel, a cracker of a place, best of everything. So first day, he gets the towel and he's out on the beach and he gets on the chat with this other guy. Turns out this guy's from Edinburgh as well. Turns out he's a lawyer. So he says to the doctor, "Isn't this just what the doctor ordered?" "Absolutely," says the doctor. "I tell you, I needed this," the lawyer says. "The fire came at the right time." "How do you mean – fire?" the doctor says. Have you heard it?'

'Not me,' Paton said. 'What about you, Jim?'

Meldrum who'd been unwillingly fascinated by Gowdie's trick of being able to chew and talk at the same time, more or less without spraying, didn't answer at once since his mouth was full.

'Doesn't matter whether he's heard it or not,' Gowdie said. It came out harsh and fast, but at once he went on with a smile, 'Some folk just aren't into jokes, that right, Jim? Anyway, the lawyer says, "We'd a fire at the office. The insurance settlement was more than fair. And after all the excitement, I needed a holiday." And the doctor says, "Isn't that a coincidence! Exactly the same thing with me. Our practice was caught in a flood. But, fortunately, like you, the insurance more than covered it." The lawyer sat staring at him, didn't say a word – like Jim here. At last the doctor asks him, "Is something wrong? What is it?" And the lawyer says, "How do you start a flood?"'

Paton laughed.

Meldrum chewed another mouthful slowly, swallowed. 'Aye,' he said, 'I have heard it.'

'Bet you didn't laugh then either.' Gowdie showed his teeth, but it didn't much resemble a smile.

'Different strokes,' Paton said. By nature he was a peacemaker. 'My sister can't stand Billy Connolly. She hates the swearing.'

'He was funnier before he started swearing,' Meldrum said.

'Oh, I like him,' Paton said. He smiled. 'My father's a funny old bugger. Sunday there, we were up visiting him in the Old Folks Home. Me and the brother and the brother-in-law pay for him, best of everything, food's really good. If he wasn't in there, he'd be starving to death. Before she died, my mother ran after him hand and foot, he couldn't even make a pot of tea. And they're good to him, but he hates the place. My sister told him, you don't hate being here, you hate being old. So the old bugger's sulking and staring out the window, and my sister and I are arguing away as usual. And he looks round and says, I'm old enough to remember when Billy Connolly was funny. I swear that's about all we got out of him, and we were there for an hour.'

'I hear you went to see Pat Bannigan,' Gowdie said.

Paton looked from one to the other, gathered up his tray and left.

'How did you hear that?'

'Pat phoned me. He says, after you left him he got to thinking. He thought it was funny you coming out to talk to him like that. He wondered if there was something you weren't telling him.'

'Like what?'

'Like, had there been a break in the Chambers case.'

'He should have phoned me.'

'Right,' Gowdie said derisively. 'You didn't even know his wife had died.'

'That what he told you?'

'It came up. So is there?'

'What?'

'Don't fuck around – you know what I'm talking about. Have you come across something? What have you found?'

'Something everybody's missed, you mean?' Meldrum was beginning to enjoy himself.

'Is that why you went to see Pat? Have you turned up something about the Chambers murder?'

'If I did, it would have to be about all of them, wouldn't it?' Meldrum said. 'We're sure the same man killed Kitty Grant.'

'And your one. The Marshall girl.'

But, using Kitty Grant's name, Meldrum had seen the girl's image, a smiling sixteen-year-old, and felt disgust with himself. Losing taste for the game, he kept silent.

After a moment, Gowdie sat back. 'Bollocks,' he said. 'You haven't found anything.'

Meldrum began to put stuff on his tray ready to leave.

'That you finished? I'm going for the pudding. You'll not work up much of an appetite, sitting at a desk. Taking it easy and picking up the same pay packet as the rest of us, nice work if you can get it. Are you enjoying it? I wouldn't fancy it. Speaking for myself, I couldn't stick it for five minutes.'

'It has its moments,' Meldrum said, and because he was needled couldn't resist adding, 'Pat Bannigan was very helpful.'

Gowdie's eyes narrowed. 'Bollocks,' he said again. 'Oh, by the way, Deekers McGroarty was at the club last night. He brought your name up, late on, he'd had a bit to drink. He really doesn't rate you. I was quite surprised. I wouldn't have thought he'd even have heard of you.'

'Oh, I've heard of him,' Meldrum said, getting up. In the context of another investigation, he recalled McGroarty discussing in confidence his weakness for underage school-girls. 'The famous Deekers.'

Without realising it, he was smiling.

'The best scrum half Scotland ever had,' he said.

Gowdie looked venomous but baffled. He knew something had gone wrong with the needling, but he had no idea what.

Chapter Twenty-Two

Meldrum wakened the next morning and lay in bed unable to persuade himself to get up. Call it the Protestant work ethic, call it being a wage slave, this had never happened to him before. All his life, even when he least felt like it, he'd opened his eyes on a work day and within five minutes rolled out of bed to get on with it as best he could. One winter years ago, he'd worked on through two successive bouts of flu. When he'd tried to do it for a third time, he went down with pneumonia. Very occasionally even now, if he got tired enough, he felt a shadowy ache at the top of his right lung like the fading memory of bad times. Staying off work wasn't something he did.

This morning he couldn't face it.

He spent a long time staring at the ceiling. He lay for a while thinking that he needed to get up and piss, then that he badly needed to get up and piss, then he fell asleep for a while. When he finally got up and went into the bathroom, the bulb was out. It had been out for a week, and he'd been meaning to get another one. It was awkward not having a light, since it was an internal bathroom without a window.

Standing with his knees against the bowl in the dark, he filled the room with a hot sweet scent and decided it was probably just as well he couldn't see the colour of his piss.

Driving with one hand, he shaved in the car. It was half eleven. As he came to the brow of a street, he saw the Fife hills, and a giant oil tanker dwindled to a toy on the glittering surface of the Firth. If he intended to go to work, he was heading in the wrong direction. It was another fine day, though, and it was good to drive, taking a road that gave him occasional glimpses of the estuary.

Half an hour later, he was driving down into a housing scheme in Prestonpans. When he recognised the name of a street, he thought he'd come there by accident, but as he got out of the car he wondered about that. The other possibility was that some customary taskmaster in his head had led him this way. Maybe he'd lost whatever knack he'd ever had for stealing a day out of his life. It was an unpleasant thought.

It was the second last house in the street. At the gate, he went past, crossed to the other side, walked back to his car. What was he trying to prove? That he would consciously decide what he wanted to do? If so, as he set off up the street, it seemed he'd decided to go back to the house.

There was a little patch of overgrown front lawn. The curtain on one of the front windows was pulled halfway across. Three muddy Wellingtons were lined up on the front step. The woman who answered the door wore a skirt and a jumper that was too big for her.

'Miss Cairns?' he asked.

'Mrs,' she said.

A small fat boy peeped round her legs.

'Sorry.' He showed his warrant card. 'Detective Inspector Jim Meldrum. I was looking for Dorothy Cairns.' The woman made no response. 'This is the address I had for her.' Glancing down, he saw the fat boy screw up his face as if getting ready to cry. 'But that was two years ago.'

'Is it about Kitty?' the woman asked.

'Kitty Grant? Yes.'

'I never saw you before.'

'Can I ask, are you Dorothy Cairns?'

She gave that some thought, as if weighing the options. 'As was. I'm married.'

'I'd be grateful if you could answer some questions. It wouldn't take long.'

'But I never saw you before.'

'I wasn't one of the officers involved at the time.'

'How do you know about it then?'

So much for not dodging work, he thought. The reward of virtue seemed to amount to a conversation with a half-wit.

'I'm going back over things,' he said. 'I'm sure you'd want to help. From what I've read, you were her closest friend.'

'I was the last one to see her alive. That's what they told me. I was probably the last one to see her alive.'

'Apart from the man who killed her.'

She frowned. 'One of your lot said that too. I didn't think it was funny.'

'I'm sure he didn't mean it that way.'

'You did.'

Meldrum looked at her. 'I'm sorry.'

'Show me your card again.' She studied it carefully. 'You'd better come in.'

She went down the passage, Meldrum far enough behind to avoid stepping on the child. He stopped at the door of the kitchen. The table was covered with plates from breakfast and what looked like last night's dinner. The work surfaces were lost under boxes of cereals and tins and wrappers and God knows what. A mound of varied items reared up from the sink.

'I'll just put the kettle on,' she said.

He watched as she moved stuff out of the way, using the spout of the kettle as a kind of battering ram until she eased it under the cold tap.

When they went into the front room, neither of them had a cup. The kettle had been put on for some kind of gunge the child was now spooning out of a bowl as he sat on her knee. On balance, Meldrum regretted the lack. Coffee had to be seriously bad before an addict would prefer nothing. He asked his first question and she got up so suddenly the child began to whimper. He thought he'd touched a nerve and might be about to stumble on something worth hearing. Instead, she straightened the sagging curtain and said, jiggling the child in her arms, 'This wee rascal's always pulling at it. He's a right terror.'

Meldrum waited until she sat down. When he thought he had secured her attention, he tried again. 'How many of you went together to the Hamilton Hotel that night?'

'I couldn't tell you, not exactly. Give me a minute.' She sank into a trance of calculation.

Put her at her ease with a simple opening question had been the idea.

This could take some time.

'There was a lot of us,' she said at last. 'I was so pleased. It was for my twenty-first, did you know that? It was Kitty's idea. Now you're an old lady, she said, joking, you know. We're going to party, she said. My two sisters were there and girls we knew since school and two of Kitty's pals from

Tesco.' Her eyes filled with tears. 'If it hadn't been for me, she might still be alive.'

'It was all women. You didn't have any men with you?'

'No way. We were out to enjoy ourselves.'

'What time would you say you got to the Hamilton Hotel?'

'Half-past eight, maybe near nine o'clock, something like that. My older sister and Kitty took me out for a meal. That was Kitty's idea, too. She was just awful generous. She'd give you the coat off her back. She'd do anything for you. I met her when we were in the last year at primary school, and we were friends from then on. I really miss her.'

'And then you went on to the Hamilton Hotel? And that's where other friends joined you?'

'That's right.'

'Whose idea was it to go to the Hamilton Hotel?'

'Not me. I'd have gone to a club or something, like we usually did.'

'But it was your birthday, so something different seemed a good idea? I wonder who thought of that?'

'It must have been Kitty. It was all her idea, like.'

'Do you know why she picked the Hamilton? From Pilton, I'd have thought there were handier places.'

'We took a taxi.' She sounded faintly offended.

'She didn't say anything about arranging to meet anyone there?'

'The other girls.'

'Apart from them?'

'Do you mean a man? She wouldn't be out for my birthday and arrange to meet somebody.' Then, unexpectedly, she laughed. 'Mind, I'm not saying anybody wouldn't if they met some terrific—' She stopped abruptly.

'Did you notice her talking to anybody?'

She shook her head. 'Do you think they didn't ask us? None of us saw her talking to a man.'

Meldrum looked at her sceptically. 'A group of young women out on their own, attractive, having a laugh. It's hard to believe you didn't attract some attention.'

Abstractedly she wiped round the baby's mouth with her finger and slid it into his mouth.

'It seems more than two years ago,' she said. 'Like a different life. My wee sister — you know about this?'

'About something Kitty said to her?'

'That's right. According to Tarn, Kitty told her this guy had spoken to her and said she'd beautiful eyes.'

'An old guy. Wasn't that supposed to be what she said?'

'I wouldn't waste your time on it. Tarn was flying. She was only sixteen then. A few drinks and she was just stupid. She thought she remembered something, likely she made it up. She was always doing that. She wouldn't just say she didn't know. Used to drive my mother mad. And if she made something up you couldn't get her to admit it. She's come away with something stupid and I've told my mother, I was there, that's not true, definitely. Tarn wouldn't ever give in. I think she liked the fuss. She liked the fuss the police made of her.'

'But just suppose this time, she'd got it right. What do you think Kitty would mean by an old guy.'

Again the laugh that seemed to take her by surprise, gone as quickly as it had come. 'Anybody over thirty.'

The Sleat Bar on a Saturday night, crowded to the doors, young women round a table getting steadily drunker, in the morning memory slippery or non-existent. Little wonder Gowdie had got nowhere.

'Kitty was sitting beside you, wasn't she?'

'Right beside me. She made a Happy Birthday speech. That's the way she was. She was always laughing. I used to say to her, you don't need a drink. You've taken a happy pill.'

'Drugs?'

'No! She was just . . . cheery. We were always laughing about something.'

'You say she was beside you. Was that for the whole evening?'

'She said to me, have you had a good night? And I told her, it's been great. And she said to me, I'll just be a minute. But she never came back.'

'She didn't say about going to meet somebody?'

'She said she was going for a pish. Come away from there, pet!'

Meldrum had been so intent he'd paid no attention to the child when he scrambled down off her lap. Now, glancing down, he saw the boy smiling up at him.

'He's made a mess of your trousers.'

Stripes of gunge on each knee. 'Back to Mummy,' he said, lifting him: Without getting up, just by leaning forward, he was able to settle him gently at her feet. It wasn't a big room.

'I could get you a cloth.,' she said without moving.

'Don't bother. I'll give it a brush when it dries.'

As the child, who had decided it was a game, set off again towards Meldrum, she caught him up and held him on her lap. 'It's a skelp he needs,' she said.

'No harm done. Are you sure nobody approached any of the rest of you? I'd have thought somebody would've given it a try. What about yourself? Nobody try to chat you up?'

She shook her head. 'A crowd of lassies having a good

time. You might not believe it, but that frightens a lot of men off. I think that was the best night out I ever had. It was ages before I realised she hadn't come back. Two of us went and looked in the lavatory. And I asked this woman if there was another Ladies and she said she'd no idea. I knew something was wrong. And nobody took it seriously. She's got lucky, they said. They said, You know what Kitty's like. Not on my birthday, I said. Aye, even on your birthday, they said. And the taxi was there, and they all kept on at me, so I went. God help me, I went. If I'd just stayed, maybe it wouldn't have happened, I'll never know.'

'Don't blame yourself,' Meldrum said. 'Whoever was watching followed her out. From then on, it was going to happen. It wasn't your fault.'

'I still can't believe she'd just — it was my birthday.'

'She had been drinking.'

'A lot. But that was same as usual. We all did.'

'What would the usual be?'

'If we were clubbing, eight pints maybe. Some Bacardi Breezers. Then we'd go on to the shorts.'

'How many shorts?'

'I don't know. We drank triples.'

Christ, Meldrum thought; and said, 'I see what you mean by a lot.'

He'd spoken mildly, but at whatever she saw in his face she flared up in anger.

'We were young. We're entitled to have our fun. What did you want us to do? Be like my mammy's granny — have eight kids and make pots of jam?'

Chapter Twenty-Three

Why not? Meldrum thought the next morning, though the previous night he'd read Hector Wemyss's note and thought, No chance. It had been on the table, part of a bundle of mail, most of it junk, which he hadn't bothered to open before he left the flat.

He'd come home late and tired. The visit to Kitty Grant's friend had left a metallic aftertaste of depression. After leaving her, he'd driven on down the coast and pulled in to the lay-by just outside Aberlady. A footbridge took him across to a path that ran beside marshland down to a stretch of beach. It was a good place. He'd stood for a while on the bridge watching the wading birds stride across the sand, busy as wind-up toys. This late in the year, he'd had the beach to himself and walked back and forward beside the water for a long time, trying not to think, until the light went grey and darkness came.

When he arrived at work the next morning, no one mentioned that he hadn't been in the day before. As far as he could tell, no one had missed him. By midday, it seemed an experiment worth repeating. He got his jacket from behind the door, walked along the corridor, went up the stairs to the ground floor and left the building. He passed people, some of whom nodded, vaguely, in what might have been his direction, all of them busy. It felt like being the invisible man.

He put the car into the park behind the Festival Theatre and walked along George IV Bridge to the Lawnmarket. It was another fine day, a high blue sky, the air fresh and cold. As he crossed the road to what had until recently been the Lothian Regional Council building, an ugly structure of faded concrete, he saw Hector Wemyss in the middle of half a dozen people waiting on the steps. As Meldrum approached, the old man, an upright and vigorous eighty-two-year-old, came forward and held out his hand.

'I'm grateful to you for coming,' he said.

'I'm not sure why I have. Your note—'

'There's someone I want you to meet. You'll know why when you see him.' And turning to one of the group, Wemyss explained, 'Don't worry, I've spoken to Norman. He's happy Mr Meldrum won't be a security risk.'

'If I'd known friends could be invited . . .' a white-haired man at the back of the group trailed off querulously.

As Wemyss turned back, ignoring the complainer, Meldrum asked with a touch of irritation, 'Risk? What is this?' From the brief note, he'd received the impression Wemyss and he were going to lunch alone together.

'The Society of Authors in Scotland,' Wemyss explained, 'has an invitation to lunch here and then attend the afternoon session. Have you been to the Parliament since it opened?'

'It hasn't been top of my priorities, no.'

'I'm disappointed in you.'

It wasn't easy to find a response to something said so simply and straightforwardly. Meldrum was rescued from the need to find one by the arrival of a lean-faced, bustling man in his sixties, who apologised for keeping them waiting and led the way inside. Bringing up the tail of the procession, Meldrum gathered that the man was a Member of the Scottish Parliament and that the Society's invitation had come from him. Was this the man he was supposed to recognise? He knew the face from television and newspapers, but couldn't put a name to it. Somebody, certainly, who'd been around a long time.

They clustered in the reception area as Wemyss and the MSP went over to talk to a man in uniform at the desk. Perhaps, Meldrum thought, they were accounting for his presence as an addition to the invitation list. Behind him three or four of the group were chatting.

'It's a dreadful building,' a woman's voice asserted.

'But then it always was. For a local authority to house itself in a concrete monstrosity and set it near St Giles needs a kind of genius for vandalism.'

'Look around! Not much of a welcome. A bare space with as much atmosphere as a garage forecourt.'

'After all, it's only temporary. Once the Parliament building is completed, everything will move down the hill to Holyrood.'

'I don't,' the woman said, 'have high hopes for *that* building.'

'All the same,' the second man said, 'you have to admire Edinburgh's ability to find a building whenever one's needed. You want a Gallery for Modern Art? We just happen to have a wonderful old school that will do splendidly. And as for the Parliament – concrete monstrosity this place may be, but it does perfectly well for offices. The debates after all are what matter, and they aren't here but up on the Mound. What could be more extraordinarily fitting than that the debating chamber of the new Parliament is being housed during its first years in the Assembly Hall of the Church of Scotland? After all, the General Assembly was the nearest thing to a Parliament we had for three hundred years.'

'There speaks a Kirk elder.'

'And not ashamed of it.'

'I'm sure the Church will be glad to have the Assembly Hall back again. And the MSPs must be looking forward to getting the Holyrood building. It's taking long enough.'

'It will be an exciting day when we move,' a new voice said, the MSP having come back in time to catch the last remark. 'Not least, because the drought will be ended. You can't have a Parliament without a Members bar.'

'Norman has been corrupted by his thirty years at Westminster,' Hector Wemyss said. He spoke with the slow emphasis of a man who takes it for granted that he will be listened to without interruption. 'The job of a Labour MP during the Thatcher years was to go to his constituents every time a factory was threatened and tell them they had the hundred per cent backing of the Labour Party. And then the factory closed.'

'Time for lunch,' Norman said equably.

He showed no sign of being offended. It was hard, of course, to offend a politician. In any case, it was soon clear he held Wemyss in special esteem and even affection. The dining area was downstairs, a self-service counter facing an area of tables, some of them for four, others set up to let a dozen people eat together. Norman kept Wemyss with him, alking animatedly as they moved up the queue. Behind hem, Meldrum found himself beside the white-haired man vho'd complained he hadn't known friends could come.

'What do you do yourself?' the white-haired man asked.

And Meldrum experienced his customary moment of resitation, then admitted, 'I'm a policeman.'

'Oh,' the man said and, to Meldrum's relief, let the conversation lapse. Seemingly, he'd no curiosity about a policeman's lot, whether a happy one or otherwise. When, however, they'd filled their trays and Meldrum, seeing Norman and Wemyss settle at one of the tables for four, vent to join them, the white-haired man tagged along and ook the remaining seat.

'How often,' Norman asked, fixing his gaze on them both, 'can you say you've had lunch with a great man? I was rereading *MacDiarmid on Whalsay* the other night. It's a vonderful play. If posterity has any sense, it'll confirm that his man here,' nodding at Wemyss, 'is a great man.'

'Do you think posterity might even manage to stage it?' Wemyss asked, his tone conspicuously ungrateful for the compliment.

'Plays in verse,' Norman said. 'Never easy. Think of Shelley. Think of Browning.'

'Think of Fry,' Wemyss said in parody. 'Think of Eliot.'

'Oh, if you wanted to be rich,' Norman said, 'you should have written about cats.'

The white-haired man, turning his attention tennis natch fashion first to one then to the other, looked strained and lugubrious as if trying to memorise what was being said. For his part, Meldrum chewed and listened.

'I remember at the first night of *The Cheviot, The Stag and The Black Black Oil*, you telling me Scotland was too small to govern itself.' Wemyss waved a hand at the scene around them. The dining room was crowded, filled with a buzz of conversation. 'It could never have a Parliament, you said, because you could meet everyone who mattered on the Monday morning plane to London. I mind I wrote a song about that – *The Man on the Monday Morning Plane*.'

'The words were fine, but you needed a better tune. You should have asked me, and I'd have recommended one.'

'Perhaps I still should. There's an art in changing tunes. And here you are a member of the very Parliament you said was impossible.'

'That Parliament, the one you wanted—'

'The one I've battled for all my life.'

'That Parliament is still impossible,' Norman said with a smile. 'We deal with the details here, the big picture needs the wider view and that stays in London.'

'So you've no power.'

Norman waved a fork in denial. 'We can do lots of useful things. There's the difference – I'm a dull practical man. And you're a poet, which is to say a dreamer. Dreams are fine, but they have a habit of turning into nightmares if you try to live them.'

'And here I always thought you left the Communists and joined the Labour Party just so you could get elected to that whorehouse in London.'

'Maybe that too, and why not?' said the imperturbable Norman. 'But I saw into the future as well. My Highland grannie had the second sight.'

'The nightmare,' Hector Wemyss said, 'is living in a country with the worst health statistics and the worst slums and the worst deprivation in Europe. And this same country

ich in natural resources and with oil pouring in from its
erritorial waters for thirty years.'

'The same old parochial arguments.' It was the first time
Norman had shown a sign of irritation. 'Those of us who
have to deal with the real world know it's not so simple.'

'Will I tell you the most parochial thing I ever heard in
all my long life?' Hector pushed away his plate, having made
an old man's frugal meal, and settled back. 'There was a
member of your Party, who managed to get herself elected to
the European Parliament. And one day, Gorbachev himself
came to address them. This was when he was still in power
in Russia. And in the middle of all the seriousness of great
issues, this wee woman stood up and cried, "Beware of
nationalism, Mr President. I come from Scotland and we
know all about the dangers of nationalism there." History
does not record Mr Gorbachev's thoughts on that advice,
but in terms of what you might call the bigger picture – say
the last thousand years of European and Russian history – it
gave me a bloody good laugh at the time, and makes me
smile even now when I think of it.'

'Think of Putin instead. After all, she may not have been
so far wrong.'

'Is it possible she'd a Highland grannie?' Hector wondered, and they both chuckled.

After everyone had finished eating, they went back
upstairs and out into the street. The group began to straggle
up the Lawnmarket in the direction of the Close that gave
access to the Parliament. As the MSP, leading the way, fell
into conversation with a colleague, Hector Wemyss dropped
back and taking Meldrum's arm steered him into a bar. At
first glance as they went in, he apologised for choosing it. 'In
the old days, we drank in Milne's.' Sweeping aside Mel-

drum's offer, he insisted on buying the drinks. They carried them to a table at the back of the room.

'Slainte!'

'Cheers,' Meldrum said.

'So what did you think of Norman?'

'He seems to admire you,' Meldrum said drily. He was irritated with himself. Coming to meet Wemyss in the first place had probably been irresponsible. It didn't help for it to be a waste of time.

It didn't help that a father who should be grieving for his son was — what was he doing? — fishing for compliments, trying to show how important he was? He hadn't liked the old man, but he'd thought better of him.

'That's the best you can do?'

The rasping burr of the schoolmaster again, not a tone Meldrum responded to well.

'He admires your poetry?' Meldrum tried again. 'Does his opinion matter? I don't know about these things. Does he know what he's talking about?'

'You can take it he does. He could have been a fine Minister for the Arts, probably the best we've had. Labour was out of power too long for him to get his chance. In an independent Scotland, he might have been remarkable.'

'Well, there's another thing I noticed,' Meldrum said. 'He doesn't agree with your politics.'

Instead of rising to the bait, Wemyss frowned and then sighed. He turned his glass on the table. 'How did we get on to this?' Suddenly, he looked exhausted. Even lifting the glass to his lips seemed an effort, energy like some palpable substance draining from him. He made an odd rubbing movement of his lips, as if seeking and failing to find the taste of what he drank.

Meldrum could think of nothing to say. Under cover of the table, he stretched out his wrist and checked the time.

'Would you believe,' Hector Wemyss asked quietly, 'when I saw my baby son lying in the crib, I thought I saw the future of Scotland? Was that politics? I suppose it was. Well, disillusion was a beast with a sudden coming, and I've had my thoughts over the years . . . not being stupid. I'll tell you something I've never said aloud to another soul on earth. A part of me never stopped hoping and waiting that he might find himself. I didn't marry young, and I wasn't a young man when Archie was born. Love isn't rational or measured, not between father and son.'

'If you want to talk, I'll listen,' Meldrum said. 'But you do know I'm not part of the team investigating Archie's death now?'

The old man nodded. 'Why is that?'

'Detective Superintendent Gowdie took over. I was moved to another case.'

'Is that usual?'

'No.'

'I trusted you,' Wemyss said. 'That first day I thought if anyone was going to find Archie's killer, it would be you.'

'Detective Superintendent Gowdie's a good—'

'He's had three weeks. When I try to speak to him, he's never there – or that's what they tell me.'

'To be fair—'

'I don't trust him.'

They sat in silence. Looking the length of the room, Meldrum saw a man in the doorway, a bus moving past behind him. The man changed his mind and turned away. A girl with long blonde hair went by on the opposite pavement. He imagined Wemyss explaining to someone how he

trusted him and distrusted Gowdie. Bad enough if he chose
to say it to Gowdie; but who was to say a man like Wemyss
might not get to see Fleming or Chief Constable Baird
himself? And what would either of them, particularly
Fleming, make of the fact he'd agreed to meet the old
man? What could it seem like but another act of indis-
cipline, and worse an attempt to stir up trouble for a fellow
officer? He'd been a fool to come. But he wasn't a fool, so
what had he thought he was doing? Had he thought at all?
He'd come here like a sleepwalker. It was as if some enemy
inside was trying to destroy him.

'I'm off the case,' Meldrum said. 'I can't help you.'

'You said you would listen. That's all I'm asking you to
do. Listen and remember.'

'I'm not the right one. Even if you told me something
that might help, Gowdie wouldn't pay a blind bit of
attention, not if it came from me. I'm not trying to put
you off. I'm telling you the absolute truth.'

'That's why I trust you,' Hector Wemyss said. He
chopped at the air with his hand. 'Three weeks, isn't that
too long?'

'Some investigations can go on for months.' Years. But
he didn't say that.

'How often are those ones successful?'

'It can take time. The main thing is that a case isn't
closed. We keep on.'

Wemyss sipped from his glass, following it with the same
puzzled dissatisfied rubbing of the lips. 'But there are others
you solve at once, isn't that so?' And when Meldrum
nodded, 'How would you describe them?'

Suppressing his impatience, Meldrum said, 'Domestics.
Street fights. Brawls in pubs. Ones like that, solving doesn't

190

come into it. You pick the one with a knife in his hand. Or the man sitting on the kitchen floor beside his wife's body.'

Wemyss leaned forward across the table. His eyes were blue, not an old man's faded colour at all, but hard and intent. 'How would you describe it when a man's killed in a room rented by his brother-in-law?'

'I know you think Patrick Hennessy killed your son. You told me that, but—'

'Am I supposed to believe that it's a coincidence he died in that room? Does Gowdie believe something so absurd? Do you?'

'There are circumstances in this case.' Meldrum hesitated. The main circumstance would be the evidence given on her husband's behalf by Hector Wemyss's daughter, the dead man's sister.

'And Rannie? Is that another coincidence?'

'I don't know about coincidence. It's why Hennessy said he was there. He suspected Rannie of having an affair with his wife.'

'My daughter.'

'Yes. But Rannie was with someone else.'

'Is that supposed to make me feel better?' Wemyss asked sourly.

Meldrum had met a lot of grieving relatives over his career. There was no law that said you had to like them.

'I can't make sense of it for you,' he said. 'But I don't have to.'

'From what I can learn, Superintendent Gowdie is paying no attention to George Rannie. He seems to think he's irrelevant. Do you think he's irrelevant?'

'I don't have an opinion,' Meldrum said. 'I shouldn't even be discussing this with you.'

'Did you talk with George Rannie, though? Before you came off what you call *this case*, my son's death?'

Reluctantly, Meldrum nodded.

'Did you take the measure of him?'

'I don't know what you mean by that.'

'You disappoint me.'

That's the second time he's told me that, Meldrum thought. I wonder if it's a favourite word of his.

'Can I ask why?'

'Because you're in the business of evil,' Hector Wemyss said. 'I thought you would take his measure.'

Meldrum had taken enough. He pushed back his chair. 'I'm sorry, I'm not on this case, I'm not involved, I don't want to be involved. I shouldn't even be here. I don't see the point of it.'

'You know why I asked you. I wanted you to see Norman for yourself.'

'The MSP?'

Wemyss stared at him. 'Don't pretend you didn't see what I was doing.'

'If you're talking about Norman whoever-he-is, what has he got to do with it?'

'Whoever he is?' Wemyss repeated, and his look mixed contempt with something like despair. 'What are you, man? Don't you read the papers? Do you know nothing of what's going on in the world? Or is your world robberies and violence and horrors? Is that all it is? Do you live in a city full of history and know nothing of history? When Norman talked of my play *MacDiarmid on Whalsay*, do you know who Hugh MacDiarmid was, do you know where Whalsay is? I can see in your face you've no idea. You walk the streets in a dream, a ghost among ghosts. There's nothing solid about ou. What a fool I was to take it for granted you would recognise Norman.'

'Well, who the hell is he?'

'Norman Rannie,' Wemyss said getting up. 'George Rannie's father.'

And that was it. He was gone without another word, despite being the one who had asked for this meeting. Impulsive; an old man suddenly at the end of his tether. Disappointed.

At his lowest ebb, on the couch that night in his flat, with a half-eaten fish supper on his chest, Meldrum lay for a long time wishing that the phone would stop ringing.

When at last he dropped a hand over the edge of the couch and picked up the handset, a distinctive Aberdonian voice at his ear complained, 'You took your time.'

'Andy?'

'I hope you're not too comfortable.'

'Why?'

The thought of a disciplinary hearing went through Meldrum's mind. A stupid idea at eleven o'clock on a Thursday night, it showed how he was feeling.

'I've got a girl dead in Stockbridge for you.'

'For me?'

'You're a lucky man.'

BOOK THREE

Business of Evil

Chapter Twenty-Four

Driving down to Stockbridge to the address he'd been given for the crime, Meldrum kept thinking tonight or tomorrow someone would tell him, this is a mistake; and he'd be back in a room on his own staring at a computer.

As he pulled up, he decided he must be last on the scene, which didn't help. Among the cars double parked outside the entrance, very nearly blocking passage along the narrow side street, he recognised Bob Ross's winter car, the yellow Subaru, which replaced the Morgan kit car the medical examiner favoured when the weather was fine.

Meldrum took a moment to look at the building, a sandstone tenement, bay windows on what would be living rooms, from what he could see of them decent curtains on the windows, a glimpse into a ground-floor flat with curtains undrawn of a vase of dried grass, a round brass mirror, two or three prints. The general impression was confirmed as he went into the close, which was clean and had seen a new coat of paint fairly recently.

On the first-floor landing, a young constable stood guard outside a door that lay open like a declaration. What had been a private space had become public. As he went in he saw two SOC officers at work in the living room. A glance, though, showed no sign of a body in there. The room looked as if a hurricane had blown through it. As he went down the lobby, he heard the sound of men's voices and recognised Bob Ross's emphatic briskness. The medical examiner had his coat on and was pacing around getting in the way of two more SOCs, one of whom was dusting and lifting prints with tape from the contents of a bedside table. Working so attentively, he seemed entirely unaware of the woman sprawled on the bed. Red knickers made a stripe of colour across the body. Apart from that, she was naked.

'At last,' Bob Ross cried. 'I've been finished here the best part of half an hour, but I didn't want to leave till I saw you. What kept you?'

'I came as soon as I got word.'

'What did they do? Send a carrier pigeon?'

'I'm here now.'

'So you are.'

'All I got was an address. Who is she?'

'Your sergeant's made a start on all that. At least, I imagine he has.'

'Bobbie Shields?' Meldrum asked in surprise.

'He'll be glad to see you. He's been wandering round like a knotless thread.'

'Where is he?'

Ross nodded vaguely towards the lobby. 'Front room?'

'No, I've just looked in there.'

'If you think it's a mess, you should see the kitchen. Every drawer pulled out and emptied. Spaghetti, rice, flour, just dumped in a heap on the floor. An incredible pigsty.'

Meldrum looked round at the tangle of clothing scattered around. The wardrobe doors lay open to show it empty. All the drawers, yes in here too, pulled out and their contents dumped on the floor.

'Give me a minute. Promise, I'll be right back.'

As he went back into the lobby, the door on the other side of the passage opened and Bobbie Shields peered out.

'You'd better come and see this,' he said.

'I still have to speak to Bob Ross. You get a name for the dead woman?'

Shields raised his eyebrows in surprise. He came out and shut the door firmly behind him. 'You not recognise her?' he asked with a shade of self-congratulation. 'It's that guy Rannie's bird. The one he had in the hotel. Her name's Liz McKinnon. Remember?'

But the last word was lost as Meldrum went back in three long strides into the bedroom he'd just left.

The body was lying diagonally across the bed with the head tipped back almost off the edge of the mattress. The face was livid and congested, but when he bent close there was no doubt.

He looked up to see Ross staring at him curiously. When he explained, Ross said, 'Not surprised you didn't recognise her. Her own mother might not be too sure right now. Being choked to death does that.'

Meldrum blew out his breath. 'That how she died?' He felt slightly sick.

'Sorry,' Ross said. 'It hits you differently when you've known somebody.'

'I didn't really know her,' Meldrum said. 'Met her once. She made an impression, though. Very good looking. Lively and . . . She was serving a buffet, and she was wearing a chef's hat.' Hard to explain. 'She seemed like good fun.' He glanced at Shields, who he was sure had also been taken by her. Shields, however, returned his look with a careful blankness he couldn't read.

'In our jobs,' Ross said, surprisingly gently, 'it's better to be dealing with strangers.'

Meldrum nodded. He knew Ross as a brash hard-drinking man, an enthusiastic golfer who enjoyed telling jokes, occasionally dirty, always with a touch of the macabre. To be offered sympathy by Ross was disconcerting. It made him feel he had shown weakness. He said, 'What about other injuries. Did she put up a fight?'

'There are other injuries,' Ross said and pulled a face.

'You saw what it's like in the front room,' one of the SOC officers said. He was on his knees, separating clothes around the bed into piles for putting into labelled sacks. 'First thing I thought when I saw it was that there had been a hell of a fight. We'll take samples everywhere, but it's not going to be easy to tell what happened. Not after all this mess. Even finding out what she'd on won't be easy. Or whether she took clothes off or had them pulled off her. Half the stuff lying about been's torn or cut. We should be able to identify the pants she'd on. For the rest,' he shrugged, 'we'll just need to see.'

'You should see the kitchen,' the SOC who'd been lifting the prints said gloomily.

'I'll know better when I've done a post mortem,' Ross said, 'but I think the throat's been compressed with excep-tional force. Not big hands, going by the bruising, but strong. Once she was gripped, she'd no chance.'

Shields said, 'I know where her clothes are.'

'Where?' the SOC said sharply.

'Room over the corridor.'

'The other bedroom? I thought it was locked.'

'One of the guys in the front room found the key.'

'You might have told me,' the SOC said.

'You know now,' Meldrum said. 'Let's have a look.'

Shields went first as if he'd established rights by having already been into the room. As Meldrum followed, he was conscious that as well as the SOC, Bob Ross was coming as well. He wasn't the only one, it seemed, who'd caught Shields' muted excitement. The sergeant opened the door and stood back. Like a bloody showman, Meldrum thought. Roll of the drums—

'Fuck me,' the SOC said.

'I doubt if that would be the main item on the agenda,' Ross said.

They were looking into what seemed to be a dungeon. The cupboard set on the wall, candle flames throwing shadows up on to grimacing masks, as it turned out, had a false back. It was designed to cover up the outside window; and the candles were electric. The brick and stone, too, was only wallpaper. There was an element of theatre, too, of make believe, of commerce, in the stocks and the whipping bench, the cage in the corner, the chains on the walls and hooked from the ceiling. Even the woman's clothes scattered around the room, the torn dress, the bra, the stockings, shoes, might have seemed part of a scenario. It was the body in the next room that made it all real.

'You touch anything?' the SOC asked.

Shields nodded at the plastic covers on his feet, held up his gloved hands.

'That could explain the phone calls,' he said to Meldrum.

'What phone calls?'

The young constable, called in from his post on the

landing, explained there had been two anonymous calls to say no one was answering the door of the flat and something must be wrong.

'That could have been the murderer,' Ross said. 'He'd gone too far and panicked, but phoned to get help just in case she was still alive.'

After wrecking the place, Meldrum thought. The young constable was nodding, a respectful nod, full of controlled excitement at sharing this kind of insight. Meldrum wondered if he was under the illusion Ross was a detective.

'Or it could be a punter with an appointment,' Shields said. 'Maybe he got worried when she wasn't answering.'

'Would a punter phone the police?' Ross asked sceptically.

'A regular might. It takes all kinds.'

'Elementary, eh?' Ross said, grinning round to see if anyone caught the allusion. Dr Ross and Sherlock Shields.

But Meldrum had fixed on the constable. 'You're not telling me you broke in here because of an anonymous phone call?'

'Downstairs was getting flooded, sir.'

'Plug in the basin,' Shields said. 'And a tap on. If there had been a combi boiler, the plumber could have put the water off from the landing. And she could have lain in there for a long while. Just as well there wasn't.'

'Excuse me,' a woman's voice said.

They'd been standing in a huddle round the door. Startled, turning to look, inadvertently they gave her a view into the room.

Chapter Twenty-Five

Mrs Yolen's flat was on the same landing. Meldrum had taken her across to it and, sitting in her front room, listened as she apologised for the third or fourth time for getting so upset.

'It's a natural reaction,' he said. She'd stood staring into the fake dungeon, then started crying, great tearing sobs that were only now starting to calm. If he had been put under oath, he'd have described her emotion as excessive. Based that is on what she'd seen, assuming she'd simply come in like a good neighbour to find out why the front door was lying open. She hadn't asked what had happened, why they were there. He hadn't had a chance yet to tell her about the body. God knows, given her present performance, where she was going to find a response to fit that piece of news. Start on a high note, you've nowhere to go.

'You must think I'm a fool,' she said.

She was a handsome woman in her early fifties. As she sat sprawled on the couch, slack with emotion, it was hard not to notice how good her legs were.

'Of course not.'

'It was the unexpectedness of it. I think the world is going mad. Utterly, entirely, nothing to do with a girl like that. She's lived opposite me for three years. Such a nice girl. Have you seen her? If you've talked to her, you'll know what I mean.' He opened his mouth to explain, but she swept on. 'In the summer, my daughter took me on holiday to Turkey. My first holiday since my husband died. I didn't want to go. She said to me, you have to start your life again, I won't let you give up. We were away for three weeks, she'd taken three weeks from work. That was so generous of her. The day before we were to come home, my daughter found a purse in the street. It wasn't anything to do with us, we were on holiday, in a strange city. But she feels responsible. That's how she is. We'd passed a police station and nothing would do but that we should hand it in there. From the minute we went in, I knew it was wrong. A fat sweating man who wouldn't just take it and let us go. Polite at first but all the time as if he was laughing at us. He brought out a form. Two other men came through and watched as we were trying to fill it in. He said we'd got some bit wrong and tore it up. We should have walked out, but by then I didn't know if he would let us go. Does that sound stupid? And then another policeman came in from the street holding these two girls. They were only children. They looked like sisters. The fat sweating man said to us, they steal. And he slapped one of them across the face. My daughter protested and then – I don't know how to describe it to you. He *trampled* on the child. We waited outside for more than an hour, we wanted to make sure they were all right, the children, but they didn't come out. And when I saw that room tonight that's why I was crying. A nice girl like that. What has she to do with such awfulness?'

Meldrum hesitated, looked for the right words, but she took the fact of the murder more calmly than he could have hoped for. 'When I saw that awful room, I thought you'd arrested her for that.' Emotion spent, she shook her head as if what he told her was no more than a confirmation, something added to what she had learned of the world.

'No,' she said. 'I didn't see men going in and out. You mean, she was a prostitute. But would she have to be? Even with that awful room? I mean, people seem to me to be mad nowadays. Mad enough for anything. And I never heard a neighbour speak badly of her. But we're not people who pry and spy. I couldn't tell you how people I've nodded good morning to for ten years earn their living. It was only by accident I found where Miss McKinnon worked. I went with a friend to Setting The Scene, and there she was.'

Just after Meldrum got to bed, he heard a clock chime three and, sleepless, lay wondering where it could be coming from since he hadn't heard it before. Even in the middle of the night there was traffic in the street below, but not so much, and so there might have been a tiny pool of silence into which the sounds had fallen, perhaps from an open window in some neighbouring flat.

Chapter Twenty-Six

Not a confiding man, for some reason Meldrum told Shields about Mrs Yolen's holiday. What upset her, she'd said, coming back to the subject as he left, was the number of people who, when she shared her experience, responded by telling her about a beautiful beach at Marmara or wherever.

'Can't see why she was surprised,' Shields said. 'If hell had a beach, they'd be running package holidays to it.'

Meldrum grunted. Shields lapsed into silence. In fact, Meldrum had appreciated the joke. He wasn't without a sense of humour. He had been able to make Carole laugh, and had taken pleasure in that. Since their marriage broke up, though, his black, private humour typically went unshared. The difficulty was, as had happened before when Shields sprang that kind of surprise, a response didn't come easily to him. He wondered what would happen if he found a quick reply. Would Shields respond in kind, and so on and so forth? The image of the two of them exchanging wisecracks defeated him. Like Abbott and Costello, it wasn't funny. He couldn't imagine why it had occurred to him in the first place.

Almost as unfunny as this morning's conversation with

ACC Fleming, who'd made it clear as an etching in acid that the only reason for Meldrum being on a murder investigation was a manpower shortage, and even then, little button mouth bunching with distaste, 'Only against my better judgement.' At which it had occurred to Meldrum that perhaps the little man had been persuaded or overruled by Chief Constable Baird. Just after he'd had this thought, Fleming had thrown something perilously close to what in a child would have been described as a tantrum. This could have been a coincidence. The other explanation was that Meldrum had let some of what he was thinking show in his face; bad news for a man who prided himself on his self-control. One way or the other, not a good experience.

'That's it,' Shields said. 'You've just driven past it.'

Setting The Scene occupied a substantial corner site. Meldrum had never heard of it, but then his concept of interior design had been arrested somewhere around the pot of mushroom yellow paint stage. He did have a nose, though, for how a business was doing. Not so much the style at the front or the bustle round the drawing boards as they were shown through, but something sleek and purring behind Alistair Hewison's outward appearance of lean energy suggested that this one was doing very well indeed.

Told why they were there, he said all the right things and said them well, and when he checked the time, more than once, it was done with such practised discretion it would have been easy to miss.

'She was with us for three years. Even in her last year at Art School, she worked with us on Saturdays. I was completely taken aback when she said she was leaving.'

'Did she tell you where she was going?'

'She said she intended to look round before deciding

what to do next. She called it, taking time out. My first thought, naturally, was that she'd been, not head-hunted exactly, she was very young, call it *poached*. She did have a gift. I rang one or two people and asked them straight out if they'd made her an offer. In the end, I gave her an excellent reference and told her there would be a place here for her if she wanted to come back. And now this.' He frowned at the mystery of life. 'You say it happened at home?'

'She was killed in her flat, yes.'

'When she first worked with us — before she took her degree — she stayed with her parents. And then she got a flat of her own. She was very pleased about that.'

'Were you ever there?'

'Not inside. I ran her home a couple of times, when there was a big project and we were all working late.'

'You say only a couple of times. But she was here for three years? Was there any reason why you stopped giving her a lift home?'

'She got her own car.'

'Of course.'

'People do that once they start to earn.' Now he made no attempt to conceal his checking of the time. 'I don't think I can tell you anything else that would help.'

'I appreciate the time you've given us,' Meldrum said. Hewison smiled and eased forward as if to get up. Without any change of tone, Meldrum asked, 'From what you say, I take it you didn't have any contact with her once she left.'

'None at all.'

'You weren't curious? You didn't try to find out where she'd gone?'

'Of course not. Why should I?'

'Well, you did say you'd phoned round a few people.'

'Business rivals. When she first talked about leaving. To check if one of them had offered her a job. If anyone had, I don't mind admitting I'd have been bloody annoyed. But she left, and we heard no more of her. And we would have, believe me, if she'd been working as a designer.' Still speaking, he got to his feet. 'Like any profession, ours is a small world. She just dropped out of sight.'

Shields got up. Meldrum paused, then stood up as well. 'Since you regarded her so highly, you must have thought that was strange.'

'I suppose we all did. She had a future here. But people come and go. You know how it is. Talent isn't enough, not on its own.'

'Is there anyone she was particularly friendly with?'

'Friendly with everyone. A very nice girl. But particularly friendly, no. There's no one I could suggest you should speak to.'

'One last thing,' Meldrum said. 'Have you ever heard of a man called George Rannie?'

Setting the example, Hewison had been moving to the door of his office. Now he stopped. 'Why?'

'I take it you have.'

'What's he got to do with this?'

'He was a friend of Miss McKinnon's. I wondered if he might have met her here.'

'It's news to me.'

'You mean that they were friends?'

'He's a client of ours.'

'Did Miss McKinnon do any work for him?'

'She might have. I really can't remember.'

'But I suppose if you had to . . . There would be some kind of record?'

'At one time, we did a lot of work for him. I imagine almost everyone would have been involved to some extent at one time or another.'

'Were you doing something for him at the time Miss McKinnon decided to leave?'

'We're talking about, what? – almost four years ago!'

'All the same. Perhaps you could check your records?'

Hewison frowned. 'Yes, I think we were. Almost sure we were, now you mention it.'

Meldrum smiled. 'You've been a great help,' he said.

They walked slowly back to the car. The sun was out and it was as if, reluctant to get started again, they'd made an unspoken agreement to take their time.

As they crossed the road, Shields asked, 'Do you think he was banging her?'

'What put that in your head?'

Shields grinned. 'He said she'd a gift.'

That was the thing about a sense of humour, either you had it or you hadn't.

Chapter Twenty-Seven

'I'd expected you sooner,' George Rannie said in the tone of a host glad to see his guests at last.

This time, Meldrum had rung to make sure they would catch him at home.

'I'm sorry to have kept you waiting,' Meldrum said, falling into the spirit of the thing.

'We're sitting at the back,' Rannie went on as he led the way down the hall. 'It's my favourite part of the house when the sun's shining like today. I warn you some people find it can get almost too warm even this late in the year. But not me. I soak up the heat. Like a lizard on a rock, my father used to tell me.'

That image had an odd effect on Meldrum. The incongruous welcome they were being offered, together with Shields' suspicion of it, had given him a moment of dour amusement. That ended with the image of a cold-blooded creature basking in the sun.

Rannie took them through the flat into the kitchen and out into the conservatory beyond. Without the party and the buzz of people, it seemed even bigger than on their first visit, half a dozen chairs and a couple of coffee tables islanded in a high empty space. No long table laden with food. No redheaded girl in a tall chef's hat. They walked out, though, into the same white suddenness of light he remembered. As they did, one of the chairs moved, a disconcerting effect as if it had taken on a life of its own.

'Sorry, Jamie,' Rannie said. 'Unexpected visitors.'

'Not some of your bloody boring neighbours?'

The chair completed its half-turn to reveal the speaker. It was the kind of casual rudeness a man might commit if he was drunk. To Meldrum, however, this one gave the appearance of being perfectly sober, though squinting against the light it was hard to be sure.

'Two policemen, as a matter of fact. And my neighbours are splendid people, not boring at all.'

'Policemen,' the man in the chair said. It didn't sound like a question, more as if he was thinking about it.

'Detectives, actually,' Rannie said. 'They've come to talk to me about a murder.'

'In that case,' the man said, 'I'll leave you to it.' It was an authoritative baritone, used to giving orders, the voice, no doubt about it, of a big man, though when he stood up he was undersized. Broad shoulders, deep voice, but not much over five feet in height.

'Don't you want to know who was murdered?' Rannie asked.

'Should I?'

'Liz McKinnon. Don't you remember? I introduced you to her.'

'I meet a lot of people.' When he chuckled, that too was on a deep note, a pleasant sound. 'Most of them manage to stay alive.'

Rannie went out with him. As they waited for him to come back, they stood silently, not looking at one another. Confined to their own thoughts, it was as if the intensity of light were holding them apart. Doing the interview out here seemed to Meldrum designed to put him at a disadvantage. He wondered about telling Rannie he'd rather talk to him somewhere else. And if he refused? Why would he do that? Not that he could be forced, it was his house after all. He was still trying to decide when Rannie came back.

'Sorry about that,' he said. 'Is it all right to talk out here? It's not too hot?'

'Why not?' Meldrum said.

Rannie gave them chairs with their backs to the sun, and carried one across to face them. As he sat down, he took a pair of shaded glasses from his shirt pocket and slipped them on. 'It won't last long. That gap between the buildings for the sun to get through is a bit of luck. Lower in the sky now, though. We'll soon be in shadow again.'

'When was the last time you saw Miss McKinnon?' Meldrum asked.

'The day of the party. A birthday party I threw for two of my neighbours. But you were there.'

'That's almost a month ago.'

'So?' A band of darkness shielded his eyes.

'It seems a long time not to see someone you're sleeping with.'

He laughed. 'We both enjoyed it, the sleeping with. But we weren't all that close. I hope that doesn't shock you. Officially, that is. I suppose policemen are like ministers or lawyers in a courtroom. You all have to uphold yesterday's morality, whatever you believe privately.'

Ignoring the trimmings, Meldrum said, 'I got the impression you were close. Both Miss McKinnon and you gave the impression you spent a lot of time together.'

'No, I don't think so. Did you take notes, have you a note of me saying anything to suggest that? As you say, it's a while ago. If you feel it's necessary, please, check with my friends. You'll find most of them won't even know her name.'

'Did you know she was working as a prostitute?'

'Was she? She never asked me for money. She wouldn't have got it if she had. Sex isn't something I've ever had to pay for.' He laughed again. 'Leave aside flowers and theatre tickets and weekends in Paris. If that's deceiving myself, don't we all?'

'You had sex with her at the Hamilton Hotel?'

'Yes. Only on that one occasion.'

'And you had sex with her here?'

'Yes.'

'And at her flat?'

'Isn't this getting just a touch prurient?' But Meldrum noted the little involuntary twitch of the lips, as if he was amused, and decided it was because of the word he'd chosen to use. Prurient. Old fashioned, like a policeman's morality.

'I don't follow you, sir,' Meldrum said stolidly. 'Are you saying you didn't?'

'No, I'm not. I had sex with her at her flat. As I recall, she probably told you that.'

'Yes,' Shields said. Startled, in the way people tended to be when Shields broke silence, Rannie waited for him to go on. 'She did,' Shields said.

'Did anything about her flat strike you as unusual?' Meldrum asked, getting the tempo back.

'You mean that roomful of toys she'd got herself? Of course, I thought it was unusual. Bloody unusual.'

'Is something amusing you?' Meldrum asked.

'Why?'

'You smiled.'

'Amused, isn't the word,' Rannie said, 'not with the poor girl being dead. But how do you react to something like that? I told her it wasn't my scene. A little mild spanking, given not received. That was about my limit in that direction.'

'Did she want to use what you describe as her toys?'

'Do we have to go into this?'

'Yes,' Meldrum said.

'All right, she did.'

'How did she want to use them? As you put it – giving or receiving? Which way?'

'Oh, for God's sake!'

'I'd appreciate an answer.'

'I'm sure you would,' Rannie said.

Meldrum let the silence go on.

'I cut the conversation short, if you must know. And then we made love perfectly normally.'

Meldrum waited.

'As far as I could tell,' Rannie said, 'she wanted me to – be the active partner.'

'Could you be more explicit?'

'No, I couldn't.'

'She wanted you to be active. What did she want you to do? Whip her?'

'I suppose. That kind of thing. You've seen the room, for God's sake. I stopped her before she got started. I didn't want to know. I told her, for me it was a complete turn-off.'

'And she accepted that?'

'Absolutely.'

'And then you made love normally.' Meldrum laid the faintest stress on the last word.

'Absolutely.'

Meldrum paused, let him anticipate what might be coming next, took a different tack. 'Where were you last night?'

'At home for once. Don't ask me what was on the television. I haven't the remotest idea. I drank some malt whisky and listened to Mahler on the stereo.' He paused. 'Music, that is. He's a composer.'

Aye, cunt, but could you hum me the tune? Meldrum thought. Even if he'd never heard of Mahler, he disliked being patronised.

'You weren't surprised when I suggested Miss McKinnon might have been a prostitute.'

'I'd seen that room! Of course, I wondered. But you saw what she was like. She was lively and funny, a lovely girl. A girl like that, the idea of her being a prostitute – it hadn't remotely crossed my mind. When it did, I didn't care for it, so I put it out of my head.'

'The thing is, we haven't any evidence that she was working as a prostitute.'

Rannie regarded him quizzically. 'Expensive toys.'

'If that's what she was, one of her clients would be the likeliest suspect. We'd be looking among them to find whoever killed her. Your evidence, of course, suggests different possibility.'

'What would that be?'

'A lover. Someone who came to the flat to have sex with her. Who didn't find that room of hers a turn-off. Someone who went too far.'

'How was she killed? When you phoned, you didn't say

'It'll be in the evening paper. She was strangled. According to the medical evidence, it seems exceptional strength was used.'

Rannie leaned forward and held out his hand. 'Take it,' he said. 'Please.'

Curious, Meldrum took the outstretched hand. After a moment, he felt Rannie tighten his grip. As he squeezed, from behind the dark glasses he kept his eyes fixed on Meldrum's, who was reminded of nothing so much as playground trials of strength when he was a child.

'You see,' Rannie said, 'perfectly respectable, but nothing exceptional.' He relinquished his grip and sat back. 'What did you think of that?'

'Interesting,' Meldrum said.

'You're thinking it wasn't very scientific. But I was trying.'

'As a matter of fact,' Meldrum said, 'I was thinking how much our strength increases when we're excited. I don't know if there's any way science can measure that.'

'I didn't murder her.'

After a moment, Meldrum asked, 'How did you meet her?'

'She was an interior designer. I was involved with a project, she worked for a company we used. We were attracted to one another. Simple as that. I asked her out, and things went on from there.'

'She left that job. Do you know why?'

'At Setting The Scene? You're sure she did?'

'If you mean, have I spoken to Mr Hewison? Yes, I have.'

'I can't tell you why she left.'

'Quitting work is a big decision. It seems she did it just after she'd met you. Are you sure she didn't mention it?'

'We enjoyed one another's company, but she didn't confide in me.'

'But when Setting The Scene was working on your project, surely you must have noticed she wasn't around any more? You've been to bed with her and you don't look for her or ask where she is?'

'The project wasn't mine. Keeping my hand in, you could call it. As I told you, since I came back to Edinburgh, I've made a point of not putting myself under pressure. I had years of that in London.'

'So you thought she still worked with Setting The Scene?'

'At some point, she probably said she wasn't with them. I honestly can't remember.'

'Didn't you ask what firm she'd gone to? What she was doing now? The kind of questions you ask if someone tells you she's given up her job.'

'I just wasn't interested. I suppose you could blame me for that.'

A cold-blooded creature. Like a lizard on a rock.

On impulse, Meldrum said, 'You mentioned your father when we came in.'

'Did I?'

'I was at the Parliament not long ago, and your father was there.'

'No surprise in that,' Rannie said. 'Speaking in a debate was he?'

'He was having lunch. We were at the same table.'

'Well, it's where he works after all, isn't it?' Meldrum couldn't read his tone. 'What were you doing there?'

Conscious of Shields' presence, Meldrum almost made up a reason, something bland and evasive. Then he thought to hell with it, and said, 'I was meeting Hector Wemyss.'

From the corner of his eye, he caught Shields' involuntary turn of the head as he fixed on the name. He'd given a hostage to canteen gossip, by which news of what he'd done could get to Barry Gowdie, and from there by half a dozen routes to ACC Fleming.

All the same, Meldrum decided, when Rannie asked why he'd met Wemyss, he would tell him the truth. Whatever the consequence to himself, suddenly he badly wanted to see how Rannie would react to being told of the old man's determination to find Archie's killer.

'They've known one another a long time,' Rannie said. Meldrum waited, but he left it at that.

As they were going, however, just before he closed the door on them, Rannie asked, 'Remember you asked who it was I phoned? Well, you just met him. I phoned Jamie.'

'I asked you?' Meldrum had no idea what he was talking about. 'When was this?'

'The night Archie was killed. I left Liz in the bar because I had a phone call to make. You asked who it was I phoned.'

'The man who was here just now?'

'Campbell James Michie. If you want to, you'll have no difficulty finding him.' Rannie laughed. 'CJM HOLDINGS – his initials are on half the development sites in Edinburgh.'

Chapter Twenty-Eight

It seemed Harkness didn't have a ready answer to a simple question. Using one finger, he prodded a folder three or four times till he'd lined it up with the edge of the desk. Finished with that, he glanced at the phone, but it didn't ring.

'It doesn't affect how he does his job,' he offered at last.

Meldrum eased his weight in the uncomfortable upright seat. The Hamilton Hotel was large, but its manager's office was small and badly furnished. He was grateful Shields wasn't slumped on the only other available chair, taking up space and scarce leg room. Rather than risk another visit to the Hamilton Hotel, the fat sergeant had staged an implicit rebellion by suggesting he should get in touch with every firm that might have employed Liz McKinnon, and if Hewison at Setting The Scene was right and none of them had, to check whether she had even approached any of them in search of work.

'This is the fourth time he's confessed to murdering a young woman, and it doesn't affect his job?' Meldrum allowed himself a tone of incredulity.

'It's not public knowledge.'

'Is that a rule you'd apply to cockroaches in the kitchen?'

'There's no call for that.'

'I apologise. But because it's not public knowledge, that's a reason? Are you really telling me that's why he's still working here? When he confessed to killing Sylvia Marshall, confessed to me, I couldn't have imagined he'd still be playing the Highland laird out there at your front door eight years later.'

'But he wasn't guilty. You found that out at once.'

'Because you said he was with you.'

'Which he was.' Harkness frowned. 'And he couldn't drive, so there was no way he could have been the man seen getting rid of the body.' He paused, seemed to be thinking that over, then added, 'That poor girl's body.'

'So he doesn't kill girls. He just keeps confessing. That doesn't worry you? You think that's normal.'

But Harkness pushed with his hands against the edge of the desk, rolling back the chair until his arms were at full stretch. 'Why are you talking like this? I won't be bullied.' He didn't, however, get up. 'Hugh McArdle does his job extremely well. Let me tell you something. He never forgets anyone who's been a guest here. They come back years later and he'll greet them by name. People love that. He gets postcards from all over the world.'

'Don't tell me he's an institution,' Meldrum said. 'He should be *in* an institution.'

'He's harmless,' Harkness said. 'Why persecute him? I don't know why you're so angry.'

For Meldrum it had been like a replay of Sylvia Marshall's murder. The morning briefing had been dispiriting. The team he'd put on the door-to-door check had found Liz McKinnon's neighbours a match for the three wise monkeys. Since they'd seen nothing on the night and heard nothing either then or by way of gossip, there was nothing they could say. The last time Meldrum had come across so complete a veil of silence had been among six tinker families camped on a piece of waste ground who'd wakened after a night's drinking to find the elder of the tribe, a brutal eighty-year-old, lying outside his caravan with his throat cut. In Liz McKinnon's case, the silence of her neighbours seemed due to respectability and a fairly complete indifference to the world outside family and friends; a pastel echo of the tinkers' fear and clannishness. As he'd left the briefing, not in the best of tempers, reflecting it was like investigating murder in a catatonics ward, he was told Hugh McArdle was in an interview room waiting to talk to him. The confession that followed had been full of emotion, even passionate, obviously sincere (if you knew nothing of the man's history), and the absurdest yet with nothing in place, time or opportunity that fitted the shabby, violent death of Liz McKinnon.

'I've charged him with wasting police time,' Meldrum told Harkness.

'Surely that wasn't necessary?'

'God knows why it hasn't been done before.'

'Do you know he's been seeking help? The psychiatrist will speak for him. I'm sure your charge won't come to anything.'

'Put it this way, it's going to be public knowledge.' A word in Dougie Stair's ear. It was the kind of story the reporter liked. 'See how your guests feel about that.'

The tall elegant Harkness was a man who, Meldrum judged, kept his feelings firmly in check. Yet now, as he watched, a flush of blood rose from the man's neck, touched his cheeks, and even stained the high pale forehead. When he spoke, his voice was taut with anger. 'How dare you try to damage this hotel? This is personal, isn't it? You've some kind of obsession with poor Hugh.'

Contemptuously, Meldrum shook his head. 'Nonsense.'

'Why did you come here then accusing him of murder? Hugh told me, he said he felt you were going to attack him. Raving about Sylvia Marshall. Drunk, he said.'

Controlling his shock, Meldrum said, 'He's lying, of course.'

'You've done it two or three times apparently. I only saw you once, and, my God, you were drunk then.'

'When was this? You've seen someone else. I've never come here drunk.'

Shaking his head, Harkness decided the time had come to get to his feet. 'I'm willing to believe you think that's true. You were so drunk, I doubt if you would remember a thing in the morning.'

Afraid even to think about that until he was alone, like a boxer getting up off the floor, Meldrum fought back on instinct. 'One thing,' he said, getting up. 'The night Archibald Wemyss was killed. Who paid the bill for Room Four One Seven?'

'Bill?' Harkness stared at him.

'Four One Seven. It's the room Wemyss was found dead in.'

'I'm not likely to forget that.'

'It was taken by a man called Patrick Hennessy so that he could spy on the neighbouring room. But, according to Hennessy, he changed his mind and left the hotel on the Friday evening. So who paid for the room?'

'If it matters, the payment details will give the name of the credit card holder.'

Harkness opened the door and stood aside as Meldrum went out into the lobby.

'Cash,' Meldrum said. 'On your computer, it was recorded as a cash payment. I should have asked at the time, but I didn't get a chance.'

Before Gowdie took over.

'Too late now then,' Harkness said, and shut the door.

Chapter Twenty-Nine

There is a kind of Edinburgh wakening where light lies on the bedroom ceiling grey and inert, a melancholy effect. It has no connection with the previous day's weather, then the sun can have been shining, and the sky may change again before the morning's well started. Only, just at the point of wakening, it's hard to remember a different weather and it's hard to think of a reason why that light should change, just because something's always happened doesn't mean it always will, faith and experience not always being enough. On those mornings, it's important to get out of bed at once. Eyes open, roll out. Meldrum didn't, which was a mistake. He lay wondering if his anger at Hugh McArdle was because already he knew no one would be caught for killing Liz McKinnon, any more than for the murder of Sylvia Marshall. He wondered if Harkness had been telling the truth about him coming to the Hamilton Hotel drunk to accuse McArdle of murdering Sylvia Marshall, and could see no reason for him to lie. Not once, he'd said, but several times. Could that have been what he'd been doing on the night of Archie Wemyss's murder? Had he come to the hotel again, looking for Hugh McArdle? He didn't remember, but if Harkness was telling the truth there had been earlier visits and he didn't remember them either. Was it possible there was some final depth of drunkenness he'd sunk to a handful of times in the last year? But why go after McArdle? Sober, he knew McArdle had alibis. But even sober, instinct had itched at him. Drunk, had he scratched the itch? Sylvia Marshall. Madge Chambers. Kitty Grant. Add Liz McKinnon? But why add her? There were resemblances to the others, but no absolute connection.

Apart, of course, from the fact that McArdle had confessed to each of them.

With that, he swung his legs out of the bed, was up, made coffee, drank it on the move in his tiny living room, three cramped steps one way three the other, all the time circling round an idea, studying it obliquely, trying to hold on to it but cautiously in case, looked at too closely, it turned to smoke.

In so short a time, the light had changed.

Chapter Thirty

It was true, the initials could be spotted surprisingly often. They cropped up on display boards at the edge of gap sites, on boards jutting from the windows of office conversions, on all sorts of buildings in the process of demolition or construction. Yet Meldrum had never noticed them before. It was often the way, he thought as he drove down to Leith, a name was drawn to your attention, a town or a person, a movie actor maybe, a singer, a politician, and for a week afterwards you'd be tripping over it. What might have been overlooked stood out. In this case, CJM HOLDINGS. Campbell James Michie.

Always the same, and there it was again, red letters on a light green background, one of a half-dozen companies on the display hoarding. Meldrum had slowed, looking for it, and now he drew in through the gate at the side of the building. It was a big yard designed for lorry traffic, but so crowded with vehicles and stacks of material that the parking gap he found in a line of cars seemed to use up the last inch of free space. He squeezed out of the car to find a man in a gold-coloured hard hat, with, yes, those same initials, bearing down on him.

'You're on private property.'

'I phoned your head office. I was told Mr Michie wa⟨s⟩ here.'

'Is he expecting you?'

'No, but he'll know what it's about.'

'He's busy. They shouldn't have sent you here.'

'You've got a phone there. Give him a ring and see.'

The man shook his head dismissively. 'You'd need a hel⟨l⟩ of a good reason. He'd chew my ear off.'

Meldrum showed his warrant card. 'Detective Inspecto⟨r⟩ Meldrum. Try that for a reason.'

The man walked away a few steps, bending his head an⟨d⟩ muttering into the phone. When he turned back, he wa⟨s⟩ grinning. 'If you want to talk, he says, come on up. Just wai⟨t⟩ by the door over there, I'll get you a hat.'

Inside was an echoing space, a one-time warehouse tha⟨t⟩ by the look of it had lain empty for years rather than months. As Meldrum followed the man across the floor, h⟨e⟩ eased the strap of the hard hat under his chin. The lift, open-sided with bars and big enough to take a house removal⟨,⟩ creaked up, juddering and occasionally hesitating as if i⟨n⟩ protest at being pressed back into service. After a discon-certingly long time staring out into the high empty space⟨,⟩ they came to an upper floor that showed a glimpse of grey walls and a corridor littered with torn boxes. On the floo⟨r⟩ above that, the lift stopped.

'You all right for heights?' the man with the gold ha⟨t⟩ asked.

They were walking down another grey corridor, narrow⟨,⟩ enough to touch the walls on either side and low ceilinged. A place for claustrophobia not vertigo. Meldrum frowne⟨d⟩ down at the man and said, 'What's Michie doing up here?⟩'

The corridor fed into a hall about twelve feet square. A ladder had been set up, its top supported against the edge of a small skylight. Cold air leaked down from the opening.

'Checking the roof,' the man said.

Meldrum eyed the ladder with distaste.

'You want to tell him I'm here?'

'I'm sorry,' the man said. The grin had disappeared. 'If you want to talk to him, you'll have to go up there.'

'I might just do that.'

'It's your responsibility, mind. If anything happened. It's your choice, you don't have to go up there. Is it that important? Can it not wait?'

To Meldrum, though, this sounded altogether too concerned. He'd an image of Michie laughing at the detective who'd been scared to go up, to where probably there would be a platform fitted or a stretch of flat roof.

'It could wait,' Meldrum said, 'but why should it?'

He gripped the ladder. Like most people, he wasn't good at heights, he wasn't bad at heights, about average.

'It's the way he is,' the man said. 'Nobody can tell him what to do. Amount of money he has, he does as he likes.'

It sounded like a genuine apology. Oh fuck, Meldrum thought, and began to climb.

As he came through the skylight opening, he had an exceptional view across the estuary of the Forth, curling with mist, to where the Fife hills made a blur in the distance. He was very high up. Turning his head carefully, he saw Campbell James Michie about fifteen yards away walking, casually as if he was in the street, down the long rake of the roof. He was wearing a dark suit, and for some reason Meldrum noted that his black shoes were highly polished. He had his hands in his pockets.

He looked up to where Meldrum's head and upper torso poked through the opening, but when he spoke it was quietly and Meldrum couldn't make out what he was saying. He made no effort to approach, but stood waiting, head cocked slightly to one side.

With an effort, Meldrum forced his hands to let go of the ladder. He stepped up and was on the roof. Instinctively he bent slightly at the knees. The first step was the hardest. Crabwise, turned against the slope, he edged down until he'd halved the distance between them.

'You wanted to speak to me?' Michie asked.

'I didn't come for the fresh air.'

'It gets cold if you stand around.' He smiled and walked a few steps to the side then angled up until he was close to Meldrum. 'Reports are all very well, but I like to take a look for myself. I can hold half a dozen deals in my head and run rings round the moneymen. *And* I can do this. Respect's what it's all about.'

'Your friend George Rannie claims he made a phone call to you from the Hamilton Hotel—'

'The night of that murder? He called me about ten in the evening. We talked for over twenty minutes.'

'It's weeks ago. A long time to remember a friendly call.'

'Didn't George tell you we were in partnership in London? Successfully enough that he can take life easy, idle bastard. But George and I still do a little business together, so it wasn't just a friendly call.'

Meldrum's right leg, lower on the slope, had begun to ache from taking his weight. Sweat was trickling down his back. Michie smiled, as if sensing his discomfort.

'I know something about your time in London,' Meldrum said. 'You liked to pay prostitutes to let you beat them up. When some girls were murdered, the police down there interviewed you about that.'

'The policemen I talked to were politer than you. One of them's working for me now.'

'Rannie said he introduced you to Liz McKinnon.'

'At a birthday party. The one you invited yourself to.'

'Were you a client of hers? We're pretty sure she took clients. From what we can learn, she'd have catered for your tastes.'

The wind had risen.

'You're a very stupid man,' Michie said. 'You can't talk to me like that.'

I know who you remind me of, Meldrum thought. If he concentrated on Michie's face, he wouldn't a second time make the mistake of looking down on the Forth where the mist was gathering and moving towards the land. Michie had a face like Orson Welles, the American actor, but smaller in scale. Squashed Orson.

'Names of murdered girls,' Meldrum said. 'Sylvia Marshall, Madge Chambers, Kitty Grant, in Edinburgh. A girl called Elsie Richards in Aberdeen. And a girl in London called Sandra Norton. You were in London for a long time, maybe there were others. Or maybe in London, you could buy most of what you needed. Or maybe the need's got worse.'

Meldrum felt the wind cold on his face and like a hand against his chest. He moved slightly to keep his balance and, cramped from tension, his foot slipped. As he swayed, Michie reached out and caught him by the upper arm.

Without letting go, he spoke quietly, as if telling an underling something so obvious only a fool would need it explained. 'Like I said, George and I were partners in

London. We came to Edinburgh about the same time. Even before that, our business took us all over the country.' When he took his hand away, Meldrum felt his arm ache. The man had an exceptionally strong grip. 'Check all you want. You know what you'll find? Any time I was in London or Edinburgh or Aberdeen or Hamilton, you're going to find Rannie was there too.'

'Frances Deacon,' Meldrum said.

'What?'

'I didn't mention her. She was killed in Hamilton.'

When Michie laughed, his eyes crinkled and half closed. Squashed Orson.

'Yes, you did. That's foolishness — a policeman's trick.' He walked back up the roof and stopped at the edge of the skylight opening. 'You've met George Rannie,' he said. 'Look into his eyes. Can't you see he's capable of anything?'

Chapter Thirty-One

It was late on Tuesday afternoon before Meldrum got a chance to phone Hector Wemyss. The message had been on his desk when he came in the day before, after his rooftop encounter with Campbell James Michie. He'd taken a brief look at it before going to see ACC Fleming, who'd treated his theory about Michie with contempt and given a bruising refusal to any notion of spending man-hours on following it up. Since then, he'd been deploying the team on trying to uncover the details of Liz McKinnon's life. Shields had confirmed that, after quitting Setting The Scene, she'd made no efforts to find another job. A harrowing visit by the two of them to her parents, a retired couple in Loanhead, had made it abundantly clear there was no question of her having had private means. She had no savings that they had been able to trace; but no debts either, though she was supporting the mortgage on her flat and what seemed to be a comfortable lifestyle. It was possible she'd had savings that for some reason she had hidden away, but ways of doing that didn't come easily to a private individual. She had no unemployment record, and so no benefit. The likeliest explanation was that she was earning as a prostitute, but they hadn't been able to trace any contacts or clients.

And while all this was going on, Meldrum's private thoughts had been circling endlessly around the possible guilt of Campbell James Michie.

When the phone was answered, it wasn't by Wemyss himself but by his wife Frances.

'Your husband left a message yesterday that he wanted to see me.'

'It was I who phoned.' Her voice was thin but surprisingly firm. He had a sudden image, not of the old bent woman, but of her eyes, fierce and unaged. 'Will you come?'

'I explained to your husband, Mrs Wemyss, that I'm no longer involved with your son's murder.'

'Not involved. Does that mean it doesn't matter to you?'

'I'm sorry.'

'I want your help, not your pity.'

'If I could help—'

'Come and talk to us. Is that too much to ask?'

The truthful answer was yes. It was too much to ask. He was tired. There had been a time when he could work for weeks on very little sleep. In the last year, he slept and woke tired. He could move fast if he had to. None of his strength was gone. It was a tiredness of the mind rather than of the body.

'Are you there?' she asked. There was no quaver in her voice. She wasn't a woman who would know how to plead for help.

'I couldn't be there before nine,' he said. 'Would that be too late?'

In fact, it was after ten before he turned into the last and narrowest of the roads that led to the house. The headlights laid paths into a darkness made complete by heavy cloud cover. Penned in by hedges, like a walker in a maze, there was no option but to drive slowly. It was a relief to reach the gateless pillars, drive through and come to a stop in front of the house. He switched off the engine and listened to the after-sounds until they settled into something like silence. When he got out of the car, the door had been opened and the figure of a woman stood against the light. His attention was momentarily distracted from her by the red sports car he'd parked beside. It seemed an unlikely replacement for Hector Wemyss's old Granada.

'Detective Inspector Meldrum?'

'Yes. Sorry I'm late.'

He'd registered that it was the voice of a younger woman. As he came to the door, she stepped back and said, 'My mother's been waiting for you. She won't admit it, but she gets tired.'

A door lay open at the end of a short lobby. As he went into the room, it was so low in the ceiling he'd to restrain an impulse to duck. A chiffonier set sideways against the wall just to the left of the door acted as a kind of room divider, and he stepped round it before seeing the old woman Frances Wemyss in a chair beside the fire.

'You're here under false pretences,' she said. 'Hector's away visiting with a neighbour. He's not been able to sleep, and it's better he keeps busy. Lena's babysitting me.' She held up a hand bunched and knotted with arthritis. 'It's degrading to grow old. Do you think it's cold in here?'

As if signalled, the younger woman knelt at the hearth beside a basket of split logs and put two of them on to the fire. As she stirred a poker under them, licks of flame shone on her face and along her arms. It was a very smooth, young

face, oval in shape, the forehead high, not beautiful but
striking. Even in the moment of shock, now having met the
mother and the father, he could see both of them in her. A
slim woman with small high breasts; as she stretched to drop
the second log into the fire, the top she was wearing rode up
to show an inch of olive brown skin. Without having to see,
he knew there would be a tattoo on her belly, curled under
the navel, dark blue-green like a bruise. When the old lady
told him to sit down, he folded into the chair opposite her as
if his strings had been cut.

'You can't have met my husband,' the old woman said,
'without having some sense of the man he is.' He nodded,
hardly listening, watching the woman Lena as she edged
round on the floor until she sat with her back against her
mother's chair. 'I met him when I was only twenty. We were
married three years later. It was ten years after that before I
got my son. Another two and Lena was born.' Archie
Wemyss had been thirty-seven when he died. With the
looks of a girl, his sister must be thirty-five. 'I would have
liked more children. We gave our lives to his poetry, but the
poetry was rooted in all that we wanted for our country, and
so there was no choice but to give our lives to that as well.'

As she spoke, she began to stroke the younger woman's
hair, as if unthinkingly. Meldrum couldn't see the expression
on the daughter's face, as she bowed her head under her
mother's hand.

'Now we're old, they tell us the nation's time is over. But
when Hector and I were young, we heard just that from the
clever Communists, who were so much better than us at
argument. You would have laughed if you could hear how
they ran rings round us. Now everything they were so
passionate about is gone, and the world's still too big for us

o save. First we have to care for every part of our own land, feel for every corner of it as patriots. If we don't, how are we ever to tend the world?'

For Meldrum, who kept a grip on himself against the forces of chaos, and so believed in authority and order, and feared change, at the best of times this would have been empty noise. He gave up any pretence, stared at the younger woman and waited for her to speak.

'She's trying to make you understand,' she said.

It was the voice he remembered, pleasant, educated, perhaps here at home with a faint trace of a Borders accent, an echo of her mother.

'Understand what?'

'Why you shouldn't hurt my father.'

Meldrum felt the fierceness of the old woman's gaze. He said to her, 'No one could work out why Archie was in the Hamilton Hotel the night he died. But suppose your daughter was in the hotel that night? If she went there to sleep with a man called George Rannie, could that be why Archie went there? Is it possible he went there to stop her? Do you think Archie would do that?'

'I know who George Rannie is,' Frances Wemyss said. 'I knew him from when he was a tiny child. We used to visit Norman Rannie's house, Hector and he were old friends. We always took our children, Archie and Lena, with us. But when they came here – which they did only a few times – they came on their own. Left the children with a babysitter. I don't know why, maybe because we don't have a lot of rooms, maybe because Norman and Juliet enjoyed getting away without the family. George Rannie was twenty-five before he set foot in this house. He invited himself, out of the blue, I was surprised, the only time he was ever in this house. He was twenty-five and he was going to London. asked him, Isn't Scotland good enough for you? And h laughed and talked about the streets being paved with gold He slept under our roof for two nights, and when I woke u on the morning of the third day he'd gone and taken Len with him. She was seventeen years old. And Archie wasn' ever the same after that. It didn't happen all at once, but h finished up living with us again like a child. He became man who was so frightened he went round every night an locked all the doors and windows. And even then, often I' hear him getting up in the middle of the night to check i was done. And I'd lie and think it wasn't thieves he wa locking out. He was locking out his life.'

'Listen,' Meldrum said. 'Try to understand. I'm no guessing that your daughter was at the hotel. I *know* sh was. But that means George Rannie and Patrick Hennessy your son-in-law, lied about what happened that night. The claimed Rannie was with a woman called Liz McKinnon.

'I don't want Hector to be hurt,' the old woman said

'Finding your daughter slept with Rannie might hur your husband. But I'll tell you something more important t him. More than anything else he wants to know who kille Archie. And that has to be either Rannie or your son-in law.' He felt desperately sorry for the old woman, but tha was because he was so tired. Tiredness could do that to you 'Or both of them. Maybe Archie was killed by both o them.'

'No,' Lena Wemyss said. Her mother gripped he shoulder. She covered the old woman's hand with he own. 'I killed Archie.'

The story came in two parts to Meldrum, first as she tol it in front of her mother, and later when they were standin outside before he got into his car and drove back into the dark to go home.

She had been only seventeen when she ran away to London with George Rannie, the first man who'd ever made love to her. Years later at a party, he'd introduced her to Patrick Hennessy. By then she was twenty-seven and didn't take Hennessy, then only twenty-two, seriously, not for a moment, not at first. A charming reckless boy he'd seemed to her. Six months later she'd married him. They came to live in Edinburgh, and were happy enough for a time. But when Rannie came back to the city, everything she'd felt for him was still there. They became lovers again. When Patrick said he was going to be away for the weekend, Rannie asked her to spend the night with him. 'I didn't want to sleep with him in my house, and if he wanted to go to an hotel instead of taking me home with him, why not?' They made love, and were lying in the dark, making themselves hungry talking about what they'd get room service to send up. 'There was this funny little scratching noise. It must have been the key in the lock, for the door was thrown open.' There was a struggle, shapes in the dark. Rannie was on the floor calling for her to help him. She struck the man who was crouched over him, the head turning to her as she swung so that the blow took him on the temple. When the light went on, she turned to see her husband in the doorway. 'I was holding the ashtray from the bedside table. Then I saw the man on the floor was Archie.'

Everything that happened after that, the taking of the body into Room Four One Seven, getting Liz McKinnon to lie, had been done by Rannie and Hennessy to protect her.

When they came out of the house, it was country dark, her face a white glimmer though she stood so close.

'You see what's she's like,' she said. 'When we were children, there was a time when they had no money at all. A poet can't be expected to work in an office. One morning, I found rat droppings in the porridge meal. He was hundreds of lines into a long poem, and she was terrified he'd be thrown out of his stride. So she cooked it and we ate it without a word. To this day, he doesn't know. I meet people who tell me that poem is his masterpiece, but I can't read it. It makes me sick.'

'You tell a good story.' He paused to get her reaction, but she waited him out. He went on, 'Your mother believes it.'

'Don't you? It's true.'

'I have a difficulty. Where did I fit in?'

'They were carrying Archie into the other room. You appeared from nowhere while I was waiting for them. You were staggering and angry about something, I don't know what. Patrick came back, saw you and panicked. He hit you and you collapsed.'

'With his fist?' Meldrum asked. Having seen Hennessy, he was sceptical.

'No. I don't know what he used. You were knocked out. Patrick went for George and I shut the door and locked it. I wouldn't let them in and after a while they went away. I lay on the bed and fell asleep. Some time during the night you must have come round and stripped off. I found you beside me. Nothing happened, though I pretended in the morning something had.'

'Why would you do that?'

'Lock them out?'

'Yes.'

'I was afraid they would hurt you.'

Dead Man's Night

He woke in the middle of the night and knew he'd left a window open somewhere. At once he slipped out of bed and left the room. It was dark, but he didn't put on the light in case someone was waiting for him. He knew the house, so he would manage in the dark better than a stranger. Softly he went from room to room, checking each window by feeling along the top until he found the bolt and made sure that it was secure. He checked the side door, the bolts were shot home top and bottom, but although he'd locked the door he'd left the key in the lock. Somewhere he'd read that with the right tool, some kind of gripping pliers, you could turn a key from the outside. Blaming himself for his carelessness, he removed the key and hung it on a hook he'd put up on the wall by the sink. As he passed his parents' room, he heard his mother call out his name, 'Archie!' He opened the door quietly, intending to reassure her, but there was no response and so she must have called out in her sleep.

Despite the worry about the next day, he didn't lie awake for long. It was still dark when he got up in the morning, and he made breakfast and took it into his mother and ate his at the table in the kitchen, listening to his father singing to himself as he shaved in the bathroom. After a while, the singing stopped and then his father came in and they nodded to one another and his father poured a cup of tea and sat opposite. His father didn't make anything to eat, he almost never ate in the morning. Looking at his father sipping at his tea, he wondered about that. For himself, he could hardly imagine what that would be like. He began days with cereal and then an egg or sometimes toasted cheese; always something warm, even in summer. He made a good lunch too and ate too much every night for dinner. Being old, his father and mother made small meals. He couldn't do that. Meals were the high points of his days.

'I'm going to do the blackcurrants,' his father said.

'It doesn't look a bad day. The sun's shining. It'll be cold though if there's any wind.'

'You haven't been out?'

'No.'

'You want to give me a hand? If we both do it, we could get the raspberries done as well.'

The two of them moving along the rows, him hunkered down, his father on the rubber kneeling pad. He'd first helped his father to do that when he wasn't much more than a child.

'Don't try and do it all today,' he said. 'It's getting to be too much for you on your own.' He smiled. 'You're not eighty any more.'

'So what are you going to be doing instead?'

And what he wanted to say, suddenly more than anything else in the world, was that he would spend the day with his father. Every three years, the blackcurrant bushes needed to have about a third of the main stems cut away at ground level. That kept the bushes producing good fruit year after year. Rasps were even simpler: cut out the wood that had fruited that summer together with the broken or feeble canes of the new growth. Together they would work away, pruning the bushes, laying the wood aside for burning, taking their time and talking a wee bit to and fro. That would be a good day.

'I've to go in to Edinburgh,' he said.

His father looked surprised. What business would take his son to Edinburgh or, come to that, anywhere?

He said, 'Take the car.'

'That's all right. I'll get the bus.'

'There's the doctor's appointment for tomorrow for your mother. But I don't need it today.'

'I might' – he paused and looked at his hands, still clutching knife and fork either side of his emptied plate – 'stay in town overnight.'

Now, his father's surprise intensified. There was no risk of him questioning this decision, however. Not asking came naturally to him as a point of honour; after all, his son was a grown man.

Archie was still at the table when his father came back. Ready for the garden, he'd put on a jersey and was zipping up a fleecy jacket.

'We'll see you when we see you,' his father said. 'Take care of yourself.'

Walking across the field path to meet the bus, he wondered how he would put in the long day.

He walked from Princes Street to the Botanic Gardens, where some of the trees had lost their leaves to show that architecture of branches he almost preferred to the bunched busy greenery of summer. He walked back in to the city

249

centre, distances were nothing to him, he could have walked all day without tiring. He tramped from one end of Princes Street to the other looking into the shop windows. At the far end, he went into Frasers department store and took the escalators to the top floor looking for the restaurant to have lunch. He took his tray to a table at the far end and then moved when he realised he'd sat in the smoking section. Once settled, he ate the soup, which was country vegetable, and the hotpot of lamb and potato he'd chosen as a main course. Then he went back to the counter (fortunately, since it was coming into the afternoon, there wasn't a queue) and got coffee and a Danish pastry. When he came out, the sun was still shining and he walked quite slowly back along the street the way he'd come till he was almost at Leith Walk. On impulse (it was a long time since he'd been in a bookshop), he went into Waterstone's and looked at the new novels piled on tables near the door, then he looked at a book of walks in the Pentland Hills and a book on skiing, and then he went upstairs and took a book from a shelf and found a seat and read. The book was called *The Yale Dictionary of Art and Artists*. It was an odd choice for someone like him, who was capable of leaving a room without noticing the colour of the wallpaper. At university, he'd studied history and philosophy. All the same, once started he opened its pages at random over and over again, his interest seemingly held by the brief accounts it gave of lives, predominantly the lives of men. Some were successful, many had been poor and only gained recognition after their death. The accumulation gave an impression of the part played by accident in these outcomes. There was a painter, for example, called Adolf Holzel, whose life he puzzled over, and as with many of the others mostly he wondered about what the article didn't tell.

Holzel, born in 1853, studied in Vienna and Munich and visited Paris more than once. He taught that painting could be related to music, and through his students his ideas had an influence on the artists of the Bauhaus. In his last years, he made a series of studies in pastels, abstract as music necessarily is, but like music able to touch the emotions. The article, of course, being brief couldn't give examples of what he'd written to explain why he'd come to certain conclusions as to what was important in painting; and didn't say whether he'd ever married or had children, that not seemingly being important for his art, though often things like that must affect real lives as they are lived and so have a bearing on what is painted or whether a man could get up the energy to paint at all. In fact, as Archie sat with the book open on his knee thinking about it, he realised that he hadn't learned anything about what Holzel was like as a man; and that perhaps what had fixed his attention was that Holzel had lived in Dachau. While he was there, it seemed he'd established an influential painting school, which wasn't what Archie associated with Dachau. He'd died too in 1934, which made Archie think of what had happened in Germany the year before and wonder if Holzel had been pleased or dismayed to have Hitler, by coincidence also called Adolf, become Chancellor of Germany, though as an old man by that time perhaps what might happen next didn't matter to him one way or the other. At eighty, it might not have been easy to believe in the reality of the future, and still harder to take seriously a choice of possible futures, glistening ahead somewhere like a cluster of haemorrhoids, an indignity of parallel universes shrinking under God's ointment smeared finger. Somewhere about seven o'clock, he went into a pub thinking he might get something to eat, but the glitter and noise turned him back at the door. At some later time, he encountered a public phone box, but once inside with the receiver in his hand realised he didn't know the number of the Hamilton Hotel. There wasn't a telephone book, there never was. He was about to try directory enquiries when a woman tapped on the glass and said if he wasn't going to phone would he let her in since she was tired of waiting. He came out and watched her through the glass, waiting in his turn. Finished one call, though, she put in more money and began another. When she did that, he wandered off. He could have waited. He could have complained to her as she had to him. The truth was he didn't want to phone Patrick Hennessy. He wished that he had never answered Hennessy's letter. He wished he'd never agreed to meet him, never been told Rannie was trying to take Lena back. He could have lived in ignorance, without being condemned to the hopelessness of confronting him. Let Hennessy wait at the hotel. He looked at the posters outside the Odeon cinema, then went inside and stood in the foyer pretending to wait for someone until an attendant told him that the last showing had already begun. All the distractions made no difference, none of them helped. The guilt grew until all his choices narrowed down to the only choice he'd had since the moment he chose to open Hennessy's letter. He set out back to Princes Street and along Shandwick Place and then down towards the Dean Bridge. Along the way, he bought fish and chips and ate it out of the paper as he walked.

It was an odd day for his last, and a poor meal to finish on, but by then it was almost over.

When he got to the hotel, an instinct of caution made him decide against going up to the room Hennessy had written he'd occupy. The same instinct had him use the public phone rather than asking at reception for a message to be sent up to Hennessy. From where he stood with the phone at his ear, he could see the woman as she replied and then put him through to Room Four One Seven. Patrick Hennessy's first word to him was a curse. If he was too much of a coward to come up on his own, he would come down to fetch him.

He hurried, though he was tired now and faintly nauseous from waiting too long to eat. He didn't want to add minutes to the hours he'd kept Hennessy waiting. When he got there, however, the back hall was empty. He waited in front of the lift doors, watching for one of the three to open. Dull walls seemed to soak up the light. Cold air below round his ankles, and looking round he saw the outside door hadn't been properly closed. The approaching figure of a man swayed and stumbled across the car park.

When he turned back, Hennessy was beckoning him to come into the lift. As he hesitated, Hennessy lost patience. He came at him in a rush. Before he slapped his face, the only clear words he said were 'your sister, it's your fucking sister'. Next moment Hennessy had been lifted from his feet and thrown back against the wall. The man who'd come in from the car park was very tall and he hit Patrick, and when Archie intervened he turned on him. A kind of fierce joy went through Archie as they fought. There was no complication in it, no shame, like the guilt and shame that would have held him still under Patrick's contemptuous slap. This was simple. He felt the stranger's blows on his face and body and in return he beat with his fists into the stranger's ribs. He took a blow in the face and felt his teeth break. As he sagged against the lift, the stranger, who seemed crazed with some anger of his own, turned again on Patrick. Archie got the lift door open, and pressed the button for the fourth floor. Everything now was simple. He was going to rescue his sister. No more complications.

Outside the room on the fourth floor, he heard a noise and saw the drunken stranger gesturing at him from the far end of the corridor. Hennessy had promised he could get a key and there was one in the lock. He turned it and the door opened. No light in the room; his body blocked light from the corridor. On the edge of a pool of darkness, stepping forward was drowning. Yet here at the last he overcame the fear that had spoiled his life. As the woman got out of bed, she said his name and he went in and took her in his arms. Holding her, a sound made him turn his head and he saw Rannie behind him with his arm raised.

And so it was over and at the price of a moment's agony he could rest from guilt and choice.

BOOK FOUR

The Second List

Chapter Thirty-Two

As Meldrum approached the close entrance, a curtain at one of the bow-fronted windows on the first floor of the building stirred. His nerves jumped at the thought someone was in Liz McKinnon's flat. Next moment, he'd identified the window as that of Mrs Yolen, who lived along the landing. Turning into the close, he smiled sourly at the idea that Mrs Yolen might belatedly be taking an interest in the world about her. Maybe they all were. Nothing like a murder for encouraging neighbourhood watch schemes.

Climbing the stair, he half expected to see Mrs Yolen waiting for him, eyes fixed on the no-admission-without-authority sticker, indicating a site sealed off for the duration of a police investigation.

He closed the door softly behind him and felt along the wall until he found the light switch.

The last time he'd been here the flat had been bustling with people going about the business of violent death. Alone now he felt like an intruder. He put the light on in what must have been an ordinary bedroom when Liz McKinnon bought the flat. Sitting on the padded bench, carefully not

thinking what it might have been used for, he looked round
at what had been made of the room. Wallpaper imitating
brick and stone, stocks, a cage, chains, whips, canes, paddles
Liz McKinnon had been trained as a designer, but nothing
here was individual. Her clients would have wanted ob
sessive repetition not imagination. Your bog standard
dungeon, in fact, for the dullards of the perverse to mock
the real cruelties of the last century by play-acting them fo
the new millennium.

As far as forensic had been able to reconstruct her death
she had been tortured in this room, then taken into the
bedroom where she'd died. The view of Shields and the res
of Meldrum's team had settled to the notion that she had
been the victim of a client who had paid for sadistic spor
and gone too far. It fitted the notion of her being taken into
the bedroom for a climactic bout of sex in the course o
which she had been strangled. It was even possible tha
despite the severity of her earlier treatment this final violence
had been intended to heighten the sex act and that her death
had been an accident. When Meldrum asked them how thi
squared with the flat being torn apart, presumably after he
death, he had been offered what struck him as half-baked
psychological theories, not least from a hired gun psychol
ogist from one of the local universities.

The kitchen had been swept and the mound of mixed
flour, rice, sugar and the rest been sifted and examined. In
the process, inadvertently the kitchen had been restored to
some appearance of normality. The same was true of th
bedroom, and without thinking Meldrum closed over th
wardrobe doors which had been left hanging open. He stood
for a while by the bed, trying to empty his mind of emotion
and reconstruct what had happened that night. Why tak

her from the dungeon into the bedroom? The obvious answer was for sex. Even the fact that no semen had been found in the vaginal canal, though some was on the dead woman's face and in her hair, didn't disprove the idea of sex. After all, the men who came to women like Liz McKinnon to abuse or be abused were unlikely to take any of their pleasures naturally. Equally, though, it fitted the theory that Meldrum increasingly held to: that the woman had been tortured for information and been killed in the effort to get it out of her. It was possible, Meldrum thought, that she had died in the dungeon – perhaps she had let herself be tied up thinking it was a session like others she had done, only to find out too late that the man was there on a different errand. If that was so, then taking her into the bedroom, laying her on the bed, even the emission of semen, might have been meant to suggest a client who had gone too far: exactly the theory which everyone had signed up for, except him. But then, if that was the case, why tear the flat apart? He'd listened to the theories on that (every detective his own Krafft-Ebbing, the psychologist had joked, piqued at the richness and variety of the competing oddities they'd come up with), but his own preference lay with a more mundane explanation. There was something the killer needed to find or recover, and Liz McKinnon either wouldn't – more probably couldn't – tell him where it was. In consequence, he'd had no choice after her death but to tear the place apart in search of it.

Meldrum laid a sheet of paper on the dressing table under the light. It was a photocopy of the one the SOC officers had found on the floor in this room. There were eight sets of initials on it – each with a note beside it. TM – and the note: cbt and electric. DC – mummy's baby. JW –

pow. KL – gestapo. BR – cookery class. DP – cruel daddy
ST – pony. WW – flogger. The strangest thing about it to
him was that no one else seemed to find it strange. Why
would a prostitute keep a list like that? As a reminder of
clients' tastes? Were those all the clients she had? Or were
they ones who came regularly? And what did the initials
stand for? He could have understood it if it had been a set of
first names, all probably false, given to her by clients. But the
sets of initials might indicate complete names, and if she had
those and was able to trace the men then that suggested
blackmail. But how could she have obtained them? Not by
herself surely; could she have had an accomplice? Accomplice spelled pimp? God knows, he thought.

The curtains were open in the front room. He stood at
the window looking down at the street. A quiet street, not a
living soul under the lamps. He drew the curtains before
putting on the light. No point in having some alarmed
neighbour call the police. There was the same unexpected
effect of a restored normality in this room. A pile of books
had been laid back on a shelf, magazines were piled on a
stool; though set down haphazardly, chairs were upright
again. At a casual glance, it would have been just possible to
imagine the owner had slipped out and might be back in a
moment. An uncomfortable thought to be alone with. There
was a framed picture on the mantelshelf of a fair-haired
grinning boy. Meldrum had placed him as being about ten
and when he first saw it had assumed he was the dead
woman's child. Being looked after by a grandmother if he
was lucky, more likely in care, would have been his guess if
he'd been asked. That was the stereotype, of course, but he'd
encountered too many to be much of a believer in the whore
with a heart of gold. In fact, the child had turned out to be

Liz McKinnon's younger brother. When he talked to him, Meldrum had seen in the man traces of the boy in the photograph; and traces, too, of the sister who had encouraged and supported him all his life. Now in his last year of medicine, he, too, looked like someone who, under normal circumstances, would be fun to have around, good natured and lively. Told the truth of what his sister had been doing, he looked first murderously disbelieving, then heartbroken. Looking at the photograph, Meldrum remembered his conversation with the owner of Setting The Scene.

Hewison had talked of Liz McKinnon being among those who'd worked on design contracts for George Rannie. It had been after meeting Rannie that she'd left her job, not sought another, become a prostitute. If it had been Rannie who corrupted her, then he had put her in the way of the death she suffered.

He was at the door of the flat ready to leave when the phone rang. The shock of it froze him in his tracks. Irrationally, just for an instant, he felt guilty, as if about to be caught where he shouldn't have been.

When he lifted the phone, a man's voice began at once. 'Liz, John here. It's been a while. Is it too late to come tonight? . . . Are you there?'

Before Meldrum could speak, the phone went down. He tried 1471, expecting to be told that the caller had withheld his identity. To his surprise he got the number. He jotted it down and, before using it, put in another call which gave him a name and address to go with it.

He listened to the dialling tone.

The same voice: 'Hello?'

'Don't hang up,' Meldrum said. 'We need to talk.'

Chapter Thirty-Three

His name wasn't John.

'After your call last night, I expected you earlier,' he said. 'First thing in the morning, in fact. You sounded so keen.'

And how were you supposed to respond to that? Whatever Meldrum had expected, it hadn't been this sprightliness or the little twinkle in the eye. There was something to be said for belonging to a brutal police force in foreign parts. No problems of finding an answer there, a kick in the balls serving for repartee.

'This is Detective Sergeant Shields,' he said.

'Come in.'

He was a tall thin man with a long face and long hands which beckoned them forward in wide gestures as if guiding planes on to a deck. Safely landed and the door shut behind them, he led the way down the hall with the undulant gait of a camel. It was a long hall, and the drawing room, which was very large, was full of fine furniture reflected in the wooden floor, darkly gleaming with generations of polishing, under a high ornately plastered ceiling. Meldrum, not usually sensi-

tive to such effects, took this one since it was caught fo
emphasis in a painting above the fireplace.

'Isn't it splendid?' the man said with another gesture s
inclusive it was hard to tell if he was referring to the room o
the painting. 'For a painter in the Scottish tradition, I can'
think of anywhere better to live and work than a flat like thi
in the New Town. Cadell's old studio is just around th
corner from here. I never pass it without thinking of tha
wonderful painting of three Edinburgh ladies in a drawin
room just like this. There's such an air of time suspended
Wonderfully elegant women. Each of them separate lik
islands in space, not one looking at another. It's as if they'r
all waiting for something to happen, for a shiver to pas
through the air and time begin. Which, of course, it did
Since it was painted in nineteen thirteen. Convulsions
Horrors. Life, like an urchin nose pressed to the glass
leering in at their bourgeois stilled lives.'

If Meldrum was lost, his consolation was that Shield
looked faintly homicidal.

Using an old tactic of his, he asked, 'Why did you cal
yourself John when you phoned? If she was blackmailin
you, she must have known your real name.'

His real name was Brian Renton. On Liz McKinnon'
list: BR – cookery class.

'Blackmail's such an ugly word. But, you know,' tuckin
a long hand under his chin to consider the point, '
wouldn't call it that. We met – outside her professiona
role – by pure accident. She turned up at the privat
showing of an exhibition by a friend of mine. There sh
was circulating, glass of wine in hand, I assure you she wa
more startled than I was. The idea of her having been t
Art School – I don't know why that touched me, but i

did. Well, it's true afterwards I occasionally gave her something – over and above, as it were. I felt it as a penance – but only in small amounts, you understand. But no, not blackmail. Can you easily blackmail anyone now? With television crammed with people letting it all hang, hideously, out? And by the way, wouldn't that be a splendid idea for a television show – The Confession Box. You wouldn't see the priest, well they don't in real life anyway, do they? Or perhaps the priest's face would be lone in those glimmering squares. The whole nation would be caught up trying to guess who he might be. Like the actor who played Charlie in Charlie's Angels, he was only a voice on the telephone. A very beautiful voice, it has to be said. Our priest would have a voice like that, and he'd ask the most probing questions, and get the most indiscreet answers. People have no shame now. And you'd hear every detail of the confession – and then the penance would be given. It would get a mass audience. Like Jerry Springer, but somehow classier.' The flow paused. As Meldrum opened his mouth to speak, Renton intervened with an afterthought: 'I went on calling myself John, of course I did. I didn't really feel Brian in that context.'

'And what do you do yourself, sir?' Shields intervened. 'Are you an actor?'

Renton winced. Inadvertently, his eyes went to the painting over the fireplace. He confined himself, however, to a dignified, contemptuous, 'No.'

Meldrum asked, 'You didn't know Miss McKinnon had been murdered?'

'Isn't it odd? I watch television, I read the papers. I'm not a snob in *that* way. You do miss things, though. I wouldn't miss news in the art world, I don't think so. And I expect

you'd snap up anything to do with crime. But, no, I didn'
know until you told me the gory details.'

'You can account for where you were that night?'

'But if I'd murdered her, why on earth would I hav
phoned her? Or would the idea be that I was hoping you'
think that? But if I hadn't, how on earth would you ever hav
found me? Oh, I suppose she might have mentioned me t
someone or written a letter. And so I forestall all that b
phoning. Is that what you'd call a double bluff? That's reall
clever, quite ingenious. But awfully silly too, don't yo
think?'

Meldrum was inclined to agree, but repeated, as he ha
to: 'Can you tell us where you were?'

Briskly then, the tone businesslike, he said, 'I'd dinne
with a friend. We met about half seven. After dinner w
spent the night together. I mean the whole night.'

And in a very Shields moment, the sergeant produced
notebook and asked, 'Could you let us have a name an
address for him?'

Renton snorted, a kind of laugh. 'Oh, Christ, really! He
Could I have that?' The swoop was so unexpected, Shield
surrendered the notebook without a struggle. Renton ben
over it very briefly, but when he handed it back, Shields turne
the book to let Meldrum see. Under the address and name
he'd drawn a woman's likeness in half a dozen energeti
strokes, so individual Meldrum felt he would recognise he
passing in the street. 'I make you a present of that.'

'Police property, sir.' Shields stared gloomily at the page

'For your widows and orphans, then. Auction it fo
them.'

Taking a grip, Meldrum asked, 'How did you first mee
Miss McKinnon?'

'I telephoned.' He sighed: 'This is pedestrian, it was an escort agency. I explained the kind of girl I'd like to meet. I had no expectation at all, of course. But that's how I met poor Liz, and she was more than I had any right to hope for.'

'What agency was this?'

'Pedestrian again, the Apple Agency. I can't give you the number now. Are they in the Yellow Pages, I wonder?'

'Is that where you found them?'

'I really can't remember.' For the first time, Renton looked vague. It lasted only a moment, then he began again, self-absorbed as before. 'Am I a little in shock? I don't think I could claim that. Sorry for the girl, naturally. If I let myself brood on it, terribly sorry. But a little excited, too. Isn't that shameful? I have to tell you, one thought I had is that I wish I'd seen her lying on that bed where you found her, so that I might have painted her. I know that shocks you.' His gaze passed unsatisfied from one impassive countenance to the other. 'Yet it might have meant she would be remembered. Letters fade on marble. Pictures outlast headstones. I had a dedication once, to a book of essays on art — To The Unknown Whore. And it was taken as a generality — it was even analysed, in a thesis, by a cunt,' with a glance at Shields, 'a him not a her, as it happens. But it was very particular. I spent an afternoon with this woman, and she gave me a phrase and the argument of the book came from that. But I've no other memory of her, no idea who she was — or any need to find out. And so unknown, not unknowable. Any more than a skinned orange is some kind of mystery.'

When they left, he saw them out.

Perhaps moved by some lingering irritation with Shields, as a kind of parting shot, he offered, 'Wisdom is tolerance,

don't you think? Who knows, there may be people who
would despise your lifestyle as vanilla.'

'Fuck me,' Shields exclaimed, staring at the closed door.
'What's his then? Raspberry ripple?'

A tickle started somewhere in Meldrum's chest, and he
was laughing, and then he couldn't stop, until he was
laughing with tears in his eyes.

Chapter Thirty-Four

As they went through Hennessy's outer office, Meldrum noticed the same bald stocky man in shirt sleeves, seemingly as busy as ever at his computer, chair half turned from them. Glancing back, he caught him looking up, and in the glimpse before he ducked his head, fixed the face in his memory, almost but not quite recognising it.

Hennessy closed the door of the conference room. Instead of seating them on the couch between the windows as he had before, he nodded Meldrum to a seat on one side of the long oval table, Shields on the other, and took his own place at the head of it. Wants his back to the window this time, Meldrum thought, maybe he feels less confident. Or he's playing chairman of the Board.

'Has anything happened?' he asked as he sat down, pushing back the papers in front of him.

'What are you thinking of?'

'Archie, of course. When you phoned to speak to me, I thought at once that you'd arrested someone for Archie's murder.'

'And came to see you?'

'To tell Lena. Break it to her. She's been terribly upset about her brother's death.' He looked from one to the other. 'I gather you haven't caught anyone?'

'I'm not in charge of that investigation now.'

Before Meldrum could go on, Hennessy said, 'Yes, I know a Detective Superintendent Gowdie took over. I assumed you'd be working under him. My wife's been told nothing. She has no idea if you have a suspect or are near an arrest. What is the position?'

'You can tell your wife that, as I understand it, enquiries are progressing,' Meldrum said. 'But I don't think they are close to an arrest.'

He wondered what Lena Hennessy would make of that message if it was passed on to her. Take it as some kind of reassurance he was sending her? That her secret was safe with him? Was that true? He doubted it, but wasn't sure of anything. There was always a division between the detective, asking questions, and the man inside with his own thoughts. When things were going well, though, the man inside was a shadowy presence: no more intrusive than the shadow inside the tennis player focused on returning a serve. There was comfort for a man in losing himself in the task. When you couldn't do that, you were in trouble. Meldrum knew he was in trouble. The detective went on with the routine of question and answer. It was a tool of his trade, a game of rules and tactics he'd spent half his life learning to play. The man inside fretted, an unwanted second self.

'So why do you want to see me?'

'I'm investigating the murder of Elizabeth McKinnon. I think you know her.'

'No. I can't imagine where you would have got that idea.'

'But you do know who she is?'

270

'I know of her.'

'Have you ever met her?'

'Absolutely not.'

'You sound very sure of that.'

'She was a prostitute. If you choose that way of life – no, I don't even mean that, poor woman, it must have been a terrible death.' Meldrum was at once reminded of the feeling he'd had on their first meeting that being *nice* mattered to Hennessy. He was a man who wanted to be liked. That was important to him. 'I feel sorry for her. But I wouldn't have wanted to meet her, or anyone like her.' He smiled, glossy, handsome, fleshy necked with good living. 'I'm not a policeman or a journalist. And sex isn't something I've ever had to pay for.'

'I'm interested that you call her a prostitute,' Meldrum said.

Hennessy looked wary. 'According to the papers.'

'Never mind the papers. She worked for the Apple Agency—'

'I've already told—' Hennessy glanced at Shields, 'Weren't you here with Detective Superintendent Gowdie?'

'No.'

'He'd someone with him rather like you. Anyway, I told him that my wife runs the Agency. I have nothing to do with it.'

'So you're saying it's your wife who lives on immoral earnings?' Meldrum allowed himself a touch of distaste.

Hennessy flicked the fingers of both hands, as if physically pushing away something offensive. 'You must know better than that. The Agency provides escorts for clients. It arranges meetings and takes a fee. Its books are open to inspection. It pays its taxes. Everything above board.

It meets a need – for social occasions, for company. My wife was appalled when she learned what the McKinnon woman was doing.'

'Who thought up the name?' Meldrum asked.

Hennessy blinked. 'What?'

'The Apple Agency. Who came up with that?'

'Why?'

'Last time we were here, you explained why Schwert Associates was a good name for your firm. I wondered if you'd thought of calling your other business the Apple Agency, since you're good with names.'

'I don't have another business,' Hennessy said. He smiled. 'Suppose I told you my wife thought of the name Schwert Associates? She did German as well as French at school. I tell her it's a shame she didn't go to university.'

Meldrum waited, letting silence dwindle Hennessy's response.

'When you saw Elizabeth McKinnon with George Rannie at the Hamilton Hotel, you didn't know who she was?'

'No. I've told you.'

'But once you were told who she was, I suppose you told your wife. Did she tell you Elizabeth McKinnon worked for the Apple Agency?'

'Yes. But, however he met her, it was nothing to do with the Agency. To be fair to him, I can't imagine him as a client of an escort agency.'

'Would you say you know him well?'

'We're not close. He's fifteen years or more older than I am for one thing. But the families know one another. I was at Fettes with a cousin of his. Edinburgh's like a small town in some ways. Everybody knows everybody else. Don't you find that?'

Shields hummed a single sceptical note, perhaps unconsciously. He might have felt his chances were low of knowing anyone from a public school, and, given the size of its fees, lower than most for Fettes.

'But he did introduce you to your wife. Didn't you tell me that?'

Hennessy paused in his turn. Elbows on the table, he rested his lips against the tips of his fingers. They were beautiful hands (an embarrassing thought put into Meldrum's head by the Hamilton Hotel receptionist): well shaped with long fingers, a pianist's fingers, with strength as well as grace.

Looking up, he said, 'Let's go and talk to my wife. Wouldn't that be best? I'll phone to make sure she's at home.' As he stood up, he added, 'You can tell her about Archie yourself.'

Meldrum was left with the feeling that he was the one who'd fallen into a trap.

Chapter Thirty-Five

As they pulled up, Hennessy's red Ferrari was drawing into a resident's parking space ahead of them. Crossing Princes Street, they'd had a glimpse of crowded pavements. Late in the year sunshine was welcome, and it seemed as if these days the tourist season never ended. Getting out of the car, Meldrum saw the terrace on the other side of the street was in shadow. Hennessy was already out of his car and striding across the road. He ran up the half-dozen steps between the heavy stone balustrades. Looking over the balustrade as they followed him up the steps, Meldrum was struck as he'd been before by the rubbish scattered in the area below and the blank unwashed windows behind their guard of iron bars.

Using his key, Hennessy let them into the dark wood panelled hall. He'd tapped the doorbell as a signal and, as they went in, his wife appeared from the back of the house.

'Still no news about Archie,' Hennessy said.

She didn't say anything to that, but then presumably he'd already told her when he phoned.

In the front sitting room, they sat in the leather chairs, placed in a half circle in front of the empty hearth. Facing north, the room was cold. Lena Hennessy's legs were bare under her skirt and her erected nipples pressed against the light fabric of a polo top. Meldrum wondered if she'd come from some snug room at the back, perhaps having to desert a roaring fire to join them.

'Your husband tells us,' he said, 'that you had no idea Elizabeth McKinnon was working as a prostitute.'

Perhaps for warmth, she hugged herself, arms crossed, palms covering her breasts.

'If I had, she wouldn't have been working for the Agency.'

'By the Agency, you mean Apple, the escort service you own, isn't that right?'

'It's the first time we've ever had the slightest trouble.'

'You've been lucky. How many girls do you employ?'

'It varies. "Employ" isn't the right word. They pay a percentage of their fees. In return, we talk to the clients, put them in touch with the right girl. And if we haven't dealt with the client before, we can run a credit check and arrange perhaps for the girl to phone us, or be phoned, during the evening. It gives the girls a sense of security.'

'You say "they" and "we". Do you mean your husband and yourself?'

She shook her head.

Hennessy had been sitting back, staring into the empty fireplace. He looked up and said, 'I thought we'd covered that.'

' "We" means me,' she said. 'There isn't anyone else.'

'How long has the Agency been going?'

'About four years. Not long after we came back to Edinburgh.'

'Did you have any experience of running something like that?'

'No.'

'Perhaps your husband suggested it?'

He looked up again, but left it to her.

'Patrick enjoys being a businessman,' she said. 'In my own family, everyone was bookish. All with their head in the air, you know? It was a revelation how much fun business could be. I suppose you could say Patrick inspired me.'

'Do you keep a record of all the girls?'

'Sorry?'

'These girls you use. Can you provide names and addresses for them?'

'I thought we'd covered that, too,' Hennessy said. Speaking to his wife, he went on, 'I told them Apple has always kept proper records. Tax and all.'

Glancing at him, Meldrum noticed the man in the painting on the wall behind him. A great-grandfather, for a bet. Leave aside the mutton-chop whiskers and the wing collar, there was no mistaking the family resemblance. Something about the eyes, something about the nose; something about being well gathered and well fed for several generations.

'There have been changes over the four years. Girls come and go,' she said.

'When did Elizabeth McKinnon come?'

'When did she come?' she repeated.

We know when she went, he thought, and nodded.

'Not too long after we started, it must have been. Three years or so ago, or a little more.'

'How did she get in touch with you? Did you advertise?'

'We did to start with. Then we didn't have to.'

'Girls contacted you? Or somebody recommended a girl? Did someone recommend Elizabeth McKinnon?'

'Three years ago,' she sighed, as if to say ancient history. 'It might be in the file. Like Patrick said, I keep a file.'

'I wondered if George Rannie might have recommended her. But I suppose you would have remembered if it had been him.'

'I'm sure he didn't,' she said.

With the eyes of the three men on her, she spoke calmly enough, a trace only of indignation, not too much. But she couldn't stop the flush that came and went on her cheeks at the mention of his name.

'When she met Mr Rannie, she was working as a designer. A good job, from what we were told. And she seemed to be well thought of. But she left it. And then she joined your agency. After that, did Mr Rannie ever give you a ring? I mean, to ask for her services?'

'Certainly not.'

'So she wasn't working for Apple the night she went to the Hamilton Hotel with him?'

'Isn't that what I said?'

Meldrum nodded agreeably. 'I wonder if Mr Rannie was sleeping with her before she left her job.'

'I imagine you asked him.'

'There are so many things to think of. Like this, for example.' He took out the photocopy of the list found at Liz McKinnon's flat, and passed it across to her. 'Do you recognise that?'

The woman stared at it. 'What is it?' When her husband reached for it, she passed it across.

'It was found in Miss McKinnon's flat. It wouldn't be anything to do with her work for the Agency?'

'I can't imagine how,' she said.

278

'Why show it to us?' Hennessy asked. He held it out to Shields who sat nearest him. 'We've no idea what it is.'

'A list of the punters she had up in that place of hers,' Shields said, looking at the list but making no attempt to take it from him. After a moment, Hennessy drew it back. 'Like those would be their initials and she's written what they like beside them.'

'It reads like nonsense,' Hennessy said.

Meldrum studied him, wondering if he was being deliberately naïve. He glanced at the woman, but found she was watching him. He couldn't read her expression.

'I wouldn't say that,' Shields said.

'Without going into what the notes mean,' Meldrum said, in case Shields felt tempted to explain, 'if those initials stand for names, the first question would be how she got their names. Men going to a prostitute don't usually give names, at least not their own.'

'Particularly if they're after what she was offering,' Shields said. 'That kind are as nervous as cats. They even lie about their first names.'

'Why should you be sure they'd all be men?' Lena Hennessy asked.

Meldrum looked at her in surprise. He'd long ago got over the notion that doctor or professor or judge automatically implied a man. This, though, was an odd context for feminism. 'Maybe not all of them would be. Do you have many women phoning to book someone from Apple?'

'I told you, whatever she was doing it had nothing to do with the Agency.'

'You mentioned running credit checks on clients,' Meldrum said. 'That would be if someone was paying by credit card?'

'Lots of our clients pay by credit card. Why wouldn't they? It's a respectable business.'

'So you've got names, addresses. It would be interesting to see if any of the names matched the initials on that list.'

'Oh, come on!' Hennessy said. 'JW, TM, and all the rest – I could think of a dozen names to fit initials like those. What would Lena's clients think, if your people come plodding round asking questions about a murder?'

'If they're good citizens,' Meldrum said stolidly, 'they're often glad to help. You'd be surprised.'

'I would be,' Hennessy said. He held up the list. 'What did she want with this anyway?'

This time Shields leaned across and took it from him. He passed it to Meldrum.

'Blackmail would be a possibility,' Meldrum said. 'Of course, it's not easy to see how she'd get their names without someone helping her.'

'Blackmail,' Hennessy said thoughtfully. He glanced at his wife.

'Is that why she was killed?' Lena asked.

'It would be a risky business,' Meldrum said. 'Particularly if she was working on her own.'

'I'll show you the records,' Lena Hennessy said.

As she stood up, Hennessy made a noise as if to protest, which she ignored.

Meldrum followed her into the hall. On the left, halfway down, there was a curtain she pulled back to reveal a door. Oddly, it opened inwards rather than back into the hall. She put on a light. He saw an uncarpeted flight of stone steps and realised this must be the way down to the basement.

At the bottom of the steps, there was a passage with a

ncovered stone floor, two doors on either side and a single
aked bulb leaving the far end in shadow.

It was a surprise when the first door led to a room fixed
p as an office with an overhead strip light, a desk, a filing
abinet and a calor gas heater in the corner.

'Look for yourself.'

He pulled open a couple of the drawers of the cabinet,
anging files neatly labelled, four of them for the current
nd previous tax years.

'Can we take these away?'

'Of course not.'

'Can I have someone come in and go through them? You
an be here while they do it.'

'I was going to say, I've nothing to hide, but saying that
o you would be pretty stupid.' She shivered, it was even
older down here, rubbed a hand across her breast. 'I
vondered if I would see you again.'

Over her head he stared at the barred windows.

'I don't think I can do this,' he said.

'You know it was an accident. Archie was my brother.'

'I'm a policeman. I've never concealed evidence.'

If she'd told him going to his superiors would mean
rouble for him, he would have taken the consequences. If
he'd offered herself, even that would have made it easy for
im to go to ACC Fleming. She didn't make either mistake.

'Even though I saved your life?' she asked.

Before he could respond, Patrick Hennessy spoke, com-
ng into the room. 'I had to get away.' There was no way of
elling if he'd heard anything. 'Your sergeant insisted on
xplaining that list to me. CBT! Don't ask me!' he exclaimed
o his wife. 'I'll tell you later.'

It was a slightly camp performance, out of character for

what Meldrum had seen of him so far. Cock and ball tortur
though, as an idea might have that effect on some men.

Later, going back to the car, Shields objected, 'Blood
liar. It was him asked me.' Then, moved perhaps by som
association of ideas, he grinned and said, 'Wasn't wron
was I? That's some bloody woman, eh? Wouldn't min
getting her into bed. You not agree?'

And, despite everything, Meldrum did.

Chapter Thirty-Six

'When I saw you going out, I said to myself, bet he's away for a drink.'

Sandy Torrance was referring to the last time he'd seen his father-in-law, the night Meldrum, his ex-wife Carole and her new husband Don Corrigan had been invited by Betty and Sandy for dinner.

'It seems a long time ago,' Meldrum said.

'It's a fair while at that. You should drop in more often. Betty'll be sorry she's missed you.'

Meldrum had turned up at the Torrances' flat in Bruntsfield unexpectedly. It wasn't something he did often. He had a horror of imposing himself, though he'd never been made to feel unwelcome.

'But you said she'd be back?'

'Sooner or later. She likes going round Safeway. Bit sad, eh, when you do that for excitement?'

They were drinking lager Sandy had got out of the fridge. As Meldrum looked at his son-in-law, slumped on the other side of the fire with a can balanced on his chest, he wondered if he'd already been drinking. It didn't seem likely, though. Sandy wasn't like that. And, anyway, he'd been left in charge of the baby.

Meldrum tipped the can and poured half of it down his throat. It felt good.

'I don't mind shopping,' he said.

Sandy shook his head. 'What a night that was. Poor Betty, she worked hard at that dinner – made not a bad job of it. She's not much into cooking. And then that – bastard, that's what he is – shot his mouth off all night. I could see how you felt about him. I'll bet your dad's away to get pissed, I told Betty, and I don't blame him. She flew right off the handle. But I wasn't criticising you. I was just wishing you'd asked me to go with you.'

'Too late for a man with his work in the morning.'

'You'd your work.'

'I was late.'

Sandy laughed. 'I can't believe it. Don't tell Betty. She thinks you're perfect.'

'She knows better than that.'

'Want another one?'

Meldrum hesitated. He'd been more or less on the wagon since the disastrous night of Betty's dinner party. This was about as relaxed as he'd managed since then. He liked Sandy

'Right. And that'll do me.'

Sandy brought another two cans cold from the fridge.

'I'm a bit down tonight,' he said. 'It's stupid, but they set up a Committee on the Teaching of Art – new initiative from the Scottish Executive stuff – and I buy a paper this morning and there's Mr Corrigan grinning out at me like a bloody ape. What's he know about art, for Christ's sake?'

'Committees,' Meldrum said wisely, popping the tab on the can, 'are like that.'

'Come again?'

'You don't want people who know what they're doing on a committee. You want a lord, some folk with good jobs who can get off for the odd afternoon, a civil servant maybe. You'd be no use on a committee about the arts – you're a painter. And it's not Mr, it's Dr Corrigan. He may be a bastard – but he's a clever bastard.'

Meldrum was laughing, but the look on Sandy's face brought him up short. It was a look of self-absorbed misery.

'They've got a painter, bloody good painter. I'm not a painter,' Sandy said. 'I used to be a painter. Even that's not true. I was on my way to being a painter. I could see being a painter just ahead of me – like something I could reach out and touch. Not now. I'm not a painter, I'm a schoolteacher.'

Meldrum was sorry about the misery, but he disliked the self-absorption.

'No point in feeling sorry for yourself,' he said, meaning it as good advice.

Sunk deep in the chair, Sandy looked up from under his brows and managed a pale smile. 'You're one of the good guys, Jim. Sorry about this,' he said. 'Don't think I blame anybody but myself. God knows, I don't blame Betty – and I love wee Sandy. I don't know how to explain it. You're good at your job, I know that, everybody knows that. And you love your job. I don't want to embarrass you, I know it's not the way you'd put it, but it's true. I'm not talking any shit, pretentious shit about being an artist, being an artist.' Staring into the fire now, there was a tremble in his voice. 'It was a job I wanted to do. Maybe that's all a vocation is, the only job you want to do. And don't tell me about them, I know about the folk that work all day and get up at five in the morning and paint or write or whatever. A wife and

children doesn't stop them working. Whatever you put o
their back, they stand up and walk with it. Thing is, Jim,
thought that was me. And I can't do it. I'm not stron
enough.'

From the lobby came the sound of the outside doc
being opened. At once, Sandy straightened up. He wiped
hand across his face, though there were no tears.

'Pay no attention,' he said. 'There's worse things tha
being a teacher.'

Betty came in with shopping bags and she and Sand
went back down to the car to bring up the rest. Meldrun
thought about offering to help, but he wanted a moment t
himself. The truth was he'd come to Betty's house as a kin
of substitute for the way he'd gone to see Carole in the year
after their divorce. Married young, he'd been closer to h
than anyone else in the world, and it was a feeling that didn
go away because of some papers and a visit to court. Thos
visits had to stop, of course, when she married Do
Corrigan. So what had he thought he was coming to Betty
for tonight? A quiet haven? A few hours of peace?

'Sorry I was out.' Betty, full of energy as usual, came int
the room in a rush. She kissed him on the cheek and aske
'Sandy's been looking after you?'

Meldrum held up the can. 'Perfect host.'

'You'd be better with something to eat. You war
toasted cheese?'

'You having some?'

'After the baby, I'm trying to take weight off, not put
on.'

'Don't be daft,' Meldrum said. 'You're perfect as you are

'And you're a partial witness. Evidence wouldn't stand u
in court. Is it toasted cheese, then? Last offer.'

'I'll have some, if Sandy's having some.'

'He's away for a walk. Apparently, he's got a headache.' Her smile faded, came back. 'You're on your own for the cheese. I'll only be a minute.'

When she came back with the laden plate and a cup of coffee, she caught him with his trouser leg rolled up peering at his calf.

'What's wrong?'

'Nothing.'

'Let me see. That's nasty looking.' There were half a dozen angry red scaling spots. 'Have you been to the doctor?'

'I didn't even know they were there. I only felt it itching just now.'

'Is it anywhere else? Are you itching anywhere else?'

'I'm not doing a striptease.' He took the coffee, married two half slices of toasted cheese and took an enormous bite. Speaking with his mouth full, he said, 'There's enough here to feed an army.'

'You're not looking after yourself,' she said. 'It's a nervous rash. Kind of thing you get when you're run down.'

'More likely I've bought the wrong soap.' He laughed. She'd picked up one of the toasted cheeses and started to eat it. 'You want to half them?'

'I wasn't thinking.' She laid it down, picked it up again. 'May as well finish it now I've started it. See what happens when you worry me?'

They ate companionably, talking about nothing much.

At one point, when she saw him absent-mindedly scratching his leg, she shook her head and said, 'Tell you something funny. I don't think I ever told you this. When I was in Primary Two, the teacher read us a poem about an

avenging angel. Can't remember which poem, they all ha
angels, you know what our schools are like.' As a Catholi
Carole had brought Betty up to be one. If it left Meldru
out of one part of their lives, it was something he'd accepte
'Anyway, I put up my hand and said, My daddy's a
avenging angel. He catches bad people.'

After a while, it was late enough that he had to go.

With his coat on at the door, he said, 'That's a long wal
Sandy's having.'

'He'll not be long now.'

'Does he often take a long walk?'

'Leave it,' she said.

On the way to the car, he stopped at a couple of pub
standing just inside the door to check faces. He didn't se
Sandy, and so it was possible he was still walking aroun
somewhere.

Chapter Thirty-Seven

The red numerals on the dial read 6.08, when Meldrum opened his eyes. He hadn't got to sleep for a long time, and now he woke tired. He lay trying to remember, it felt as if he'd thought of something then wakened. It seemed, for a while, as if the thought was gone beyond recovery. He lay half-awake, and then perhaps he'd dozed and come round, it was as if he jerked back into consciousness, and there it was, something Sandy Torrance had said. *A Committee on the Teaching of Art.* And he'd made some kind of joke, but Sandy had been too full of self-pity to care – and he almost lost the thought entirely there, wandering off into thinking about Sandy, unhappy thoughts about someone he'd always had a lot of time for – before forcing himself back to the point. *They have a painter*, Sandy had said.

The thought that had come to him so early in the morning stayed with him for the rest of a day of plodding routine of the kind that came with the territory of a murder inquiry. In the middle of it, however, he found time for a phone call to the Scottish Arts Council in Manor Place. Although the Council wasn't directly involved, a friendly official gave him an educational contact and, when he said he'd rather not use that one, offered another at the Scottish Office which again, given the likelihood of a cautious bureaucrat checking up on enquiries, he declined. Third time lucky, he was given the name of a gallery owner who had conducted a running polemic in the newspapers over the composition of the proposed Committee on the Teaching of Art.

At that point, he'd run out of time and privacy, and it was four o'clock before he managed to make the call to the gallery owner. It gave him what he needed to know.

At five o'clock, he phoned Brian Renton, but it took another two hours before he was able to turn up on his doorstep.

'You work late,' Brian Renton said. 'I'm due out to dinner. I can give you twenty minutes.'

'I shouldn't need that long,' Meldrum said, following the painter as he hastened with his odd loping gait down the hall.

In the drawing room, Renton stationed himself by the marble fireplace, hand tucked under his chin, waiting to learn his visitor's errand. No twinkle in the eye tonight, Meldrum noted. Perhaps the novelty of a murder inquiry wore off quickly for him. Or maybe he'd been hanging around in front of a canvas all day tiring himself out. Meldrum had gone off painters.

'Well?'

'I want to ask you again how you came to know of the Apple Escort Agency. I should tell you that it isn't in the Yellow Pages. I checked.'

'I see. When you were here, did you ask me that?'

'Without getting an answer. It was my impression you

290

learned about the existence of the Apple Agency by word of mouth. I'd like to know who told you about it.'

'I have a feeling I said I didn't remember. Or does my memory deceive me?'

Meldrum took a sheet of paper from his inside pocket. On it, he'd copied the initials from the list found in Liz McKinnon's flat. TM DC JW KL BR DP ST WW. Nothing else.

'Clients of Liz McKinnon,' he said. 'She made a list and added notes on what each one liked.'

'Oh dear. Isn't it sad how people make it hard for you to think well of them?'

'I've left off the notes,' Meldrum said, handing the paper over.

'BR. Was there a note for that?'

Meldrum nodded. 'But that's not why I'm here.'

'I'd love to know what the others were.'

'Sad and boring,' Meldrum said, 'believe me. I think whoever told you about Apple is on that list.'

'They're only initials!'

'One of them fits.'

'I always thought policemen were like cream jugs, they came in pairs. But you come here by yourself. I wonder why?' He wafted the list back and forward. 'You know who he is, is that it?'

'If I'm right, you're on a committee with him.'

'I'm on so many. The price of success. Like scientists having to write grant applications, instead of doing experiments.'

Meldrum took a step closer to him. He lowered his voice confidentially, though they were alone in the bright spaces of the room. 'There are reporters who would give their eye-teeth for that list. When I came here before, you behaved as if it was all some kind of joke laid on for your entertainment. I think you were bluffing.'

'Look round you,' Renton said. One long pale hand joined with a curving gesture the room, dark furniture reflected in the polished wooden floor, and the painting above them which held the room as if in a mirror. 'I can't bear to paint people any more. To make my paintings, I ate my world. I ate my lovers, and I ate my mother. Framed and under glass, all of them. And I can work out that's why I wanted to be cooked and eaten myself. I'm not ashamed of it, though I see your disgust. But it's not a fetish I'd enjoy to see discussed by some cunt in a thesis. That would be so *un*fastidious.'

'If I get the name, there shouldn't be a need for any of this to be made public.'

'And if you don't?'

'Leaks happen.'

Renton folded the list, folded it and folded it again. 'Which committee were you thinking of?'

'Teaching of Art.'

Renton held up the paper; folded, it showed only one set of initials.

'Don Corrigan,' Meldrum said. His ex-wife's husband.

Renton smoothed out the paper and handed it back. 'Now I'm going for dinner.' He stepped round Meldrum and went all the way to the front door without a backward glance.

Outside, Meldrum turned on the step. 'One last question.'

'And then I hope I never have to see you again.'

'Why did Don Corrigan confide in you?'

'We play golf at Gullane together.'

Let me guess the club, Meldrum thought. A club as exclusive as that, why shouldn't one member confide in another?

'That was it?'

'He liked me. I liked him. He can be witty, and he's a good listener.'

Meldrum had never heard Carole's husband joke or stop for breath, which only went to show it was true what they always said. Golf was good for the character.

Chapter Thirty-Eight

It would have been difficult to explain to Shields why they were making a detour to see a woman called Redmond, so he didn't bother. That was wrong and Meldrum knew it was wrong, but Shields didn't ask, so he left it at that. In Blackford, though, as they got out of the car, Shields looked at the bungalow's unpainted windows and overgrown garden and asked, 'Live on her own, does she?'

It seemed, however, that she didn't. She was a pale woman in her thirties and, as she showed them into a little cramped front room filled by an overstuffed couch and two chairs, a man's querulous voice called from the back of the house. Meldrum saw a kitchen through a half-open door at the end of the hall and assumed the sound came from there.

When she came back, the woman said, 'My husband wanted a cup of tea. Do you want one?' Neither of them did. Somehow she didn't have the air of a woman who'd make a good cup of tea. She explained, 'My husband's still in bed.'

'Is he on the night shift?' Shields asked in a tone Meldrum recognised. It meant: poor wee thing, I'll bet the skiving lazy bastard's waiting for his next giro.

'He'd an accident at work and damaged his spine. Ever since then, he's in pain more or less all the time. The doctors do what they can.'

Sinking its occupants and tipping them back, the couch seemed to have been designed with discomfort in mind. Battling gravity, Meldrum said, 'I appreciate you agreeing to see us.'

A little defeated woman, sitting on the edge of her chair, she brightened as she asked, 'Have you got him for something?'

'Do you mean Mr Michie?'

Even before he shook his head, the flicker of brightness faded.

'What have you come for then?'

'I wanted to hear your version of what happened five years ago. When you left CJM Developments.'

'I don't have a version. I was dismissed. Nothing else to say.'

'You did try to bring a charge against Mr Michie.' As he said this, Meldrum was conscious of Shields' head turning sharply.

'I shouldn't have done that.'

When she didn't go on, Meldrum asked gently, 'Can you tell us why?'

'Nobody believed me. Except my husband. He believed me, in a kind of a way. He thought Michie'd been messing about with me, and I'd been letting him.'

'But it wasn't true.' He made it a statement not a question, offering her support, understanding, whatever it took to get her story.

'He never said a word out of place to me – before' – she nodded her head up and down like a bird in distress –

'before then. I thought the world of him. He'd made me his Personal Assistant and I was determined not to let him down. He was well pleased with me, I know he was. You were never in any doubt if he wasn't. He was a dictator, but we all respected him. But then Willie had his accident. I was nearly demented. I tried to put it out of my mind when I was in the office, but it was no good. Michie lost a big contract, it was my fault. If he'd just got rid of me that would've been the end of it. I could have got over that. He was entitled. But he'd no right to treat me the way he did.'

'He tried to sexually assault you?'

'That's what I said. It wasn't true.'

Meldrum felt as if he'd walked into a wall. 'I don't understand.'

'I couldn't say what happened. I was ashamed.'

Meldrum let it settle in his mind for a moment, all he had learned about Campbell James Michie, and he knew what it had to be, not the details, but he understood. 'Did he offer to let you keep your job?'

'I was so upset, I said I'd go down on my knees and beg him. And he said, Why not? And I did. I dream about that. And while I was kneeling there, he told me, I couldn't be his PA any more, because he couldn't trust me. But then he said, because of what had happened to Willie and because he didn't want me to starve, he'd let me have my old job back, the one I'd had before he promoted me. Only there was one condition. I'd lost him a lot of money and it was only fair I should be punished.'

She fell silent, staring at the floor.

'I'm sorry,' Meldrum said, 'but it could be important.'

'He wanted me to lift up my skirt and lie across his desk, so that he could beat me. I couldn't. I didn't tell him to go to hell, nothing like that. I just got up and wiped my face and went home.' She looked round the room and then at Meldrum, as if puzzled. 'The thing is, sometimes I wish I'd given in and let him. That's a terrible thing to say, isn't it?'

'Pretty terrible,' Meldrum said.

When they got outside, however, Shields' mood had been transformed. He wanted to know how Meldrum had found her, and enthused over the idea that his time in exile with the computer had paid off so unexpectedly. It wasn't that he didn't sympathise with the woman, he did; but that emotion was turned, as it had to be or the job would be impossible, into anger against Michie. When Meldrum told him the rest, about Michie being questioned in London, about the points of identity between the murders of the six girls and now Liz McKinnon, for Shields their detour to Blackford had paid off handsomely. It was the first time Meldrum had ever seen him in the grip of the hunter's instinct.

Chapter Thirty-Nine

Michie had moved his office from Northumberland Street to a new complex of office buildings on the outskirts of the city. As they headed for the Gyle, Shields' improved mood continued with the story of an arrest he'd heard in the canteen that morning.

'Tommy Cormack was telling me him and Paterson lifted these two guys. One of their business associates, you know Tommy, that's the way he put it, had snuffed it after a wee dispute over the quality of a smack delivery. But the thing is, they caught the two of them right beside the body. So Tommy says, naturally one of them rats out his pal. He says in the interview, "It was Jamesie. Jamesie hit him in the head three times with the hatchet. But the fourth time he couldn't get it out." It's just not real, Tommy said. He'd to stop himself from laughing on the tape. He says he'd a picture of this half-wit tugging at it till the police came – "Ah cannae leave it, this is a brand new hatchet."'

Back to Laurel and Hardy, Meldrum thought. He just couldn't think of anything to say to that.

Michie's premises seemed to take up the first floor of one of the new red stone office buildings. As they were shown from the impressive reception area, the corridor they went along was glassed on one side, giving a view of the main office. At a glance, Meldrum reckoned there had to be about twenty people working in there. Remembering that Pat Bannigan had said only half a dozen people had been employed at the office in Northumberland Street, it looked as if CJM Developments had expanded remarkably in the interim. One thing hadn't changed, however, all the employees in sight were women.

From the corner of his mouth, Shields muttered, 'Some bloody outfit.'

As quietly, needling, Meldrum said, 'Even millionaires are people, Bobbie.'

At the end of the corridor, the woman who'd collected them from reception opened a door bearing the legend in gold: CAMPBELL JAMES MICHIE MANAGING DIRECTOR. She knocked and, to Meldrum's surprise, followed them into the room.

They walked into a corner office, floor-to-ceiling windows occupying two walls. Cleverly slanted blinds gave a cool, undazzling light, while allowing an impression of the sky. It was a room with plenty of space, which was just as well since Michie was sitting behind a stretch of oak long enough for a ballroom dancer to fishtail. Meldrum had never seen a bigger desk and, as he sat down, the ex-carpenter in him automatically tried to estimate whether the top had been formed from a single tree trunk.

Michie didn't get up, but neither did he perpetrate the familiar stupidity of the busy executive routine, making a ritual out of the absorbed signing of a few documents.

'My Personal Assistant is going to stay,' he said. 'If she has to, she can take notes.'

Unlike Mrs Redmond, the PA was a comfortable looking woman in her middle fifties, which presumably increased the chances she could actually take shorthand. A recorder in a desk drawer would have done the job as well or better, Meldrum thought, but no doubt that wasn't the point.

'I gather you have some questions for me. If I can answer them, I'll certainly do so. I'd like to help, though I can't see how.'

This was a very different man from the figure Meldrum had encountered on a rooftop in Leith. He was relaxed in this setting, and full of an easy authority. Police officers with the survival instinct didn't tangle with the Michies of this world. A glance at Shields confirmed Meldrum's suspicion. He could almost see the passion for the hunt draining out of the sergeant. To hell with it, he thought. Go for broke.

'You'll remember when we talked before, you were good enough to say you'd let me have the relevant details for the dates we discussed. I could take them now, if you have them.'

Michie stared. As if conscious of a change in the room's atmosphere, the PA shifted uneasily in her chair.

'Dates?'

'For Elsie Richards in Aberdeen. Frances Deacon in Hamilton. Margaret Grant in Glasgow. Sylvia Marshall, Madge Chambers and Kitty Grant in Edinburgh. We've already talked about Elizabeth McKinnon, of course. And I wondered about a girl in London called Sandra Norton. I'm sure there must have been at least one in London.'

He caught the PA hesitate over her pad, a stutter of the pen, at the name of Madge Chambers. He wondered if she had come from Northumberland Street, if she had known the sixteen-year-old who had been murdered. If so, Michie's calculated risk in having her present at this interview, a bully's risk to face him down, had gone wrong.

'Did you send me these dates?'

'If you haven't got them, I'll send them again.'

'What did you do? Fax them, e-mail, post? Things don't usually go missing. If you sent them, I can't imagine why I haven't got them. Anyway, try again. I'll put someone on to it, and get back to you.' His tone was casual and matter-of-fact. The PA settled back in her chair. There was nothing to argue about. Whatever it was had been settled. Michie shot his cuff and checked the time. 'So, was that all?'

In a spirit of nothing to lose, Meldrum asked, 'Did you know Elizabeth McKinnon worked as a prostitute?'

'I only met her once. I was introduced to her at a friend's house. But didn't I already tell you that? I think so.'

'Did you meet her after that?'

'I've said I didn't.'

'So you weren't ever at her flat?'

'Obviously not. Why do you ask?'

'My impression was you might share certain interests.'

'Interests? Would you like to tell me what those would be?' The tone just perceptibly sharper, throwing out an unmistakable, if discreet, challenge.

'She had been an interior decorator. I believe at one time she worked on some projects you were associated with.'

'That's a misunderstanding.' Michie smiled for the first time. 'I can do any job on a building site. That's why the men respect me. I leave picking the wallpaper to other people.'

There seemed to be no way through the armour of the man's self-confidence. The only thing that might be brought in evidence against him was that he had made no objection to being asked about the murdered girls. But that was not enough. Now Meldrum had the feeling that he was the one who had gambled and lost.

'As I suggested, I can't be much help,' Michie said. 'You could have saved yourself a journey.'

'It's not a problem. On a murder inquiry, whatever time it takes is the time it gets.'

'That's a luxury we can't afford in business.'

This again, though, was said as a statement of the obvious with no particular emphasis. Like any other public servant, Meldrum had often enough experienced rougher rides from those anxious to draw the contrast between spending private money and that of the taxpayer.

'I appreciate the time you've given us.' Meldrum leaned forward as if to get up, paused and said, 'Oh, just one other thing. Has anyone ever mentioned the Apple Agency to you?'

'Apple, did you say?'

'It's an escort service.'

'Is it really? No wonder I've never heard of it.'

'Elizabeth McKinnon found some of her clients through the Apple Agency.'

'So why ask me about it?' Again, an edge in his voice challenged Meldrum to stick his neck out even further.

'For what you might call its more specialised services, my guess is it would have relied on personal recommendations. In the business community and elsewhere.'

'Why don't you ask this Agency to tell you what you want to know? Or would that be too simple?'

'One of my officers has been given access to its records. She's going through them today.'

Meldrum let it go at that. From his reaction, Michie ha[d] genuinely never heard of the Apple Agency. And, after all the question wasn't whether or how he'd met Elizabet[h] McKinnon. There was no reason to doubt he'd met her a[t] George Rannie's. The question was, had he met her afte[r] that? For, if he had, Meldrum was persuaded he was the on[e] who had killed her. In the same way, he'd killed the others.

Asking about the Agency had been no more than anothe[r] trawl. Time to give up. Nothing he'd tried had succeeded.

Campbell James Michie seemed to share that opinion. I[n] good spirits, telling the PA to stay where she was he'd wor[k] for her, he seemed to be allowing himself the satisfaction o[f] showing them off the premises in person.

'Satisfy my curiosity,' he said cheerfully. 'What was a[ll] that about the Apple Agency?'

Shields glad to escape was pacing halfway up the corrido[r] ahead of them.

'It's owned by a man called Hennessy – or his wife, she'[s] the one who runs it. He has a debt collection firm.'

As he finished he was caught round the upper arm, [a] painfully strong grip that jerked him half round so that h[e] found himself side by side with Michie, both of the[m] looking through the glass into the busy office.

'I could have any of them,' Michie said.

Shields was through the door into reception and out o[f] sight.

'And I could buy a woman to do anything.' Eve[n] Michie's voice had changed. It was thinner, with a glin[t] of something like the shine of metal where a covering ha[d] been stripped away.

'But you'd be paying,' Meldrum said. He tried to contro[l] his breath, which came in gusts as if he'd broken into a rur[?]

What's set him off? What's happened? His heart hammered in his chest. Whatever this is use it, he told himself. 'I think maybe you did buy what you wanted for a long time. But you couldn't ever be sure the fear was real.'

Some of the women in the room were looking towards them. One of them smiled, and glanced away quickly. As she did, Meldrum had an image of Michie, head and shoulders smaller than him, Napoleon dwarfed. And Michie must have had the same image, for his fingers uncurled and released that ferocious grip.

As he walked back towards his office, Michie turned and said, 'And I know you've got people watching me. Do it round the clock, as far as I'm concerned. It won't do you any good.' And he nodded and wagged his finger, as if performing for the benefit of the women on the other side of the glass.

Shields was waiting outside, leaning against the car.

Shaking his head with a kind of reluctant admiration, he said, 'I don't know about him, but you frighten me. You've got balls of brass.'

Meldrum didn't answer, and Shields scowling went round and got into the passenger seat.

The truth was Meldrum had hardly heard him. Fiercely concentrated, he was trying to understand.

What had happened back there?

Chapter Forty

It didn't help that, going through the records of the Apple Agency, DC Mary Preston had been able to find only one of Elizabeth McKinnon's clients whose initials matched those on the list found in the dead girl's flat.

'TM – Tom Martin. I wasn't hoping for miracles,' Meldrum said, looking at the notes she'd laid on his desk, 'but that's a lousy strike rate.'

'It's worse than that,' Mary Preston said. 'I've just spoken to Mr Martin on the phone. Long distance.'

'Don't tell me.'

'Denver. I traced him through the credit card he paid with three years ago. His wife answered the phone, which was a bit difficult. On the other hand, he didn't waste time arguing. He probably wanted to get off as quickly as he could and explain why a strange woman was calling him.'

'I really don't care,' Meldrum said, 'how he felt.'

'Sorry.'

'Just tell me when he was last in this country.'

'Six months ago.'

'You got enough details about him to check that?'

'I got the firm he works for.'

'Surprised he gave you it.'

'Like I said, he wanted off the phone. And I promised to be discreet.'

'There'll be nothing in it,' Meldrum said gloomily. 'What did you make of the Apple Agency?'

Mary Preston leaned back to think about it. He looked at her, then swung round in his chair so that he sat side on to her. It wasn't her fault that she was young, good looking, ambitious, unattached. He protected himself against all of that by moments of abrasiveness, and then ashamed of being unfair overcompensated. He'd been told she complained, You never know where you are with him; and he was happy to keep it that way. Although there was usually a faint tension between them, he trusted her intelligence.

'It seems to be run as a legitimate business. You know, background on the girls, credit checks on clients, a kind of log she uses for noting where they are when they're out on a job, all that kind of thing. I didn't go through the tax stuff, not with her sitting there, but they've a wad of papers in those files.'

'Did Mrs Hennessy stay with you all the time?'

'She made a cup of tea about eleven o'clock. Apart from that, she never budged. Didn't talk much, let me get on with it. She read a book, but she didn't miss a thing. Fair enough, I suppose, wanted to keep an eye on what I was doing.'

Meldrum grunted.

'If these Apple girls are half as sexy as she is,' Mary Preston said, 'I'm not surprised her Agency's busy.'

Before Meldrum could respond, his phone rang. An internal call. ACC Fleming was ready to see him.

It was a nasty surprise to find Detective Superintendent

Barry Gowdie, Fleming's protégé, already there, hands on knees, enormous thighs spread, scowling like a hired body-guard.

A believer, clearly, in the army maxim, Never explain, never apologise, Fleming didn't account for Gowdie's presence.

'Sit down,' he said. 'You asked to see me.'

When Meldrum took the available seat, he found that it had been set so that he faced both of them. Disliking the kangaroo court feel of that, he took a moment to move his seat back, adjusting it as he did just enough to let him ignore Gowdie.

'I interviewed Campbell James Michie today.'

'Why?' Fleming let the single monosyllable escape through little pursed lips.

Court in session.

'You'll remember I asked if I could have one or two more people so that we could dig into his past. You described that as a waste of resources.'

'I *remember*,' Fleming said, 'that you couldn't give me any proper reason for doing it. Apart for an interview with him. At which you'd neglected to have anyone with you for verification. And which, for some incomprehensible reason, you decided to conduct on a roof. Does that cover it?'

'His name came up when I was working on the computer records for Sylvia Marshall and the other girls killed in Edinburgh. After the same kind of killings in London, men who went to prostitutes who catered for clients into violence were pulled in for questioning. Michie was one of them.'

Gowdie said, 'If you'd checked, you'd have found there was a lot of doubt about whether the murders down there really were connected.'

'So you checked?' Meldrum asked. He looked at Fleming What was going on?

Directing a frown at Gowdie, Fleming said, 'When you were assigned to the McKinnon murder, Detective Constable Maxwell took over the case files on Sylvia Marshall and the others.'

'So he's followed up on Michie?'

'DC Maxwell's been doing a very thorough job. Of course, he's had computer training, and that made the difference. I find older officers aren't so comfortable in that area.'

'When I spoke to Michie yesterday,' Meldrum said, 'he told me he was under police surveillance. Is he?'

'I hope you told him he wasn't,' Fleming said. 'If he asks again, tell him so.'

Before Meldrum could work out a politic response to that, Gowdie shifted from one ham to the other and rumbled, 'You were out of order going to see witnesses of mine without telling me.'

'What witnesses?'

'Mrs Cairns for one. She was a friend of Kitty Grant and that was my case.'

Meldrum looked to Fleming, expecting him to intervene. As the ACC returned his gaze expressionlessly, a number of questions lined up wanting an answer. How had his visit to Mrs Cairns come to Gowdie's knowledge? Had the computer literate DC Maxwell also been to see her? If so, what did that mean? What was going on?

'Of course it was your case,' Meldrum said agreeably. 'That's why I sent you a memo. Did you not get it?'

'I did not,' Gowdie said, his tone expressing profound scepticism about its existence.

'There you go,' Meldrum said. 'I should have sent you an e-mail.'

'In this building, memos don't usually get mislaid.' Fleming leaned forward, a faint flush of anger showing on pallid cheeks.

'I agree, sir. But it must happen. I mean, I didn't get the one DS Gowdie sent me.' He glanced at Gowdie. 'About Elizabeth McKinnon. She was with George Rannie the night Archibald Wemyss was killed. You must have checked up on her, the Apple Agency, all of that. So, I suppose, when she was killed, you sent me the information you had about her.'

He had the satisfaction of seeing Gowdie squirm. On the other hand, it never paid to take liberties with an ACC. They didn't get to the top by being fools; and, seeing Fleming give one of his rare thin smiles, gave him a bad feeling.

'I see the point you're making,' Fleming said. 'The connections between the deaths of Mr Wemyss and the McKinnon woman are quite striking. I'm wondering whether it would make sense to put the two teams together. You know it probably would. We could set it up within a day or two. With Barry in charge, of course.'

Chapter Forty-One

Meldrum didn't know when Directors of Education started their day's work, so he arrived outside Don Corrigan's house in Barnton before the sky had started to lighten. He didn't mind the early start, though. He was sleeping badly, and he was as well there, switching the engine on and off, letting the heater run, listening to the radio, as he would have been awake in bed staring at the ceiling, brooding over the prospect of being part of a team led by Barry Gowdie. Once he'd worked out the formula: years of service over X into annual salary, and the pension that would give him, and then asked, What do I do then? the best thing was to roll out of bed and hit the road.

There was a long hedge, a scrollwork iron gate, a glimpse of house at the end of a stretch of lawn. He annoyed himself by working out what the house might be worth. It was a big house and this was an expensive district. It was the first time he'd seen it, though he'd learned from Betty that her mother had sold her house in Sciennes and put that money together with what Corrigan had got for selling his. They'd moved into this one when they married. More than likely, it was

carrying an enormous mortgage, he thought, and chance
were Corrigan couldn't afford it. He was that kind of flash
bastard. Meldrum wondered if the house was in both their
names, or if it was conceivable that Carole could have let
Corrigan buy it as sole owner. That would have been foolish
and Carole wasn't a fool, but he'd seen how she let herself be
bullied by her second husband. For a while, he tormented
himself with memories of Carole and the house in Scienne
and the two of them sitting either side of the fire, and when
he'd finished with that went back to worrying about
Gowdie.

Before he realised it, the gate had opened and was closing
again behind a black BMW520. Luckily, he'd the engine
running and, slamming into gear, caught up and gestured
that the car should draw into the side.

As he walked back to the passenger side, the window
purred down.

'It *is* you,' Corrigan said, leaning across. 'What on earth—'

'Ten minutes,' Meldrum said. He opened the door and
got in. 'I can talk to you at home, or I can make it official
and come to your office with my sergeant. I thought you'd
prefer this.'

He expected Corrigan to bluster or be perplexed
instead he flushed and sat silently staring ahead. It was
as if he'd been waiting to be caught, and perhaps he had
waiting all his life for some dirty hollow place inside to be
uncovered.

'I've reason to believe,' Meldrum said, 'that you were
seeing a prostitute called Elizabeth McKinnon.'

'Are you going to arrest me?'

Meldrum looked at him in astonishment. 'Why? What
have you done?'

Corrigan made an odd gasping sound, as if he'd stopped breathing and had just started again. 'Nothing. Have you any proof I went to this woman — whatever her name is?'

'Now you're being silly. We'll get through this more quickly if you don't waste my time. You know she was killed?' Corrigan nodded. 'Can you account for your movements that night? It's routine, but I have to ask you.'

'I saw it in the papers on the Friday. The night before I'd been to the theatre. We were with a party of friends and we went on for a meal afterwards. Then Carole and I came home.' He glanced sideways at Meldrum. 'You'd take her word, I suppose?'

'Did Elizabeth McKinnon try to blackmail you?' And, as he saw Corrigan hesitate, 'Before you answer, I should tell you, we have a list.'

And again, Corrigan caved in; asking no questions, which was fortunate, the list of initials as proof carrying about the same weight as a laundry list.

'I gave her money.'

'Blackmail money?'

'Yes.'

'Can you give me an idea of the sums involved?'

'About two thousand pounds.'

'About?'

'It was two thousand.'

'A single payment?'

'No. A few hundreds at a time. Over three months.'

'It's not big time blackmail,' Meldrum said. 'But if it had gone on like that it would have added up. Would you have gone on paying?'

'Probably. It was well calculated. It was a strain, but I could manage it. Just about.'

And if things had got tight you could have asked your wife to go for a promotion, Meldrum thought. At a guess, Carole had been persuaded to give up her headteacher's job before the blackmail started.

'Was anyone else involved?'

'You mean apart from McKinnon? She told me if I tried to do anything, I'd have to deal with someone a lot worse than her. When I asked about that, she said there was a man. I thought she was lying, but I couldn't be sure.'

'You could have told her to go to hell.'

Corrigan put his elbows on the wheel and held his face with the tips of his fingers. He said, 'Do you know what I went to her for?' His driving gloves were very nice, a soft yellow leather.

'The list has you down as "Mummy's baby".'

Corrigan groaned. 'How could I face that being known? She would—'

'I don't care if she wiped your arse or your nose,' Meldrum said.

Corrigan sat up. 'Are you going to tell Carole?'

'Don't insult me. I wouldn't be seeing you this way if I wanted Carole to know.'

'Do you know what I thought, when I heard that woman had been killed?' Corrigan asked. He seemed to have recovered some of his confidence. 'I hoped it hadn't been an easy death.'

Wish granted.

Meldrum said, 'One more thing, and I'm finished. How did you first meet Elizabeth McKinnon?' And when the other man hesitated, added, anxious to be done with him, 'Was it through an Agency?'

'Apple.'

'Somebody told you about it?' A careful half-nod in reply. 'Who told you?'

No hesitation this time. 'Brian Renton,' Corrigan said. 'He's a painter. You won't have heard of him, he's not a household name.'

But according to Renton, Corrigan had told *him* about the Agency. It would be difficult, and probably not worth it, to discover which was the liar.

'I've heard of him,' Meldrum said. 'She tried to blackmail him, but he treated it as a joke. Among the people we've traced, you're the only who paid.'

No point in telling him that made one out of two.

A good point to finish on, but as Meldrum was getting out of the car, Corrigan had something of his own to add.

Leaning across again so he could speak through the open window, he said, 'Speaking of arses to be wiped, did you know Carole folds the toilet paper?'

Meldrum gaped in at him.

Switching on the engine, Corrigan went on, 'Or at least she did. It's wasteful, we can't afford it. I said to her, the toilet paper is being used up too quickly. Do you fold it? Don't fold it, I told her.'

Meldrum wasn't violent man. He'd seen too much of it not to hate it. But, watching the BMW pull away, there went one man he could imagine beating to a pulp.

Chapter Forty-Two

The receptionist, a woman he hadn't seen before, making a perfectly reasonable effort to do her job, wanted to tell the manager he was there. As she picked up the phone, however, Meldrum was already halfway down the corridor, going in like the cavalry, towing a reluctant Shields behind him. The aggression came from being told by Gowdie to stay away from the Hamilton Hotel, and even more from the undischarged anger of his early morning encounter with Don Corrigan.

His knock on the door was perfunctory, and he went in without a pause, ready to claim he'd heard a call to enter.

Harkness, in fact, was putting down the phone and getting to his feet. Presumably, he'd just taken the call from the receptionist.

Meldrum began without preamble. 'He's done it again. I arrive this morning to be told McArdle was on the phone half a dozen times yesterday.'

Intent on being unobtrusive, Shields had taken his stance by the door.

Harkness sat down heavily. 'Phoning the police? But what about? There hasn't been another murder?'

Standing in front of the desk, Meldrum towered over him.

'Not yet. But according to McArdle there's going to be one soon. He's got tired of confessing to murders and moved on to predicting them. I remembered this morning you told me he was seeing a psychiatrist. Is that at the Royal Ed?'

'I couldn't say.'

'I want the name of the psychiatrist.'

'That would be up to Hugh.'

'What are these? Private consultations? Who's paying for them? You?'

'I'm helping. What's wrong with that?'

Meldrum's voice quietened. The effect of intimacy was disturbing. 'Just recently an idea occurred to me about McArdle, and then I wasn't sure. I lost confidence in it. You know how that can happen?'

He stopped, as if thinking about that. Unable to cope with the silence, Harkness asked abruptly, 'What idea?'

'He's confessed to four murders. Somebody confesses, you check whether it's true or not. And we know, with him it's not true, he hasn't killed any of these women. The times or the places or whatever don't fit. Or he was with somebody. One time, he was with you, isn't that right? So we say, he hasn't done it. He's a nuisance. Or he's mad – so you get him a psychiatrist. A psychiatrist to find out why he keeps doing it. Why's he doing it? What reason could he have. Can you think of one?'

Harkness had been sitting under strain, his head craned back to stare up at Meldrum. Suddenly, he stood up. What he had to say, though, came with an effect of bathos. 'I'm not a psychiatrist.'

'You don't need to be,' Meldrum said. 'It started with Sylvia Marshall. He didn't kill her, but suppose he knew who did. Confessing might have made some kind of sense to him. Maybe he would have been trying to tell us something. I don't know. But if that was what happened, I can imagine why he went on to confess to killing Madge Chambers and Kitty Grant. And Elizabeth McKinnon. He'd be telling us the same man who killed Sylvia Marshall committed all four murders.'

'How could he know that?'

'If he knew who the man was, there might be ways. I don't worry about that. What's been sticking me all this time is what happened at the beginning. And Sylvia Marshall was the beginning.' Meldrum leaned close to Harkness. Now he was speaking so softly that Harkness could barely hear him. 'I was sitting in a car this morning. I'd just had a meeting with someone, and I was just sitting, getting ready to go, and it came into my mind the way these things do. Sylvia Marshall was a student, very bright, a girl with everything to live for. But her family didn't have a lot of money. And it just came into my head what this woman said at the time of her murder. The medical examiner, I think. She was looking at the body. And she said something like, looks like the usual student gear, but it's designer version, it must have cost a bomb. Nobody followed that up. Everyone had a good word to say for her. I met her father and I liked him, I liked him a lot. So I didn't follow it up – the obvious question – how does a poor student get clothes like that? It's a puzzle, isn't it? What do you think? Tell me what you think.'

Harkness stepped back. 'It's eight years. I don't think about it.'

'I do. I've had this nice girl in my head so long I'm ashamed of what I'm thinking. But it makes sense of so many things. I think Sylvia Marshall was doing a little prostitution on the side. I think she met clients here at the Hamilton.'

'That's outrageous.'

'I think a lot of the girls did their business here. I want to ask McArdle about that. And other things.'

'You'll have to wait then. Superintendent Gowdie will be talking to him first.' Wearily, Harkness indicated a chair in the corner. A blue anorak lay folded on it. 'It was hidden in a cupboard in McArdle's cubbyhole. Simms found it, and phoned Superintendent Gowdie. Apparently, it's the wrong size for McArdle. Superintendent Gowdie thinks it might have belonged to Archibald Wemyss. He was supposed to have been wearing one.'

The night he was killed. Meldrum stared at it.

'Where's McArdle now?'

Harkness shook his head. 'He didn't come in today. That's the first time in fifteen years.'

He sounded oddly sad, a man signalling the end of an era.

Chapter Forty-Three

Dazzling light. Did it ever rain in this shaft sunk from blue sky to the grassy earth between high Edinburgh tenements? Whatever grey skies fact held, for Meldrum an accident of the day and the time of the day on each of his visits meant that it would be this dazzle of light striking off glass which would stay in his memory, glass of the conservatory itself, frames of three Mackintosh flower paintings, the bright molten rim of a glass on the table in front of Rannie. Still other glasses, curiously, made the only darkness, black pools that hid Rannie's eyes. Campbell James Michie's words came back to Meldrum: *Have you looked into his eyes?*

They were there because of Michie.

'If he comes, will we hear him from back here?' Shields asked as he sat down.

It wasn't the smartest question in the world, but Rannie answered seriously, 'The front door bell rings all over the house. Including here.'

'When are you expecting him?' Meldrum asked.

'Half an hour ago. I was getting worried he'd be here before you arrived. Do you want something to drink?'

'No,' Meldrum said for both of them. 'If he's overdue, he could be here any moment.' Above the sliding doors to the kitchen, he could see a bell, presumably one of those connected to the front door. 'Have you thought about his reaction when he sees us?'

'Isn't that why you're here? To see what it is?'

Shields stirred, an irritable rearranging of his bulk that made the chair groan under him. 'We're here because you asked us.' He'd taken the call.

'I was concerned. Didn't I sound concerned?' Hidden behind the sunglasses, Rannie turned his gaze on Shields.

'You sounded frightened,' Shields said bluntly.

'I'd settle for concerned.'

'I took a note,' Shields said. 'You talked about the possibility of violence.'

'I've had time to think,' Rannie said. 'Perhaps I over-reacted.'

'Do you want us to go?' Meldrum asked.

'No!' After a moment, he smiled at his own vociferous-ness. 'That's definite enough,' he said. 'The truth is Jamie isn't someone you'd want to get on the wrong side of. On a building site, this is years ago, one of the workmen thought he'd a grievance. He was a big brute, looked as if he'd have made two of Jamie, started shoving him and yelling. Next moment, Jamie had him on the ground with his hands round his throat. I thought he was killing him. But when I tried to pull him off, Jamie just laughed up at me. Think of it as judo, he told me. I've put him to sleep, he'll be calmer when he wakes up.'

'If you'd told me,' Shields said, 'I'd have borrowed a truncheon.'

Meldrum detected an unexpected undercurrent of cheerfulness. Shields might be overweight and getting on, but no one had ever doubted his courage. The chance to overcome his wary respect for authority and kick the shit out of a millionaire wouldn't come along every day. It was also true, of course, that any policeman learned to take stories about the prowess of fighting men with a pinch of salt. What interested Meldrum wasn't whether the incident was true or not, but that Rannie had chosen to tell it. Possibly it was only coincidence that had led Rannie to tell a story about Michie choking a victim. But if it wasn't, how did Rannie know the murderer of Sylvia Marshall and the others had to be a man with exceptional strength in his hands?

He looked at his watch. Going by what Rannie had said, by now Michie was three-quarters of an hour late.

'Why was he angry with you?' Meldrum asked. 'You said he was angry with you, but you didn't say why.'

Rannie nodded. 'It's difficult to explain. Something's wrong with him. You'd need to have heard him to understand. I picked up the phone and he was in full flight, not very coherently. It seemed to have something to do with Patrick Hennessy.'

There was a long silence. To prompt him, Meldrum said, 'Hennessy?'

'Jamie knows him through me. Patrick's a lot younger than I am, of course, but family connections, school connections, you know what Edinburgh's like. When he came to London, he got in touch. Jamie and I were in partnership then, so they came across one another, a few times, quite casually.'

He fell silent again.

Meldrum said, 'They met through you. And didn't you introduce Hennessy to the woman he married?'

Rannie smiled. 'I suppose you could say I was the link that connected them. And all of us finished up back here.'

'We know you and Michie kept in touch.'

'And did a little business, as I told you.'

'What about Hennessy? When they were both back in Edinburgh, did Michie meet him here? Or did he meet Hennessy's wife?'

'Lena? Why ask about her?'

'She runs an escort agency. We know that at least one of the girls who worked for her specialised in violent sex.'

'You're talking about poor Elizabeth?'

Meldrum nodded. 'Elizabeth McKinnon.'

'But what would that have to do with Jamie?'

'You know so much about him,' Meldrum said. 'Didn't you know when the two of you were in London that he used prostitutes? He paid them to let him beat them.'

'Have you a brother?' Rannie asked.

Into the silence, Shields volunteered, 'I have.'

'Men keep their sex lives to themselves. Even from their brothers.' Rannie sipped from his glass. 'But not it seems from the police. Do you think Hennessy was blackmailing him about visiting prostitutes? People don't care about that nowadays, do they? But Jamie would hate to look foolish, maybe if it made him look foolish . . . Stupid to try that on Jamie, though. He'd be more likely to kill you than pay.' At once, in a gesture that was almost camp, he covered his mouth with his hand. 'Oh dear. Do you think he killed Elizabeth?'

If he was being manipulated, Meldrum disliked the feeling. He let the silence run on. What Rannie said next might be revealing. Gently Rannie swirled what was left in his glass and sipped and swirled again. It seemed silence didn't bother him.

Outwaited, Meldrum asked, ' "Something's wrong with Michie"? What did you mean by that?'

'The way he was talking. Everything pouring out. I couldn't get a word in.'

'You haven't heard him like that before?'

Rannie shook his head.

'He strikes me as a pretty dominating character,' Meldrum said. 'And you've known him for a long time.'

'He's an egomaniac. Men who come out of the gutter and make a fortune aren't usually nice people,' Rannie said. 'But I've never heard him like that.'

'What about mood swings?'

'What about them?'

'In the middle of an ordinary conversation, where he seemed in control, getting angry or upset for no obvious reason. Have you seen anything like that?'

'Not really. But it sounds as if you might have.'

It would have been easy to evade that with some vague generality. Meldrum almost offered one. Instead, on instinct, he said, 'He didn't seem to know what business Hennessy was in. He got upset when I told him Schwert Associates were debt collectors.'

Rannie thought about that. 'All builders overreach themselves, but I shouldn't think a prostitute would learn much about Michie's business problems, if he has any. Blood and semen flow maybe, cash flow, I doubt it. I shouldn't think pillow talk was in Jamie's line.' He held up his glass. 'I'm having another. You want one?'

Meldrum refused again. Shields asked for a soft drink.

While Rannie was in the kitchen, Shields said quietly, 'See the brother's wife, ugliest bitch you ever saw. Non-bloody-existent, that's my brother's sex life.'

Rannie came back and sat down. A silence settled, which Meldrum couldn't find the inclination to break. He amused himself with the idea Shields' brother and his wife might be going through the Kama Sutra behind drawn blinds. He depressed himself with the likelier image of the brother whining to Shields in some bleak pub about his rotten life. He watched as the filaments of a spider's web in the corner of a pane shone gold in the sun.

'He's not coming,' he said at last.

Rannie took them as far as the front door of his flat.

As Shields followed Meldrum out of the close, there was the blare of a car horn.

Tracing the sound, Meldrum saw a Range Rover parked across the street.

'Is that Michie?'

'Looks like it,' Meldrum said.

Chapter Forty-Four

I wouldn't,' Shields warned.

'You're the only one I'll talk to,' Michie said again. 'Just you.'

'Why not?' Meldrum said. 'I'll give you a ring later, Bobbie.'

Climbing in, he caught the smell of new leather. Four-wheel drive, video pack for television in the back seat, the car of choice for someone like Michie. Not a car you'd lose in traffic, he thought. He assumed that Shields would be somewhere close behind.

'I saw you going in,' Michie said. 'You were a long time.'

'We were waiting for you.'

'Why would you do that?'

'According to Rannie, you were in a threatening mood when you phoned him.'

Michie's laughter sounded genuine. 'High-powered pro-tection. Don't they usually send a constable?' Meldrum watched broad hands turning the wheel. 'You shouldn't listen to George. He's not a man you can trust.'

'Is that why you broke up the partnership?'

'No. We did well together. As partners, we made ou
pile. Then he wanted to put his money in stocks and share
and bonds and sit on his arse. I outgrew him. He didn't hav
the stomach for what I wanted to do. I'll use you, I told him
If I need you, I'll use you.'

'What did he make of that?'

Michie gave a sideways glance, as if taking measure of th
man beside him. 'Haven't you realised yet you can never tel
what George is thinking?' His tone suggested contempt fo
that kind of obtuseness.

'I'll tell you one thing he thinks,' Meldrum said. 'H
thinks you came out of the gutter. If you want to count that.

Probing for a response, he was disappointed to se
Michie smiling. 'Wishful thinking. Typical George, tha
is. His dad went to a *good* school and sent him to it as wel
and these people never grow up, so you get this he's-from
the-gutter stuff. My dad came out of the Second Worl
War a sick man. He was a builder, and building's a har
game. Everything went wrong for him, and I grew up
watching it happen. If you want the family history o
George and me, it's simple. I had a lot of time for m
dad. And he hated his.'

As they took a curve, Meldrum said, squinting at th
wing mirror to catch a view of the road behind them, 'Bu
he's not the crazy one.'

'That colleague of yours isn't much of a driver. I'm
having my work cut out not to lose him.'

'Thoughtful of you.'

'Next roundabout, we're on the A1. We'll fly and see if h
kills himself trying to keep up.'

But already, Meldrum realised, as if in response to th
words said aloud, their speed was increasing. The Rang

330

Rover overtook one car on the inside, cut in on another and without slowing took the roundabout at what couldn't have been less than sixty miles an hour. By some miracle, they hit a gap in the heavy traffic.

'Christ!' Meldrum cried.

'Tell me that doesn't take skill.'

Meldrum could taste salt in his mouth. He wondered if he'd bitten his tongue. 'Skill had fuck all to do with it. You gambled our lives.'

'I'm an exceptional driver.'

They were surging up the hill in the fast lane. Fields flicked past. Meldrum didn't even want to guess at their speed.

He took a slow breath, another, made himself be calm. He said, 'The man who dumped Sylvia Marshall's body in a ditch was an exceptional driver.'

'What did he do?'

'Drove backwards up a country road in the dark without lights.'

'You should pay attention when I talk to you,' Michie said.

Meldrum held his breath. He could see the next round-about. At the same instant, Michie was braking. The speed coaxed down, they joined the line of vehicles and went round in their turn.

'I'm an interesting man.'

'Not to me,' Meldrum said, his tone deliberately flat and ironic.

'You think I don't know what you see with your policeman's eyes? The man from the gutter with builder's hands. You don't know what I read. You don't know the music I listen to. When I was a child, I'd ride a white horse

331

across an endless plain. Night after night the wind in my face would waken me. It didn't seem like a dream. You can't cram me into your notebook and say that's Campbell James Michie.'

'I'll buy a bigger notebook,' Meldrum said.

'Doesn't it matter what's in my head? If you could know for certain what my body had done,' he glanced slyly across, 'it would be different, of course. I mean for an arrest and going to court.'

'There's always an insanity plea.'

'You're a good listener,' Michie said. He gave no sign that the suggestion of madness had disturbed him. 'Not many people find someone to listen to them. You're going to say a psychiatrist would, but that's not listening. He has a rule book that tells him what he's supposed to be hearing, hasn't he? But a detective, he'll listen to every word and think about what it means. If he wants to find the truth, he has to listen.'

'Not for too long. The budget wouldn't run to it.'

'You wouldn't care about that. Listen to yourself, talking about Sylvia Marshall. That's eight years ago. Everybody's forgotten her.'

'I haven't.' And what do I matter beside her father, Meldrum thought. He remembered the grey lined face of the retired schoolteacher, the asthmatic's savage struggle for breath, and wondered if he was still alive.

'I was at the theatre last night. I know your men were watching me. What did they see? Me, sitting in a seat watching the stage. In my head, though, they couldn't get in there. I'll tell you, though. I sat down and brushed at my arms. Like this.' Terrifyingly, he took both hands off the wheel. 'They must have thought it strange seeing me do that.

Brushed them down from the shoulders to the wrists. It took me by surprise too, a clinging like threads holding on to me. Shaving before I came out, I'd seen a black spider in the bath. It was enormous. I took a handful of tissues and gathered it up, and squeezed the papers in my fist. Some people are afraid of them. Are you afraid of them?'

'No.'

'I've never been afraid of them. But when I felt those threads, I thought of the spider I'd killed. And it occurred to me that in bed ready for sleep, I'd feel those threads renewed, folding about me till I couldn't move. At the interval, were your people there? Right into the hospitality suite, I mean, in evening dress, mingling with the sponsors and their guests? I spoke to this one and that one, some of them I'd known for years, and I couldn't be sure of any of them. And after a time it became very difficult because I couldn't follow what they were saying. I went back into the auditorium. It was filling up, but slowly, and I couldn't make out a word I understood anywhere. If you untune your ears, all the talk sounds like a foreign language. The same language shared by everyone except you. Swedish perhaps.'

And the speed had built again, one lane to the other, just missing, almost hitting.

Meldrum cracked. 'Double fucking Dutch, unless you slow down.'

From the fast lane, Michie took them with a single wrench of the wheel across the inside lane to the hard shoulder. He jammed on the brakes and slammed to a stop. In the same instant, he gripped Meldrum by the arm.

The action explosive, with the effect of anger; but when he spoke, it was confidingly.

'In the last act, I became aware of how fine the singer

playing Butterfly was. No one expects great acting in opera and this was acting so good that it wouldn't earn applause Its effects were so contained, on such a scale of perfection they were like the works of the smallest watch that could be made and still keep time exactly. For her effects, you needed not an audience's eyes, but a watchmaker's glass. It was like a child in a playground giving chase, and there's no malice in it, for if another child crosses her path she'll swing off in an arc and pursue her. And at the end she'll do something subtle, so subtle no adult watching could follow her movement. Thinking that, I went down and climbed on to the stage. Like a child in the playground, I began to chase Butterfly. And the stage was enormous — big enough for our ballet. And empty except for the two of us and no matter how she swooped and turned I matched her. Until at last the time came for the moment of the perfect subtle gesture. Do you know what I did? I put my hands round her throat. And as I did I thought, Now do you understand? But in the instant of doing it, I was in her mind. And what I heard, like a sentence of death, was, *You've spoiled it all.* Did your plods catch any of that?'

Chapter Forty-Five

The strange thing was that as he started walking along the hard shoulder towards Edinburgh, not having seen any useful purpose in refusing a pressing invitation by Michie to leave the Land Rover, Meldrum was immediately on the look-out for Shields. His only concern was that the pursuit might have gone astray at one of the roundabouts. He didn't doubt for a moment that Shields would persist with the chase; and shortly afterwards, in fact, he spotted the car. As he waited, watching it signal to pull off, realising the faith he'd had that this would happen came to him with a measure of surprise.

It was this fresh appreciation of the man he'd worked with for so long that made him keep his decision to confront Hugh McArdle to himself. If it was likely to lead to trouble with Gowdie, or more importantly Fleming, it would be unfair to involve Shields.

Getting home after eight, he found the fridge almost empty and didn't want to waste time going out for something to eat. Half an hour later, he came out on to Leith Walk, having dined on the heel of a loaf and a slab of aging cheddar. He badly wanted a drink, and stood at the door of a pub, staring into a bright interior oddly striped with shadows. It was a bad idea, and he set out instead to walk to McArdle's flat. It was a long walk, to one of the streets behind Comely Bank Road, long enough to be what Betty would have called doing penance. He called it clearing his head on the way there, and on the way back would call it being a bloody fool.

When he found the road, it was further up-market than he'd anticipated. It was possible that McArdle had been here long enough to buy cheap, sit tight and watch prices float up on Edinburgh's rising tide. Meldrum took the stairs three at a time, checking names as he went until he came to the third floor.

He couldn't see a bell, and banged on the door with the side of his fist. At the second blow, a dog began baying in response. Meldrum went on banging to the dog's increasingly frenzied counterpoint.

The door opened just wide enough to show Hugh McArdle's face. His eyes were tiny, and his face slack and blurred. Unmistakably at an advanced stage of private drunkenness, he looked bloated and unwell.

'Where's the fire? Oh, it's you.'

'Can I come in?'

'I wasn't expecting company.'

'I'm not here to be company.'

As Meldrum moved forward, McArdle stepped back out of his way. It was the first time Meldrum had seen him without the kilt. Accompanied by jeans, bare feet in trainers and a T-shirt spotted with food stains, the belly hanging over a straining belt seemed twice as big. When he shut the door, the only light showed in a strip under a door at the end f the hall. The barking had settled into a barrage of threat nd panic.

'Better let me go in first,' McArdle said. 'Raja's not used o visitors.'

As he opened the door, the barking stopped only to start gain as the dog saw Meldrum. It was a big Alsatian with omething odd about the head that suggested a hint of wolf on the wrong side of the blanket.

'Let that brute near me,' Meldrum said, 'I'll break its jaw.'

McArdle, however, was already on his knees in front of the dog. As he cupped its head between his hands, it quietened.

'Stop it, you silly big bugger, big bugger, silly silly ougger,' he crooned softly. 'You're just upsetting yourself.'

The dog whined and let itself be settled to the floor, where it stretched out panting and nervously watchful.

'He's more frightened of you than you are of him,' McArdle said, his voice slurred and careful. 'He's got epilepsy. Sometimes he has three fits in a row. He needs so many tablets, the animal care insurance ran out. But I pay or them myself. He wouldn't hurt a living soul. He's nine – hat's old for a big dog.'

'I'm surprised you're still here,' Meldrum said.

McArdle lurched to his feet and fell into a chair.

'I live here.'

'I thought you'd have been taken in for questioning.'

'In and out again. Doing the hokey-cokey.' He giggled. When I was in the army, this other fellow and me were working in the general's garden. The general asked us, Are you doing that with a hoe? And this fellow said, With a hey! and a ho! and a hey, nonny nonny! sir. If I'd said that, I'd've been in the glasshouse. Not this fellow, he'd the right accent. But a hell of a drinker.'

'That anorak you'd got hidden away, did it belong to Archie Wemyss?'

'Yiddo nose Simms — sticks it in everywhere. What the hell right had he to go into my cupboard?'

'If it belonged to Wemyss, why'd they let you go?'

'I told them I found it.'

'Where?'

'I told them out in the car park.'

'Where did you find it?'

'Out in the car park.'

'Where did you find it?' Meldrum repeated.

'Out in the car park.'

'Where did you find it?' Meldrum asked for the fourth time.

'Outside Four One Six. Like somebody had thrown it out the door.'

'What were you doing there?'

'This woman in the Sleat Bar said two men were fighting outside the lifts. I went to look. Nobody there.'

'So why go up to the fourth floor?'

'Check they weren't wrecking the place. Go up there work my way down.'

'And you found this anorak. Why'd you keep it?'

'I told them I didn't mean to. Meant to hand it in, in the morning, but I forgot.' McArdle began to weep. The dog lifted its head and growled. 'Do you know who I miss? I miss my grandmother. I'd be a terrible person if it wasn't for her. She was the only one I ever cared for. And my father, he was all right. He never did me any harm — apart from getting me born.'

'What did you think when you saw the anorak?'

'I thought, there'll be blood on it.'

'Because of the fighting?'

'I thought, that's somebody else been killed.'

'Like Sylvia Marshall. What did you see that night? The night she was killed.'

McArdle pressed his lips together in a tight sealed half-bow, making a glum clown's face.

'Did the killer ask you in to watch? Or had you been drinking with him? Did you hurt her as well? Was it because there was two of you, is that why it went wrong? Did you get one another excited? Which of you strangled her?'

'It wasn't like that.'

'Under Harkness,' Meldrum said, 'that hotel was a fucking knocking shop.'

'I would never hurt anybody. Not in real life.'

'Why should I believe you? I think you're the same kind of scum.'

'If I had been there, he'd have killed me too! Or killed me by this time.'

'Who are we talking about? Give me a name.'

As McArdle shook his head, drops of glittering sweat flew off his face.

'A man with three names,' Meldrum said. 'He likes to be given all of them. Campbell James Michie. You think I didn't know it? I was giving you a chance,' he finished so venomously the dog began to growl, a hysterical mutter at the back of its throat.

'I did my best. I went every time a lassie was killed and said it was me. If you hadn't been useless, the whole lot of you, you'd have seen what was going on.'

Meldrum bent over him. The growling at his back suddenly got louder.

'And if you'd had the guts to come and tell us about

Sylvia Marshall, three young women would still be alive. That's just three that we know about, you piece of shit.'

Smiling foolishly, McArdle said, 'So you could say I killed women after all.'

Crouched over, Meldrum didn't get a full swing, but his backhanded slap knocked the man sprawling over the side of the chair.

At his back came a noise like a scream. It was so shrill, human and unnatural, Meldrum swung round in a panic to defend himself.

The dog, however, was helpless on the floor, foam bubbling from its lips, its feet rowing in the throes of a convulsion.

Chapter Forty-Six

———•———

By the time Meldrum walked back to his flat, he was tired into his bones. As he fumbled for his keys, the door to his close opened and an elderly woman carrying a black bin sack came out.

She startled at the sight of him, then said, 'Mr Meldrum?'

'That's right.'

He recognised her as one of his neighbours. He'd passed her on the stairs, though he'd never spoken to her.

'It's not right, you know,' she said.

He watched as she sat the bin sack on top of a pile of them grouped round the base of a lamppost. Tomorrow was collection day. He thought about that and decided the chances of his carrying rubbish downstairs tonight to face going all the way back up again were not good, not good at all. He wondered why, when she seemed to be paying no attention to him, he was hanging around waiting for the woman to speak again. Courtesy to the old was one possibility. Like McArdle, once upon a time he'd had a granny. Everybody should have a granny. On the other hand, it was possible he was too tired to face climbing the stairs.

'What isn't right?' he asked.

'The idea of having locks on the close door is to keep us safe.'

'So it is.' Slowly, weighing it up, no arguing with that as fact or philosophy.

'Forty-five pounds was the estimate to have the lock repaired. And when we put a note through the doors only four of the flats replied. I don't think you did.'

'I work long hours.'

'To be fair, I think you paid when I arranged to have it done. I said, if we go ahead, people will pay. I divided up the bill and everybody paid. Except the Traheys.'

'I hope you didn't pay their share. If you did, let me split it with you.'

Anything to get to bed.

'There's no point in going to all that trouble, if people can just walk in. We could be murdered in our sleep. Either someone let her in — that's what happens, they ring a bell at random and the person lets them in. Where's the security in that? Or people hand out keys to all and sundry. I hope you didn't give her a key? Anyway, she's waiting outside your door.'

He saw the old woman into her flat on the first floor. Squinting up, he made out the figure of a woman on the landing above. Dressed in a long cloth coat of some dark colour, she leaned against the banister with her back to him. Though she must have heard them coming up from the close, she didn't look round.

She turned her head at the last moment, as he stepped on to the landing, and said without reproach, almost dreamily, as if to herself, 'So here you are at last.'

When they went into the front room, the air had a touch

of ice as if cold were leaking from the old stone walls of the tenement.

'What are you doing here?'

'Don't you have heating?'

She stood in the middle of the room clutching her shoulders, abstracted, as if considering whether to give herself the luxury of shuddering.

Coming in late so many evenings, without a detour for eating or sitting, he'd fall into bed. For days at a time, he might not be in this room. He switched on the electric radiator on the wall by the door.

'Have you anything to drink?'

'I could make a coffee, but I'm out of milk.'

'A whisky?'

'I don't keep it in the house.'

'If you were a horse,' Lena Hennessy said, 'it would be a kindness to shoot you.'

He went out along the lobby, closing the door carefully behind him. In the kitchen he boiled a little water and held a couple of cups under the tap. Not finding a dishcloth, he shook the cups over the sink to dry them.

When he came back with two black coffees, the room was warm. It was a small room, and he'd put the radiator to maximum.

'You don't have a television. Do you have one in your bedroom?'

He'd had a television. He looked at the empty table by the window where it had stood. At the beginning of the summer, all its colours had been dominated by red and green, then it had gone dark. It hadn't been worth repairing, and he'd never got round to buying a new one.

He didn't feel like explaining all that.

'So what do you want?'

She put the cup on the carpet in front of her chair, and slipped off her coat.

'To stay the night.'

'I don't think so.'

'I'm not trying to seduce you.' She put her hand to her mouth as if to hide a smile. 'It's not as if we haven't spent the night together.'

He stared down at her. He'd drunk some of the coffee and it tasted bitter in his mouth.

He said, 'You mean the night you killed your brother?'

When she took her hand away, there was no smile. It was possible she hadn't been smiling at all.

'That was the night I was thinking of,' she said.

'If you did.' Through the light top she was wearing, he could see her nipples. It was no wonder that she had felt the cold. The word she had used hung in the air, *seduced*, a word that filled the mouth, soft like a slightly rotten fruit, in his tiredness coming between him and his thoughts. 'If you did kill him.'

'Whatever you think, I can't go home.'

'Why not?' He held up a hand. 'You want me to guess. Your husband killed Archie. And you've found a signed confession. He felt he had to write it all down. Just couldn't resist the impulse. Tell me that's how it was.'

'What makes you so angry?'

He stared at her in amazement. What was he supposed to say? How do you feel about murder? Whose brother was it again?

'I liked your father,' he said, which wasn't exactly true. Or true at all.

'My father isn't someone you like,' she said. 'You can

344

admire him. Or hero-worship him. Or just worship him. But you have to be able to read without moving your lips.'

'That's me disqualified,' he said.

She tugged her coat out from under her and laid it over her knees, and he thought she was about to put it on and go. Instead she slid her hand into the pocket and pulled out a folded slip of paper held between her two longest fingers, the pickpocket's grip. 'I didn't find a confession,' she said.

It was a list of initials, longer than the one he'd previously seen, and with the same kind of notes as before. As he ran his eye down, he saw that Renton was there and Don Corrigan. It was the last entry that mattered: CJM, no mistaking those initials, you saw them on hoardings all over town. Beside them, someone had written: house of cards.

CJM house of cards.

'Where did you get this?'

'It was hidden among the tax files for the Agency. I was tidying up after that woman you sent, otherwise I'd never have found it. It was in a file for three years ago.'

He remembered how once she'd sighed at the idea of three years, as if to say ancient history.

'Why bring it to me?'

'I couldn't stay at home tonight. I'd have been afraid. If Patrick knew I'd found it – I've seen him use violence.'

'You could have left it where it was.'

'Is that what you'd have wanted me to do? As soon as I saw it, I knew what it had to be.'

'What's that then?'

'For God's sake! Don't play police games with me!' The flare-up of anger seemed genuine, but she calmed at once. 'Blackmail. You were the first one who said it might be happening. Patrick got information through the Apple

345

Agency to blackmail men. Maybe he only used Liz McKinnon, maybe he used other girls as well. I knew nothing about it.'

'House of cards . . .' Meldrum said thoughtfully. 'Is that a sexual perversion?'

She looked at him with contempt. 'Is that what you want to talk about?'

He studied her in silence. 'What about barking like a dog? When I wakened that morning in the Hamilton Hotel, you told me I'd been crawling on the floor barking like a dog. I've been thinking about that, and wondering why you said it?'

'Because it was true?'

'No.'

'You're so sure.'

'Pretty sure. But if I wasn't, it might have given me another reason for keeping my mouth shut. When you think about it that doesn't seem much different from this.' He held up the list.

'Whatever you think of me,' she said, 'I've been telling the truth. I'd nowhere else to go tonight.'

'Not even to George Rannie?'

Her reply was emphatic, almost impulsive. 'Not to him!'

Why couldn't she spend the night with Rannie? he wondered.

Everything else burned away, great tiredness could bring moments of clarity. 'For his sake,' he said. In case it put Rannie at any kind of risk or under any kind of suspicion. 'But then everything you do is for his sake, ever since you ran away from home with him, isn't that right?' He crumpled the list, holding it up as he crushed it in his fist. When she reached forward to stop him, he held it higher, out of her reach. 'Did Rannie write this for you?' She sat back, watchful as a cat. 'I think your husband could have used the Agency for blackmail. It's possible, I'm willing to believe that. And I'm willing to believe that you didn't know about it. That takes a little more believing, but it's possible too. But I've spoken to two of the people who were blackmailed. Whoever was pulling her strings, Liz McKinnon was the one they dealt with – and they didn't pay much. It was a small-time, shabby operation. About what you'd expect – men who were ashamed of what they'd done, but not ashamed enough to pay a fortune. If it had gone on, sooner or later somebody would have come to us. We'd have persuaded him into court as Mr X, and that would have finished it.' He dropped the crumpled list over the side of his chair. 'What the hell's Michie doing on the same list as those people? Am I supposed to be some kind of fool?'

'You think because a man's rich, he won't go to a prostitute?'

He contemplated her thoughtfully. 'Maybe you're the fool.' He yawned widely, and she gave a little hiss of anger. The yawn, though, had come up from deep inside and overwhelmed him; it hadn't been calculated. 'When I first thought Michie was being blackmailed, I was absolutely sure I knew why. Things he's done, terrible things. But then I changed my mind. House of cards . . . I think it's to do with his business. Something that could ruin him, if it was made public. I don't think he could stand being seen as a failure. I think he'd hate that more than anything else in the world.'

'You know about Schwert Associates,' she said eagerly. 'If it's money problems, Patrick could have found out about them.'

'So he could. On the other hand, Rannie was Michie's

347

partner in London. Why shouldn't it have been Rannie who uncovered some debt, or crooked deal Michie was hiding? Rannie would have the nerve to go in for serious blackmail. And if you'd told him what Hennessy was up to, then it might have amused him to persuade Liz McKinnon into helping.'

'Do you think Patrick killed Liz McKinnon?'

She always surprised him.

'Talking of killings,' he said, 'you told me how Rannie carried Archie into Room Four One Seven at the Hamilton Hotel. And that this was after you'd struck your brother on the head.'

'It was an accident. And after it happened, George was only trying to protect me.'

'Oh, I got the idea,' he said. 'It's not a bad story. Except that you never saw the room where Archie was found. Your brother's blood was splashed halfway up the tiled walls. How do you think that happened?'

'I don't believe you.'

'But I wanted to believe you. I saw the walls. And then I was taken off the case, and I forgot them.'

'I lied to you,' she said. 'It wasn't George who carried Archie into the room next door. It was Patrick.'

He was tired suddenly of being surprised by her.

'Let's go and ask him,' he said.

It was cold out of doors; after the hot little room colder than before. Their feet struck with a hollow sound like hammers on the stone stairs. In the side street, two merged shadows stretched under the lamp. He was content to travel in her car. A taxi could bring him back again. Or maybe before the night was over, there would be police cars at the Hennessy flat.

They crossed Princes Street, and went up past the bright empty foyer of the Festival Theatre and past the Royal College of Surgeons, where he'd stood once as part of a group in front of a jar holding a foetus waiting for the life that would never come. It wasn't far from Leith Walk to the house near the Meadows.

When they got out of the car, everything looked different. He'd only been there in daylight. The street looked wider. The carriage lamp over the door spilled light down the steps.

'He'll be sleeping,' she said.

'Not till you come home.'

He took her by the arm and drew her with him. As they began to climb the steps to the front door, he glanced over the stone balustrade into the area. Behind the iron bars on the window a blind had been drawn down.

'Look, he's waiting up for you.'

The shadow of a man moved across the blind. The light went out.

'Something's wrong,' she said.

He took the key from her and opened the door. When he closed it behind them, the hall was in darkness. Stretching across him, she pressed her body against his. He heard the soft click of the light switch.

Halfway down the hall, the curtain was pulled back to show the door to the cellar. Michie stood in the opening, cradling a gun against his shoulder. A long barrelled handgun, heavy calibre bullets; Meldrum was no expert, but it didn't take an expert to recognise a gun that could tear off your face. With his free hand, Michie gestured them to come closer.

'Don't do anything stupid,' Meldrum said. 'There are police outside. Some of them armed.'

Michie shook his head. 'If there was, she wouldn't be here with you. Making her share the risk, a man like you, I don't think so.' To Lena, he said, 'I'll shoot him first. So you can watch.' The barrel of the gun moved from one to the other, not smoothly, jerking to and fro. 'Or will I kill you and get it over? Would that be kinder? Tell me what you want.'

As she whimpered, Meldrum stepped in front of her. Michie pointed the gun at him. Gripped in one hand, he held it at the full stretch of his arm, but it made no difference. He was still too far away to reach. Meldrum closed his eyes and, waiting to die, listened not for the explosion of a shot but the delicate sliding of metal on metal as the trigger was pulled; and heard instead the beat of a great drum and men's voices calling out.

He opened his eyes in time to see Michie put the barrel of the gun in his mouth and pull the trigger. Like a leaf snatched by the wind, the impact knocked him tumbling back out of sight.

Behind him, he heard the door splinter as it was hammered open. Police, not bluff after all but real, poured in on an adrenaline high, yelling instructions as they came, trained bedlam, using noise to freeze opposition, noise to confuse. He glimpsed Gowdie among them, and Lena running to them in panic, arms outspread, getting in their way. Turning from all that, stiff jointed as an old man, he began slowly to make his way down the steps into the basement.

In the dark, he stepped on Michie's hand, then felt his way along the wall until there was a gap and he stepped through it into the office of the Apple Agency.

A dim light from the street showed the figure lying in

front of the filing cabinets. But he had to put on the lights to see the cheap carpet, and the mess where the beautiful hands had been that Hennessy must have held up to hide his face.

Chapter Forty-Seven

In his exhaustion, Meldrum clung to one clear idea. A statement had to be got out of Hugh McArdle. With Campbell James Michie dead, they didn't need the level of proof that would persuade a Procurator Fiscal to send a case for trial or a jury to convict. What Meldrum needed was the kind of proof that would let him go to the relatives of the murdered girls, above all to Sylvia Marshall's father, and tell them, It's over, now you can begin the process of healing.

What he hadn't expected was that Gowdie would insist on coming with him.

Each time he looked away from the night streets, he found himself under observation. In front, beside the detective sergeant who was driving, Gowdie had twisted himself round to watch him. Soon Meldrum tired of returning his stare and went back to gazing out of the window. They had nothing to say to one another. The darkened entrance of the Film House slid past and the lights of the Sheraton in Festival Square. Gowdie was with him because there was no one to arrest or charge, Hennessy and

Michie being dead. Lena Hennessy was in hospital being treated for shock, and couldn't be questioned until the following morning. They turned out of Shandwick Place went past a mute church and an expensive hairdresser's and round to the lights at Queensferry Street. Meldrum resented that he'd been kept in ignorance of the surveillance operation on Michie. When those following him recognised Hennessy at the open door of the flat, they'd reported back to Gowdie. He'd come at the head of a team, and dithered over what to do next until the unexpected arrival of Meldrum accompanied by Hennessy's wife. Shortly afterwards, the decision had been taken to break in. The report would say 'because gunshots were heard'; which was fair enough, since 'because DS Gowdie hoped to catch D Meldrum in wrongdoing' might give a bad impression. For whatever reason, the cavalry had arrived just in time.

Watching the shop fronts go past, Meldrum said, ' should thank you for saving my life.'

Not getting an answer, he looked round, but Gowdie had swung about to face front and all he could see was the back of his head.

McArdle's road still looked a nice place to live, even a three in the morning. Meldrum let Gowdie and his sergeant go ahead of him up the stairs. He was content to follow. I there was any credit to be gained here, let Gowdie have it When he got to the third landing, they were standing in front of McArdle's door.

'There isn't a bell,' Meldrum said. 'You'll have to knock.

As Gowdie pounded the door with the flat of his hand Meldrum waited with the pleasant anticipation that the dog would start to bark as if all hell had been let loose.

'Are you sure he's in there?'

'I can't think where else he would be.'

Gowdie shook his head in disgust. 'If he is, he doesn't want to know.'

'We could get a locksmith,' the detective sergeant suggested.

At three in the morning. Bed like a mirage receding in the distance.

'For fuck's sake,' Meldrum said. 'Give me room.'

His first kick jarred up his spine to the crown of his head. His second tore the lock out of the door.

'You bloody lunatic,' Gowdie said. 'That's down to you.'

With a sneer and a little scoop of the hand, Meldrum invited them to go in ahead of him.

As a result, he was the last to witness what was waiting for them in the front room. McArdle lay on the floor beside the dog. Seeing the two bodies like that, there was no way of telling which had died first. As worked out later, the likeliest explanation seemed to be that the dog had died in a fit. Afterwards, McArdle had consumed a bottle of whisky, and lying down with his head on the dog had died of sorrow and vomit blocking his throat.

'That's you in the clear,' Gowdie said.

'What?' Meldrum's lips were stiff. He was afraid they would hear the pounding of his heart.

'He's past complaining about getting his door booted in.'

Hamesucken

In the middle of the night, he woke convinced he'd left a window open somewhere. At once he slipped out of bed, trying to make as little noise as he could. He made his way methodically from room to room, checking each window was secured. He checked the side door as well and the Yale and Chubb locks on the front door. When he'd done all that, he thought – so many locks! and stood for a time trying to add up their number. He realised his feet were cold and, blaming himself for being an old fool, made his way back to the bedroom. As he put back the blankets, his wife sighed, and called out, 'Archie!' in her sleep. He kissed her on the cheek and lay down at her side.

Then, for what seemed like hours, he lay awake. Reading would have helped, reading always helped. He'd a book on the bedside table, Kenneth White's *House of Tides*, which had been sent him by the publisher. His wife, though, was restless and he didn't want to risk putting on the lamp in case it wakened her. It was good that one of them could sleep.

Later, though, he must have dozed, for he dreamt that

the bright morning sun laid a golden curve of light across his
face. He heard the bedroom door open and thought it was
Archie, then knew that wasn't possible, but kept his eyes
shut all the same. As he waited, he had an image of curtains
in the lavatory at the back of the house stirring in a draft.
The window must be open at the bottom. How could he
have overlooked it? Easy enough to explain: he had been
going through a ritual, for Archie, and for his wife's sake
now word was out they were two old people and alone in the
house. As for himself, he knew you had to leave a space
despite everything, for life to enter in.

As in an eclipse the sun is occluded, a shadow moved
down across the golden light. A hand pressed down on his
mouth, and then his nostrils were clipped shut. It was as he
imagined it must be to drown. He had never been afraid of
drowning or dying. All his life, he had been a fighter. An old
man's strength wasn't much, but in writing or life you used
what you had.

With an old man's strength, he fought.

BOOK FIVE

———◆———

All Things Human

Chapter Forty-Eight

Meldrum slept for thirty-six hours after the night of the murder and Michie's suicide. Like everyone else, once back at work he found new files on his desk, the caseload heavier than ever. Lena Hennessy after being questioned and released had disappeared. Twice he'd gone to the house near the Meadows only to find it curtained and seemingly empty. Before the Michie file could be closed, however, there were some loose ends to tidy up and, with that as an excuse, one morning he went to Hennessy's office.

The bald stocky man, who'd been so careful to avoid his eye on earlier visits, opened the street door. Far from seeming disconcerted, he broke into a wide smile.

'DI Meldrum. You not remember me? You did me for GBH a few years back.'

The change of attitude was explained as he led Meldrum across the uncarpeted stone slabs of the hall into the big ground floor front office.

'I was getting melancholy here on my lonesome.' He nodded at the filing cabinets and computers. 'I'm waiting for somebody coming to uplift the lot of it. This place is finished.'

'Is Mrs Hennessy selling up?' And, getting a nod in reply, asked, 'Has she been in?'

'No, haven't seen her. A friend of the family, fellow called Rannie, came in to arrange things. That's how I learned what had happened. He paid off the rest of the staff. Squared up with me, and I said I'd see this place cleared. Which is what I'm doing. Check with him if you want to, it's all on the up and up.'

'Did Mr Rannie take any files?'

'Aye, all of them. Emptied them out the cabinets into boxes, took them out to a van, that was it.'

'Did you ask if he'd any authority for doing that? Did he have anything in writing?'

'He'd three big blokes with him. No, I'm only joking. He was from Mrs Hennessy. The files couldn't stay here; I mean, a lot of that stuff's confidential.' He'd sat on one of the computer chairs, and now he swung it side to side and paddled it backwards with his feet. 'This was a great job. It's just a disaster. All right, I'm thinking of myself. But don't make any mistake, I really liked Patrick. He was a charmer. More of a wild boy than a wild man. Did you know his father's rich? He'd never a day or a minute in his life when he was short of a bob. That makes you soft. He wasn't bad at chasing folk up, but he didn't mean them any harm. People without money weren't, like, *real* to him. And he'd me there for the dirty work. So for him, debt collecting was just another stupid game.'

On his way back to keep the appointment with ACC Fleming that he fully expected to end his career, Meldrum stopped by Rannie's flat on the edge of the New Town. As at the Hennessys, no one answered when he rang. Because he'd left time to make the detour, he was early for his appointment and, too tense to work, went to the canteen to put in the half-hour of waiting. No one offered to join him as he sat over a cup of coffee. Perhaps he looked too forbidding. Certainly, his thoughts were grim enough. Trying to work out successively clearer accounts of his part in events on the night of Archie Wemyss's murder brought him up hard every time against an image of Fleming's disbelief. All the same, it had to be done, though he had not the slightest doubt that when he'd told his story he would be dismissed from the force. It was strange, sipping coffee, surrounded by familiar faces, to think he might never sit here again. He was so absorbed in his thoughts a young constable had to tell him twice that Chief Constable Baird had sent for him.

Baird had a letter on the desk in front of him.

Looking up from it, he asked, 'Have you ever heard of a Mrs Kravitz?'

'No,' he said without a pause for thought.

'She's written from New York.' He turned the letter in his hands. 'Rambles on a good deal. She was staying at the Hamilton Hotel when Archibald Wemyss was murdered.'

Oh, that Mrs Kravitz. The mind worked in odd ways; coming from Baird, the name had meant nothing to him.

'I didn't see her,' Meldrum said. 'But her son-in-law came to speak to me.' A moon-faced young man. Called himself a financial analyst. 'Tulley.' Wore a blazer. Kept taking his glasses on and off. 'Desmond Tulley.'

'That's right. She says here that when Tulley went down to talk to you, he left her in her room.' His eyes ran down the sheet. 'She went down to have coffee in the lounge with

her daughter, then changed her mind and went out to collect
a bit of shopping from the trunk – boot, she'll mean – of the
hire car. When she came back, she bumped into a man and
dropped her parcel. She asked at the desk who the man was
and then told her son-in-law she recognised him as the man
she'd seen fighting the night before. He told her not to be
foolish.'

Baird pushed the letter across the desk. Meldrum saw his
own name, that was the first thing, and then: *I had to be wrong
and if I went to the police then we could forget about catching the plane. I
knew he had important business to attend to, and weakly I agreed.
Desmond's a difficult young man to argue with. But my conscience has
been troubling me ever since.*

He looked up. Baird, who had been watching him,
glanced away.

'I can't imagine she's got this right,' he said. 'I gather she
felt you'd insulted her daughter. A bit of malice or a genuine
error, eh?' And as Meldrum hesitated, 'Don't you think
What else could it be?' Stretching out his hand, he took the
letter. 'In my book, you did as much as anyone could on the
McKinnon murder. You were the one who picked Michie
out from the files. Even if we can't prove he killed the other
women, you persuaded me. And who knows, we might get
the credit for it yet. DNA testing gets more sophisticated all
the time.' He slid open a drawer of the desk and dropped the
letter inside. 'Anyway, I'm not going to have you – and this
entire force with you – crucified by the Dougie Stairs of the
gutter press. You understand?'

It was an odd feeling, like a reprieve, a burden lifted from
his shoulders, but he was too sceptical and confused for any
simple rejoicing. From nowhere there came into his head a
forgotten saying, a favourite of his mother's eldest brother

typically deployed at the funerals of those who'd endured long illness, It's all mixed with mercy. Leave it at that.

All the same, he was cheered enough to return an uncharacteristic grin for the frown offered by Barry Gowdie when they met in the corridor.

Gowdie broke step. 'You'll not miss him then?'

'What?'

'I'm saying, you look as if you're not sorry to see the back of him.'

'Who would that be?'

'Bobbie Shields.' Gowdie's frown was slowly replaced by a look of sly surprise. 'He'd his retiral do last night. Fuck me, don't tell me you didn't know he was retiring?'

'He might have mentioned it.'

'But didn't, eh? I keep hearing this great detective stuff. Me, I can't see it. As far as I can tell, you know nothing about what goes on here. Who's fucking who. Who's in line for promotion. You walk about with your eyes shut.'

'You mean I miss all the arses I should be licking?'

Gowdie gave three solemn nods. Like a man pronouncing a curse, he said, 'It's not healthy for anyone to be as detached as you are from this place.'

Walking on, Meldrum thought about Shields. For himself, there had been a time when he'd have been glad to be rid of him. Not so much lately, though. He'd been contributing more, or at least occasionally it had seemed that way. Maybe, he'd got the odd charge of energy from knowing he was on his way out. Finished with all of it. On the pension. Inside, he must have been counting the days. Anyway, no point in brooding about it. That was how it went with people you knew on the job. They were part of your life and then one day they were gone.

As he left the building, grey clouds covered the sky and a thin rain had begun to slice down across the car park. He remembered it was the day of Frances Wemyss's funeral, but knew it must be over by now.

Chapter Forty-Nine

As Meldrum got out of the car, Hector Wemyss was coming out of his front door. He was wearing a sheepskin jacket and boots, and despite a torn scar across one cheek and bruising round the eyes didn't look as bad as Meldrum had feared.

'I need a breath of air,' he said. 'Will those shoes of yours stand up to a walk?'

They made their way down the garden to a gap in the hedge. On the other side, there was a wide space between the hedge and a stock fence.

'This bit's cut up underfoot,' Wemyss said. 'They use it for walking horses.'

'I'm sorry I couldn't make it to the funeral.'

'I appreciate you coming at all.'

'I gather they caught them. Just an appalling thing to happen.'

'Hamesucken.'

'What?'

'And you a policeman,' Wemyss mocked. 'It's the old Scots word for it – breaking in to a man's home and doing him violence. It came to my mind while they were knocking me about. Looking for money, the damned fools. I could tell by their voices they were local, and I thought they'll not have the right word for what they're doing.'

'Did your wife—'

'I'm holding to the belief she died in her sleep. I think she must, I think she must. She looked very peaceful.'

Where the field ended, they climbed over a gate into the wood.

'It wasn't a big funeral,' Wemyss said. 'I'd have liked more folk there for her sake.'

'You'd have your daughter there.' Despite himself, a questioning note crept into that to Meldrum's shame.

'No.' The single dry monosyllable. Meldrum thought he was going to leave it at that, but said nothing, and perhaps it was that decent silence which started the old man talking. 'She's in London with George Rannie. I saw Olivier doing Richard III many years ago. "But I who was not made for sportive tricks . . ." I've never forgotten him doing that speech. Shakespeare understood the anger of those in the dark against those in the light. The ones who have to sit out the dance because they have no ear for the music. And yet they can see the dance shaped before them and know it exists and feel how they are shut out from it. That was George Rannie. From a child, that was him.'

It was dark under the trees and, even where the path widened so that they could walk side by side, Meldrum couldn't clearly make out the old man's face.

'There was a minister I knew in Glasgow, this is a long time ago. He cared for the poor with a kind of passion — maybe because he came from a home that was comfortably off. He lived in the slums as a worker minister — you know, the worker-priest notion? He was a man who embraced the

370

drunk who vomited on him and picked the beggar from the gutter not to give him a pound but to take him home with him. He died young of exhaustion and overwork. I was thinking of him this morning. If he'd been in a different church, he might have been canonised and called a saint. But the world doesn't change. If the Kingdom of Heaven came to earth and we had gentleness and plenty for every man, woman and child, the grass would cry out its pain under our feet.'

Mud sucked at the light shoes Meldrum was wearing as if trying to hold him back; it had rained overnight. Thinking about that, he almost walked into barbed wire, stopped barely in time. A post hammered in at either side, three lines of wire strung across the path.

'I wanted to see the loch,' Wemyss said. 'The children and I used to go rowing there.'

Meldrum was glad, however, that they were turning back, for Wemyss seemed to have grown weary quite suddenly and, in the way of the old, as they made their way back along the path his mind ran on the past.

'I'd been wounded and was convalescing, not worrying about going back since the war had just ended. I was lying on a park bench in the sun. I raised my head and saw this girl walking towards me. Seventeen or eighteen years old she was, and I was fresh from war. She had wonderful breasts — this was before you had to worry about whether they were real or not — and men and boys on the grass were watching her and, oh, she knew it. Her mouth was a little open as she walked, as if her breath was coming a shade too fast. I rolled up off the bench and followed her out of the park, and just when I was catching up and going to speak to her she turned into the gate of a large house. Would you believe I stood outside that house for a week and never saw a sign of her?'

He turned and smiled. 'I can see you do. Every man has a girl in the park. Suppose that girl had come out, I might have gone off to Paris with her and everything been different.'

When they came to the gap in the hedge, they pushed through and back into the garden again. Brushing dew from his shoulders, Wemyss said, 'I used to tease Frances with the idea that at a certain age you should change your opinions, just go into reverse on all of them. Like being born again. But she would never stand for it, she was too fierce on what she believed. I haven't spent a night alone since I was married. Do you know what you think when you're alone? You wonder, and now what of mine? What of this unconnected life of mine? What will happen to this atom that is me? And you feel for a second the joy of being irresponsible.'

You're too old, Meldrum thought, to fuck that girl in the park again.

Wemyss insisted that he come into the house for a drink, and Meldrum agreed, both of them perhaps moved by some notion of funeral rites.

Alone in the living room, Meldrum looked out of the window at the view. When he tired of that, he picked up a book from the desk. He read the title, *Darkness in my Hand*, and wondered what kind of sense that made. Opening it at random, he read:

> Heed now in blood and bone
> What time will rub from stone:
> *All things human come to ruin.*

A sound made him glance up. Hector Wemyss had come back into the room and stood near the door watching him.

'Have it!'

'I'm not much of a one for poetry.'

As soon as he'd spoken, he regretted that as graceless. And might afterwards have regretted it for other reasons.

But coming forward, Wemyss cried, 'Put it in your pocket, man. It's a gift.'

When Meldrum came home that night, he sat on the edge of the bed and read half a dozen pages and was disappointed to make nothing of them. It seemed to him that, despite everything, there had been something brave and even optimistic about Wemyss, and he couldn't find those emotions in the poems.

Yet when he read the book again, one night near the end of another year, it was as if those things had been there all the time waiting to be found. Turning the pages slowly, the sweet smell of a neglected whisky on the air, an ambulance clamouring from the street below, he came upon them almost by accident, for they lay not on the surface but were to be discovered in the connection between one thing and the next and even somewhere under the words. Perhaps he had read too quickly the first time, and that wasn't the way to read poetry.

In any case and whatever the truth of it, he was grateful to the old man who, turning his refusal aside, had made him take a gift for the future.

A selection of bestsellers from Hodder & Stoughton

Kissing Judas	Frederic Lindsay	0 340 69534 X	£5.99 ☐
A Kind of Dying	Frederic Lindsay	0 340 69536 6	£5.99 ☐
Idle Hands	Frederic Lindsay	0 340 69538 2	£5.99 ☐
Death Knock	Frederic Lindsay	0 340 76571 2	£6.99 ☐

All Hodder & Stoughton books are available at your local bookshop or newsagent, or can be ordered direct from the publisher. Just tick the titles you want and fill in the form below. Prices and availability subject to change without notice.

Hodder & Stoughton Books, Cash Sales Department, Bookpoint, 39 Milton Park, Abingdon, OXON, OX14 4TD, UK. E-mail address: orders@book-point.co.uk. If you have a credit card you may order by telephone – (01235) 400414.

Please enclose a cheque or postal order made payable to Bookpoint Ltd to the value of the cover price and allow the following for postage and packing:
UK & BFPO: £1.00 for the first book, 50p for the second book and 30p for each additional book ordered up to a maximum charge of £3.00.
OVERSEAS & EIRE: £2.00 for the first book, £1.00 for the second book and 50p for each additional book.

Name . . . .

Address . . . .

. . . .

. . . .

If you would prefer to pay by credit card, please complete:
Please debit my Visa / Access / Diner's Club / American Express (delete as applicable) card no:

Signature . . . .

Expiry Date . . . .

If you would NOT like to receive further information on our products please tick the box. ☐